WHERE
THEY LAST
SAW HER

WHERE THEY LAST SAW HER

A Novel

Marcie R. Rendon

BANTAM

NEW YORK

Published in the United States by Bantam Books, an imprint of Random House, a division of Penguin Random House LLC, New York.

BANTAM & B colophon is a registered trademark of Penguin Random House LLC.

Trade paperback ISBN 978-0-593-97487-2
Library hardcover ISBN: 978-0-593-49652-7
Ebook ISBN 978-0-593-49651-0

Printed in the United States of America on acid-free paper
randomhousebookclub.com

2 4 6 8 9 7 5 3 1

Book design by Caroline Cunningham

For all the kwe whose hearts will never touch the ground

WHERE
THEY LAST
SAW HER

CHAPTER ONE

Quill ran the snow-covered trail. In her right hand she carried bear spray and in the left she carried a long stick to ward off the rez dogs that often ran in wild packs. Her breath formed frozen clouds of white air that drifted back over her shoulder. Winter brought its own deep silence to the woods. Dead leaves from the poplar trees and dropped twigs sodden with fall moisture were frozen under the recent snowfall. They didn't crackle and crunch under her running shoes. While the pines were still lush, the deciduous trees had no foliage to rustle. The winter-dead underbrush, bare of leaves, made it possible to see a hundred yards in either direction. The winter forest wasn't as dark and lonely as the summer forest could be.

Quill had run Duluth's 26.2-mile Grandma's Marathon the previous June, and after that run she had become determined to train every day all year round to prepare for the Boston Marathon, if not this year, then the next.

Out of the corner of her eye Quill spied a rabbit, rusty

brown in color, sitting not three feet off the trail. A cottontail. The cottontail stared without blinking or twitching a nose or ear—its survival instinct. Quill kept running. She saw a horned owl sleeping in a tree. Surrounded by forest, the bird's natural habitat, Quill mainly ignored the superstitious fear of owls—the fear that said hearing or seeing one meant death. A lone sparrow quietly hopped from one tree branch to another. Quill ran. Breath in. Breath out. Acutely aware of the life in the trees around her, hitting her stride where she barely felt her feet touch the ground.

Deep in a meditative runner's trance, Quill instinctively dropped to her knees and swiveled around, looking in wide-eyed terror in all directions, as a high-pitched scream pierced the air. The scream did not repeat. Quill crab-walked to a large jack pine and sat on the cold ground, her back on the tree, pepper spray and stick ready to attack. *Why did you wear the neon-pink running suit, fool?* she thought as she scanned the forest around her, noticing that both pink knees were dirty from the forest floor. She slid around the tree and scanned the forest in all directions. The forest was even more silent than it had been. Every living creature and plant went to hush with that scream. *It was a woman's scream; I swear to god.*

When the scream didn't repeat, Quill scooted around to the trail side of the tree and quickly scanned up and down the trail. No one else was on it. Quill crouched, keeping her back to the tree trunk. Nothing moved in any direction. She pulled her winter cap off, tilted her head as if that would help her right ear hear better. She was sure the scream came from the right because when she dropped to the ground, she instinc-tively turned to the right first.

Quill felt a chill down her back. The chill that happens when folks say, *Someone walked over my grave.* She checked her watch. When she'd decided to train for the Boston Marathon, she'd splurged and bought herself a running watch. Her friends teased her about being bougie and getting a "white runner's" watch. But it told her the time, with a GPS system, heart and oxygen status, and music, and told her how many miles she ran. Now it told her her heart was beating way above normal at two-fifteen in the afternoon and that she was three miles into the woods, which meant three miles back to the gravel road everyone called Cemetery Road, where her car sat. And another fifteen miles of reservation road to get back home. She glanced in all directions, cautiously took her time to raise herself to a full standing position, and took off running to her car.

CHAPTER TWO

"I'm telling you, I heard a woman's scream." Quill stared into her husband's dark brown eyes. She slapped the butcher knife she held in her hand hard on the kitchen counter. She grabbed cube-sized pieces of cut deer loin and threw them into the crockpot. "It wasn't no damn cougar. And no, not a barn owl. I tell you I heard a woman screaming."

Crow took a sip of coffee. An auto mechanic who worked from home and spent hours out in the cold Minnesota winter changing tires, pulling folks out of snow-filled ditches, or jump-starting cold engines, he wore a blue flannel shirt over a long-sleeved thermal shirt. His feet, encased in thick wool socks, were crossed at the ankles as he leaned against the kitchen counter. He wore a stocking cap on his head, and a lone black braid hung down his back to mid-shoulder. He ventured, "A fox?"

"It isn't even mating season yet. Wasn't no damn fox."

"Did you call the tribal cops?"

Quill attacked a whole deer loin with the knife. She whacked raw meat off the bone. Sliced the red meat into two-inch chunks and threw them into the crockpot. "I did. They said they'd drive out that way and look. I should have driven around and looked myself, but I was too freaked out. I came right home. Wanted to make sure the kids were okay."

Crow nodded. He looked at their two children lying on the living room floor. Quill followed his gaze. Their daughter held a game controller in her hands. Chasing some alien-world character through a maze on the big-screen TV. Niswi Anang, named for one of the three sisters of the sky, clamped her tongue between her teeth in concentration. Her ten-year-old eyes scrunched almost shut. Her hair in a single braid, a replica of her dad's. Her elbows were on the Navajo rug Crow's mother had given them years ago as a wedding present.

The rug was a beautiful burnt red, with woven geometric designs. What Quill loved most about the rug was a small strand of dark brown yarn that ran in one line from the inner design of the rug to the outer edge. Her mother-in-law told her it represented a spirit line woven in by the artist so that her creative spirit would not be trapped in the rug.

Niswi's hands moved side to side as she maneuvered through the game. Jackson, the three-year-old of the family, still called Baby Boy, sat next to her. Crow had fashioned his son a makeshift controller from a piece of wood with drawer knobs attached so he could pretend to play video games with his sister. He was too young to notice it didn't really work. He moved his hands side to side, imitating his big sister.

Crow looked at his wife. "That makes sense."

"I want you to drive out there with me tomorrow morning. Take a look around." The look she gave him didn't leave room for a no. "Will you dish up the kids' meals while I finish cutting up this meat?" She went back to chopping venison. "That scream scared me, Crow. And I don't get scared."

"I know. We'll go look." He reached around her to grab plates out of the cupboard. Dished up four plates of rice, sliced fried chicken and onions, with other vegetables stir-fried in. He set the food around the wooden kitchen table. "Come on, kids. Food's on."

The kids ignored him.

"Before it gets cold."

"Turn that thing off and get over here," Quill told them. "Crow, can you make a spirit plate before they eat? Put out prayers for whoever was scared out in the woods."

Crow got a paper bowl from under the kitchen sink where Quill stored their powwow supplies. He put a small amount of rice, chicken, and vegetables into the bowl. He went to the kitchen windowsill, where a cylindrical birch-bark basket sat. From it he took a pinch of tobacco and put it in his left hand. He didn't bother to put his winter coat back on, but he did stuff his feet into a pair of winter boots that stood in the entryway.

Quill leaned against the kitchen counter and watched him walk outside into the dark night. She knew he would put the bowl and tobacco out on the east side of the small pine tree growing in the front yard. In her mind she said a prayer for the woman she'd heard in the woods. She asked the Creator to please keep her safe.

When Crow came back inside, he gave Niswi a gentle shake

on the shoulders. Told her to pause the game and get up to the table and eat. He picked up Baby Boy and brought him to the table. Quill ran water to clean the venison blood from her hands in the kitchen sink. The dark woods outside the kitchen window didn't seem as friendly as they had the night before. She sat down to eat with her family. With her soft brown eyes, she drank in the faces of her children and husband. They were her life. Her heart. Her reason for being. She felt relief wash over her for the second time that evening.

She felt guilty every time she went out for a run and left them home with their games or movies streamed on a tablet or the TV screen. Crow worked from home unless he made a service call somewhere else on the rez. Folks tended to drive used cars and there was always one thing or another going wrong with someone's mode of transportation. Neither she nor Crow worried too much about leaving the kids alone for an hour or two. Niswi was a good big sister. And in the village of Red Pine, everyone knew everyone. And even though the houses were secluded, each in its own stand of pine trees, families on either side or across the road were in hollering distance.

That sense of safety disappeared now; the scream in the woods had shaken Quill to the core. Her only thought getting home was *Please let my kids be okay*. Her racing heart slowed at the sight of them in front of the game console, where they were safely ensconced when she got back from her run.

Tears welled in her eyes. And then she took it out on the deer loin until Crow came in from outside. After dinner they worked together silently to clean up the kitchen. Quill got the vegetables into the crockpot on top of the deer. Crow washed the dishes and wiped the table. They shooed the kids to bed. Quill dealt with Niswi. Crow was the softer parent. He let his daughter get away with longer game times. Skip homework assignments. Play outside after dark. Quill, the athlete, was more disciplined. More into schedules and accountability. Get them to bed. Turn out the lights. Quick kiss on the forehead.

Meanwhile, in his parents' bedroom, where Baby Boy theoretically still slept in a crib on the far wall from their bed, Crow sang an Indian lullaby to his son while holding him close in the oak rocking chair that sat in the corner of the room. When Baby Boy conked out, Crow laid him in the middle of the mattress where he and Quill slept.

Quill sat on the living room couch, TV turned to an old crime show about some government agency that tracked down killers. Crow sat down next to her and pulled her into his arms against his chest. "We'll go out and look around in the morning. I planned to change the brakes on one of the tribal pickups, but I'll text and tell them I'll do it around ten-thirty, eleven, all right? Stop worrying. Let's go to bed."

"Will you come outside with me first?" Quill jumped up and grabbed her winter coat off a hook on the wall by the front door. She pulled a stocking cap down over her ears. "Come on." She pulled on a pair of mittens.

Crow put on his coat and followed her outside. Their breath created clouds in the cold night air. Their house stood in a grove of pine trees with a gravel driveway leading to it. Quill stood between their two vehicles parked there, with her arms wrapped around her chest. Crow wrapped his arm over her shoulders, holding her close. "What's up?" he asked.

"We grew up here. I remember Old Man Jigs talking at Big Drum ceremony about not letting your kids be outside after dark. That spirits walk at night and you never know what danger might be out there. But we always ran around out here. Nothing scared us. It's beautiful to run at night around full-moon time. The moon is bright, brighter than the yard lights. Especially in the winter when all the animals are sleeping. I run on those backwoods trails and imagine I am alive before anyone else arrived here and cut down our trees. Before they dug in the earth for oil or minerals. That scream made me drop to my knees and put my back to the trees. That was in broad daylight. We've all heard the stories about what happens when these pipelines go through. The man camps. The kidnapping and trafficking of our women. All the missing and murdered relatives. It hurts my heart. I don't want to be afraid of the night. And I don't want to be afraid to run in broad daylight. I never have been. This is our land. Our woods. Look how beautiful the stars are. How the snow glitters in what little light there is."

Crow tightened his hold on her shoulders. "It's not the night we have to be afraid of. Not even the animals. But I don't want you running out there by yourself."

"I won't. After today I won't. I'll call and see when someone can run with me. We can start running in pairs. Or as a pack."

"Come on. Let's go. My feet are starting to freeze."

Quill laughed and poked him in his ribs. "Thin-blooded shinaab. You wouldn't have done me much good a hundred fifty years ago. You can't even stay out long enough to get us a deer. You'd have been out there crouched with a bow and arrow and suddenly you'd think, *I need to get home and warm up. Too damn cold out here.*"

Crow laughed. "We don't have swear words in our language, remember?" His arm was still around her shoulders as he steered her back into the house.

CHAPTER THREE

The next morning, Quill and Crow fed the kids breakfast and sent Niswi off to school. They dropped Baby Boy off at Crow's brother-in-law's house. Quill didn't tell her sister-in-law the story of what happened the day before. On the phone she only said that Crow was going to help her check out a new running trail and asked if they could drop Baby Boy off for a couple hours.

Barbie, Crow's sister, was a stay-at-home mom who loved all children, not just her own. She also had a love for Korean soap operas and cotton candy. Where Quill had a thin and toned runner's physique, Barbie was soft and round, with the contours of a woman who baked cookies and set out plates of tortilla chips and melted cheese for midday snacks. Her long brown hair was pulled back and stuffed through a hair tie. It hung down her back, with loose strands framing her curved face. She smiled and laughed at everything and everyone. After a quick hug from his aunt, Baby Boy ran into the living room ready to roughhouse with his four cousins. "He'll be fine," Barbie teased. "Go do your *thing* in the woods."

Crow and Quill laughed, nodded, and left.

They rode silently back to Cemetery Road. The sky was overcast with thin gray clouds, adding to the ominous chill Quill felt as Crow stopped the vehicle. "I parked here and, according to my watch, ran three miles in. The trail swerves to the right and then connects with a hunting road in about a quarter of a mile. It's a big U-shaped trail. I usually run back on the hunting road, but yesterday I ran back this way."

"Well, let's drive up and see how far we can get on the hunting trail." Crow was driving an old beat-up Dodge Ram from the nineties that someone gave him in exchange for replacing a transmission in one of his cars. The truck was full of rust and dents and wouldn't run when it was first towed to their yard, but after a month of long summer evenings Crow had a hunting truck that he named Betty Boop. A parking lot crash had left the paint scraped off in a pin-curl shape on the left fender. Since Crow was the backyard mechanic for most people who lived in the village, his pickup named Betty Boop, along with an unnamed tow truck, received special recognition among folks on the reservation.

Quill pointed at the turnoff into the woods, and remarked, "Look at those tracks. A couple folks have driven down here recently."

"Maybe Patrick came down here yesterday with a couple guys and looked around." Crow turned in to the hunting road and they jounced around in the truck, even though he tried to drive around the ruts in the path. "You were three miles in?"

"Yep."

At a mile in, the tire tracks showed where one set of tires turned around and drove back out. Another set of tire tracks kept going.

"I bet this is when the tribal cops turned around. Right here. Rather than going farther in," said Quill.

"I'll go up as far as Betty Boop will take us. Maybe we'll be able to approach the three-mile mark and see if anything is different, okay?"

"Yep." Quill hung on to the "Oh god" handle above the passenger door as the truck tires hit more ruts.

After a bumpy couple miles Crow stopped. "Look at that," he said. Quill was already getting out of the truck.

Quill stood at the edge of the disturbed snow. From looking at the tracks it was evident to her where a vehicle had parked and a scuffle occurred. It reminded her of the chaos left in the yard when the kids went out and wrestled around in the new snow. Here, on the road, snow was scraped up and dirt exposed. Something or somebody had been pulled along the ground.

Quill looked at Crow. "It was a woman who screamed."

"Whatever vehicle was here turned around and went back out this way. Did you see anyone else on the road when you left yesterday?"

"No. But I wasn't looking either. I was so scared I high-tailed it home." Quill paused and looked around. "It's so quiet out this way. I would remember if a car was on the road with me. They must have driven back out and up toward Brookston instead of toward the main highway."

"Come on, let's go back and talk to Patrick. It's a tribal

cop's job to figure out what happened here." Crow walked to his truck and hopped back in.

Quill walked to the right of where they stood. Something in the snow caught her eye. She bent down and picked up a small beaded earring. Tiny glass beads were sewn round and round into a delicate flower design that fit on the head of the post earring. *These are the style of earrings Giigoonh Jones makes,* she thought. Without thinking she put the earring in her pocket. She stood up and got into the pickup with Crow. Fear and concern on her face. "Where is the woman who was here? Who is she?"

"Come on. Let's get out of here. Go talk to Patrick."

"Don't be so goddamn calm with me." She leaned against the door, her eyes on the trees hugging the edges of the hunting road. " 'We'll talk to Patrick,' " she mimicked. "Tell 'em to not be so goddamn lazy. They only came halfway down this trail before they turned around and went right back. Assholes. Stupid on-the-take tribal cops can't do the job right."

After years of marriage, Quill was accustomed to Crow ignoring her passionate outbursts. A typically quiet man, he now said, "Calm down and I'll get us out of here."

Quill continued to stare out the window. "There are between two thousand and five thousand missing and murdered Indian women in this country. Nobody gives a shit. And now we have man camps getting set up all around the rez here for the men working on this goddamn pipeline." She ranted the entire ride back on the hunting trail. By the time they reached the tribal cop headquarters, she was silent and once again stared sullenly out the truck window.

When Crow didn't get out of the pickup, she said, "You go in. Tell 'em about the tracks out there. Tell 'em to go check it out more thoroughly. If I go in, I'll end up making matters worse. Leave the car running so I don't freeze to death."

She watched Crow enter the tribal building. Woodland flower designs in red and yellow arched over the doorway. Even though Crow's patience got on her nerves at times, she knew his calmness and matter-of-fact approach to life balanced her out. She knew he would relay the information to the tribal cops without antagonizing them. He could convince them they needed to be more diligent in finding the woman.

She put her hand into her jacket pocket and rubbed her fingers over the tiny beads on the earring still hidden there. She imagined a woman forced from her home or grabbed from her vehicle. Forced into a man's truck and driven into the forest. Whatever evil occurred was enough that even in the middle of nowhere the woman gave a desperate scream in the hopes that someone would hear her. A chill ran through Quill's body. She had heard her. She reached over and locked the driver's door and then her own. She sat staring out the window. She ran her thumb and pointer finger softly over the beaded earring as she rolled it between them in her pocket. *I will make them find you*, she promised the unknown woman. She opened the glove box and found the stub of a yellow number-two pencil and an old gas receipt. She wrote, *I'm gonna run home. Pick up Baby Boy.* ♥ *Q*

She slid the note into the binding of the steering wheel so Crow would see it right away when he came out. She unlocked the driver's door. No one would be stupid enough to steal Betty Boop. Too many on the rez relied on Crow's help, and besides, banged up as it was, it would not be an easy truck to hide. Quill did a couple stretches and took off running.

＝

Quill came out of the shower and found Crow standing there, glaring at her. She walked into the bedroom and stood by the queen-sized bed with a geometric Indian-print towel wrapped around her naked body. Water pooled at her feet.

Crow followed her. "What the hell were you doing, running off alone like that?" If Crow were a man who yelled and threatened, he would have been yelling. Instead, his voice was quiet as he ran his hand over his black hair, flicking the single braid against the shirt on his back. He put his arm across the doorway as if blocking her in. He was a head taller than Quill's five-foot-four frame and stockier.

Quill tightened the towel around herself, arms crossed over her chest. "I couldn't sit there any longer. What did you find out from Patrick?"

"Don't give me that crap. Don't make me drive out into the woods where you heard a woman screaming. Where you were out alone for god's sake, and where clearly a struggle took place. You insist on going to the cops and then you run off by yourself? What the hell!"

"Sorry."

"Sorry doesn't cut it."

"I couldn't sit still, waiting."

"Then you should have come in and talked to the cops with me. Not go running off by yourself. You're done running by yourself."

"What?"

"You heard me."

"Maybe you forgot. You're my husband, not my dad." Quill dropped the towel. Stood defiantly naked before him for a second. Pulled on the pink panties that were lying on the bed. Pulled on a running bra.

"Nice try." Crow let out a harsh laugh. "I mean it. I am the father of your kids and you are not going to leave me to raise them by myself."

Quill pulled on a T-shirt. "What did the cops say?"

"Not much. I talked to Patrick. We were right. A couple of their guys drove out there yesterday, only went as far as where we saw their tire tracks. They turned around and came back and reported nothing of importance. Patrick is going out there himself. He left when I left. Took one of the new guys with him, the one who recently returned from the Middle East. Said he'd call once they have more information about the circumstances."

Quill, now fully dressed, slipped under Crow's arm. "I see you have the boy planted in front of the TV. If I die, he'll grow up a TV zombie, unable to read or write or know how to talk to a human." She walked over, scooped him up into her arms, and snuggled his neck. "Come here, Baby Boy. Did you have fun at Auntie's?" The little guy, eyes bright, with a grin on his face, nodded yes. Then, looking over Baby Boy's head, she said to Crow, "I'm sorry. I understand that you're worried. I am too. This scared both of us. This isn't a fight between you and me, you know."

Crow again brushed the loose hairs that escaped his braid away from his face. "I know. But you promised me last night you wouldn't go off running by yourself."

"I thought you meant at night."

"Run in pairs. Run as a group. Don't be going off by yourself anymore. I mean it. Day or night."

"Okay. Okay." She gave Baby Boy a kiss on his neck. "Go

watch TV. Fry your little brain, little big man. Mama's gotta make us all some lunch."

"I still have to fix the brakes on that pickup for the tribe. Shouldn't take me more than a couple hours. I'm gonna get a bowl of that stew you have in the crockpot."

"That's for supper."

"I'll still eat it later," he said, already dishing up a bowl. He ate while Quill made grilled cheese sandwiches for herself and Baby Boy. "I'll call if I hear anything from Patrick. Stay home."

Quill laughed. "Now you're telling me to stay home. Good luck on that one."

They both laughed. She stood on tiptoes and kissed him. "Go make us money working on metal ponies, my Indian warrior." They both laughed again and exchanged "I love yous" as he left the house.

Quill stood at the picture window and watched Crow back out of the driveway. She reached into her sweatpants pocket and pulled out her cellphone. She FaceTimed her friend Punk.

On the screen, Punk's dyed-green mohawk haircut accented her eyes, also green thanks to tinted contact lenses. It was a startling contrast to her dark brown, year-round tan. She had a nose pierce and an eyebrow pierce, and a fake diamond stud strategically glued to her left cheek. Ever the artistic extrovert, Punk loved to shock and awe the more traditional folks on the reservation, some of whom still cringed and gossiped about a woman who would dare to wear shorts on a hot summer day. Quill also knew that Punk's pierced and tattooed exterior covered an earlier life of pain that she rarely, if ever, disclosed. "What's up babe?" asked Punk.

Quill relayed the story of yesterday and how Crow was now insisting she not go out running by herself.

Initially, Punk was appropriately annoyed at Crow, but she was also deeply concerned about the scream. "You know, those man camps bring trouble wherever they set up. And now that they've started work on the pipeline going through our rez, there's bound to be trouble. I hate to say it, but I think Crow is right."

Quill laughed. "Shuddup."

Punk joined in the laughter. "Serious though."

"Well, you up for running this afternoon? Revisit the scene of the crime?"

"Sure. Get back on that horse. What time?"

"Well, Crow should be back in a couple hours. And we don't want to be out there at dark. Two-thirty? You wanna call Gaylyn and see if she wants to come too?"

"Sure."

"Gigawabamin." They both clicked off the screen.

CHAPTER FOUR

Quill sipped lukewarm coffee and stared out the kitchen window. A bird in one of the pine trees behind the house skipped from branch to branch. As the bird landed on a snow-laden branch, a clump of white fluff fell toward the ground. The snow, falling in what appeared to Quill to be slow motion, triggered a memory.

The summer when she was nine years old, Jimmy Sky, an older teenager, had jumped off the railway bridge in front of her and a bunch of rez kids who were horsing around in the drainage ditch on the paved road a mile from the village.

The day began when her rowdy younger cousins came by the house. Quill's mom and dad were at work and an older cousin, Junebug, was supposed to be watching her. Instead, Junebug said, "Just stay inside. I'm gonna run over to Francie's and get some makeup she promised me."

That had been right after breakfast, and Quill's stomach said it was close to lunchtime but Junebug still wasn't back.

Quill pulled a chair over to the kitchen counter and made herself some toast with butter and chokecherry jelly, which she scraped from an almost empty jar. She was sitting outside on the front steps eating when five other cousins, younger than Junebug but older than herself, arrived. Barefoot, they wore cut-off jeans that exposed dusty knees. Some wore neat braids, others had leftover braids from the weekend powwow, hair strands sticking out all over.

"Ah, come on," they said. "No one will know. Junebug is at Francie's playing kissy-face with that creepy guy Morrey." The girl cousins made smoochy faces and the boy cousins pushed one another's shoulders, saying, "You wish she were kissing you."

"Not." Pushing back.

"Come on, Quill, don't be a baby." They all taunted her until she stood, brushed the toast crumbs off her shirt and pants, and went with them.

One minute they were laughing, teasing one another as they slid in the mud among the tall cattail reeds, catching frogs. The frogs, wet with slime, slid out of their hands into the waiting hands of the next kid. Then, a second later, time stood still. One of the older kids yelled, "Look!" And they all watched Jimmy Sky float off the bridge, his red T-shirt billowing up around his chest like a birthday balloon. His arms reaching for the sky. He fell without making a sound until his body hit the wet ground with a soft thud. While the bigger kids worked together to pull Jimmy Sky's limp body out of the ditch, up onto the side of the road, they screamed at Quill to run for help. And she did.

Up out of the ditch, the hot summer air thick with silence,

she ran down the gravel road toward the village. Normally she would have noticed the smell of the pine trees and the buzz of deerflies and mosquitoes. She would have noticed the bluejay that flitted from tree to tree following her journey. But that day, all she noticed was the hot pain in her chest and the burning muscles as she ran faster than she knew to be possible. Her scrawny nine-year-old legs took her into the village, where she ran to the first adult she saw. Bent over, hands on knees, she gasped out that Jimmy Sky had jumped off the railroad bridge and he looked dead. And then she herself fainted.

She came to in a neighbor's house, lying on a floral couch. Three village grannies hovered over her. One wiped her forehead with a cool cloth. Another said, "Here, my girl, drink some water." The third stood, nervously clasping and unclasping her hands in front of her chubby waist.

"What happened, my girl?" asked the granny with the cool cloth.

"Jimmy Sky jumped. I think he's dead." And Quill started to cry.

The granny with nothing to do with her hands sat down on the couch and scooped Quill onto her lap. "There, there." She rocked Quill back and forth.

The granny with the cool cloth said to the other grannies, "You know, that Jimmy Sky done had a hard life. Daddy in prison and his mama"—the granny lowered her voice as if Quill wouldn't be able to hear her—"she got that depression."

"His mama's never gonna recover now. And these poor kids that saw him jump." The other granny shook her head and tsked and tsked.

The three grannies mothered her while they tried by phone

to reach her own mother, who was off teaching birch-bark basket making at a summer cultural camp, so her dad was called in off his job with the highway crew. Both were upset with her needing them, or so it seemed to nine-year-old Quill. Neither mentioned Jimmy Sky again or the fact that he committed suicide in front of her. The kids never mentioned his name again either. And as far as Quill knew, no one ever went to that drainage ditch again to catch frogs. To this day everyone on the rez regarded that section of the road as haunted. People walked a little faster past that spot. She had seen car windows roll down and a tobacco offering dropped out the window. But the incident itself was never talked about, Jimmy Sky's name never mentioned. Shit happened on the rez and you just kept going.

It was one of the reasons she ran. It calmed the anxiety she seemed to constantly be on the edge of. Maybe she needed to go to work. Or enroll at the tribal college. She recalled how right she felt when she found out she was pregnant with Baby Boy as she completed her freshman year at state university. After he was born, the anxiety crept back up on her. She started running. The endorphins kept the heebie-jeebies at bay. After running Grandma's Marathon in Duluth, she set her sights on the Boston Marathon. Goals kept her focused, kept her mind on something besides the ever-present undercurrent of anxiousness since Jimmy Sky.

Quill scrolled through social media as she finished her coffee. The usual rez drama. Someone overdosed on fentanyl-laced heroin. Drug users beware. Two women were threatening to fight each other over their babies' deadbeat daddy. One person was accusing the tribal treasurer of embezzling money with no proof to back up the accusation. Jittery anxiousness crept through her body. Quill pulled her eyes away from the screen and instead watched Baby Boy run a metal dump truck around the living room floor. She added more vegetables and beef broth to the deer stew.

She texted Crow that she and Punk, and most likely Gaylyn, were going to run around two-thirty—could he come home to be with the little kid until Niswi got off the school bus? They could have PBJs as a snack. Stew was ready for supper. And, she stressed, don't worry.

She puttered around the house doing chores until she heard Betty Boop pull into the driveway. She ran into the bedroom and pulled on her running clothes and shoes. She kissed Baby Boy on the head and was out the door before Crow was out of his pickup. She jumped in her beat-up dark green Saturn and waved at him as she backed out of the driveway.

The houses in the village were set in a square of gravel roads that surrounded the tribal elder housing and the community center. Quill's home was on the first one-mile leg of the gravel road; Punk's home was on the next.

Quill drove down the road and around the corner to Punk's house. She pulled into the driveway and tapped the horn. Usually, Punk ran out immediately, but today she was taking forever. Just as Quill was getting ready to tap the horn again, Punk came running out and, like most everyone else in the village, didn't bother to lock her door behind her. With Punk, everything always needed to match. Today she was wearing a neon-green running suit. If she dyed her hair purple, she'd have to have all purple outfits.

Quill shook her head in amusement as she watched Punk trot to the car. She and Quill were about the same height, and close to the same weight, but Punk filled out her clothes with more curves. Even with her mohawk hairdo, piercings, and tattoos, she seemed more of a girly girl than Quill or Gaylyn. "What's the holdup? We still gotta pick up Gaylyn."

"Hot date on the phone, some steamy phone sex."

"Shuddup." Quill laughed. "Who'd you snag now?"

"No one, just kidding."

Quill looked at her. She could swear Punk was blushing, her head turned so Quill couldn't see her eyes. "Yeah, right."

"Really. Come on, let's get Gaylyn and get to running."

Quill forgot to continue questioning Punk when they started driving. As soon as the car pulled into Gaylyn's driveway, Gaylyn came running out of the torn screen door of her house. Her dad, who had been leaning under the hood of a worn-out car, stood up, wrench grasped in oil-covered hands that matched his oil-covered jeans and flannel shirt. "You better be back here in time to get your ass to work," he hollered at her.

"Yeah, yeah," Gaylyn muttered back at him. She was a tall, lean woman with waist-length brown hair. Only slightly younger than Quill and Punk, she always treated them as if they were years and years older. Grateful to hang out with them. To be a part of their squad. Part of their crew. Gaylyn tended to be a woman of few words—or Indiaanish, as folks called the quiet ones—whether from innate shyness or just being the baby of the trio. Although recently she entered some of their longer conversations. When she had first started running with the two women, she'd worn scuffed everyday tennies with a big toe threatening to peek through on the left shoe. Her black leggings were from Walmart and her running jacket was an old gray hoodie. But her long legs were the right amount of challenge for both Quill and Punk.

"Hey you," Quill said to Gaylyn as she hopped in the backseat. "How you doin'?"

"Good."

"We're going to go run that backwoods deer trail off Cemetery Road. About three and a half miles in and three and a half back out. You up for it?"

"Yep."

"Skoden."

CHAPTER FIVE

Quill parked in the same spot as she had the previous day on Cemetery Road. All three got out of the car and did a series of warm-up exercises. Punk, in her neon green, was a bright spot against the winter snow. Quill was wearing a lavender suit with one embossed eagle feather down the right arm and one on the right leg of the outfit. She and Gaylyn both wore one long braid down their backs. All three wore earmuffs and mittens against the Minnesota winter cold.

As they finished their warm-up routine a large, dark-colored pickup truck came barreling down the road toward them. Even with the winter snow on the gravel road, the truck was kicking up dust. The women stepped behind Quill's car, out of the truck's path. It had tinted windows, darker than allowed by Minnesota or Red Pine tribal law. There was no license plate on the front bumper. Again, required by state and tribal law. The pickup didn't slow as it approached. But when it was about even with where they stood staring at it, the passenger-side window rolled down and a deep male voice hollered out, "Why don'tcha squaws go back to the reservation where you belong?" And the driver slammed on the brakes and turned the wheel hard, kicking up loose gravel that sprayed the women and Quill's car with hard pellets. The driver quickly stepped on the gas and sped off.

"Motherfucker!" screamed Quill. "Goddamn white-ass motherfucker!"

"Get back here, chickenshit!" hollered Punk. "Kick your ass from here to downtown Duluth."

Gaylyn stared at them. Brushed the dust off her clothes. "I tried to get his license plate, but it was covered with mud. There's no mud around here."

"Asshole must be from the pipeline man camp." Quill, hand on hip, took a long drink from her water bottle.

Punk looked down the road, which was now empty. "What if he comes back? You think the car is safe here?"

"Hope so. I told Crow where we were going and what time we were running. If I don't show up on time, he'll have the whole damn reservation out looking for us, so we better get running. Nothing in the car is worth stealing, and if someone flats the tires or does other damage we can call Crow."

Gaylyn did one last stretch. "I wish that idiot would come back." She swung the stick she carried as if she was chopping off a person's head and took off running.

Quill and Punk raised their eyebrows as they looked at each other before following her.

The women ran the same trail Quill had run the day before. Feeling like protective big sisters, neither Quill nor Punk said anything to Gaylyn about the scream Quill had heard. They paced themselves to stay in sight of each other. They both carried bear or pepper spray. And Gaylyn, in the lead, ran with the stick in her hand. They ran a little more than three miles into the woods, then cut to the right on the narrow deer trail that connected them with the hunting road Quill and Crow had driven up the day before. When they came to the spot where it appeared a struggle had taken place, Gaylyn slowed and ran backward, talking loudly to them. "A car or truck got stuck here. Look at all these tire tracks." She turned around and kept running forward.

The hair on the back of Quill's neck rose as she ran through the area. She could see where not only their pickup had turned around the day before but what must have been Patrick's police car too. She took off her left mitten and put her hand into her jacket pocket. As she continued running, her fingers caressed the round, beaded earring she'd stuffed in the corner of the pocket before heading out. Her fingers felt each tiny bead. In her mind's eye she could see the soft greens, the pale white and purple beads that created a tiny flower design in the ball that covered the earring post. It would have been a tiny purple rosebud against a woman's earlobe.

Quill brushed cold tears off her cheeks with the sleeve of her jacket. Ahead, she could see the opening in the bare trees where the gravel road crossed the trail they were on. *I hope the asshole didn't come back and mess with my car.*

Gaylyn slowed down so that all three ran out onto the road together. The car was as they had left it. There were no new tire tracks to indicate that anyone had been down the road since they'd taken off on their run. Nevertheless, each of the women did stretches as they walked around the car, assessing it for any signs of tampering or damage. There were a couple nicks on the paint from the gravel the truck had thrown at them, but other than that everything was fine. Satisfied that it was safe, Quill unlocked the door and they all got in.

"Oh, thank god," said Punk as the engine turned over for Quill. She laughed. "I hate to admit it, but I was a bit scared there. If I snagged me a hot cop we'd have someone to protect us."

Gaylyn's soft voice from the backseat said, "Ain't scared of no redneck punk."

Quill reached under the front seat and pulled out her cellphone, unlocking it with her middle finger. "This thing is ice cold. I should have kept it on me." She handed it to Punk. "Punk, can you text Crow and tell him we're on our way home?"

"You're the only person I know who would have their fingerprint ID as their middle finger. What the heck."

"Yeah, well, if someone ever tries to force me to open my phone for them, they'll get the finger."

They all laughed.

"I'm going to call Patrick and tell him about that truck," Quill said. "If it was someone from the rez we could report it, but we'd have to have a license plate to report. Or we'd see the guy's face. No one is supposed to have their windows tinted that dark. Can't even tell who's trying to kill you."

Punk set Quill's phone on the dash. "There, I told him you were safe and sound."

"Is there a secret you guys aren't telling me?" Gaylyn asked.

Punk looked at Quill. Quill shrugged and nodded, signaling, *Go ahead and tell her.* So Punk did. "Do *not* go running without us," she emphasized.

All three were silent for a couple of miles. Although no one mentioned it, they all kept their eyes out for the pickup truck from earlier. The sky was turning a soft orange as the sun moved toward the western horizon.

Gaylyn broke the silence. "My auntie up in Fort Frances, she went to Thunder Bay. To go shopping. No one heard from her for about six months. They found her body in a canola field up toward Thompson, Manitoba. Cops said she was trying to hitchhike to Thompson. We don't even know anyone up that way. By the time they found her they said they couldn't tell how she died. They listed cause of death as exposure to the elements." She paused, then added softly, "She's the one that made my jingle dress for me."

Quill and Punk looked at each other. Gaylyn's story reminded Quill about the scream in the woods and she could tell that Punk was thinking the same. Quill looked in the rearview mirror. Gaylyn stared out the passenger window, which was all fogged up from her breathing. But she was looking out as if she could see the trees go by. Neither Quill nor Punk said anything.

Punk always talked about everything. Couldn't shut her up. Talked about details of her life that maybe you didn't even want to know, or gave too much information to begin with. Gaylyn was the opposite—a closed book as long as Quill had known her. Even on the rez, where everyone seemed to know everyone, and everyone knew bits and pieces, true or not, of everyone's business, no one seemed to know too much about Gaylyn.

She and her family lived in one of the HUD houses. Her family had lived on the reservation for as long as anyone could remember.

When Quill saw Gaylyn's mom shopping for groceries at Walmart she always seemed run down, weary, tired, worn out. A long string of words to describe a woman who with each step seemed to use more effort than necessary as she pushed the red cart through the food aisles. A cart regularly filled with carb-heavy, artificial, dinner-in-a-box meals. Salted chips of various sorts sat where people's babies would normally ride, strapped in their car seats, kicking their moms' stomachs. A large pack of toilet paper sat on the bottom shelf of the cart. All the junk food gave credence to the idea that at least one sibling was still at home with Gaylyn.

There were rumors that her dad drank and that he was mean. Quill could count on one hand the times she had seen Gaylyn's dad. There were lots of beat-up cars that didn't run that sat by houses on the rez, but Quill knew that Gaylyn got in a car that sat outside her house and drove it to work. The driver's door was red, the passenger side pale blue, and the hood a blemished black.

Quill thought back to when she'd seen him just earlier that day as she was picking up Gaylyn. He was a skinny man with a back stooped by despair or shame. She couldn't guess which.

Before that, when Gaylyn was still in high school, she stood out in front of her house and watched Punk and Quill run by. Grown folks called her "tall and lanky." The kids at school called her Sketti, short for "sketti noodle." Her skin-and-bones frame was just shy of six feet. She wore blue jeans and a dark hoodie, the uniform of all teens on the rez. Hers a bit more ragged than most.

Back then, when Quill began to run, she ran the roadway that went around the village. Punk, who wanted to lose weight, soon joined her. They would do a slow loop past the houses that sat back off the gravel roads. They ran carrying long sticks to keep the rez dogs at bay. They would pass the elder housing and wave at the seniors who peered out at them from behind curtained windows. They ran backward past the community center to wave at folks going in and out the doors. People in the village thought they were crazy. Punk was accustomed to standing out, sought out the attention. Quill not so much. But once she started running, she knew she'd found her "thing."

After about three weeks of steady running, both Punk and Quill noticed the young girl who stood outside her house each day to watch them. She would come outside as they ran past, which made the two women wonder if she was watching and waiting for them to come by. It was Punk who said, "We should see if she wants to run with us."

The next time they ran, both Punk and Quill waved at her to join them. Gaylyn quickly ducked back inside the house. Punk and Quill looked at each other, shrugged, and kept running. They weren't much farther than two houses down the road when they heard footsteps coming up behind them. They turned and looked. There was Gaylyn, in her jeans and ragged hoodie, a grubby pair of tennis shoes on her sockless feet. They slowed slightly to let her catch up and then the three of them ran two more laps around the village loop.

When they neared Gaylyn's house on the second lap, she waved and ran down the driveway to her house. In the years since, she had become a steady runner with them. They did tribal 5Ks and then longer runs in the city of Duluth. The 10K down in the Cities. Finally, Grandma's Marathon in Duluth. And they kept running.

A few months into running around the village, Punk, without saying anything, handed Gaylyn a pack of running socks. A couple weeks later Punk gave her a pair of brand-name running shoes, saying, "I ordered these in the wrong size off Amazon. If they fit, take 'em. I'm too lazy to send 'em back."

After Gaylyn graduated high school and started working at the casino, it seemed she had a little more money to spend on herself. Her running gear improved and she even bought herself a new pair of running shoes, but she still wore the shoes Punk gave her when she first started running with them. They were her everyday shoes now. Without asking, Quill figured most of Gaylyn's earnings were going to support whoever else was living in her home.

When they dropped Gaylyn off, Punk hollered after her, "No running without us! Hear?"

Gaylyn waved agreement as she bounded up the wooden steps leading into her family's HUD house. Smoke rose and tilted to the east from the chimney in the middle of the roof. Her dad was still tinkering under the hood of the car. Quill dropped Punk off next. Punk said, "Go straight home so I don't have to deal with Crow calling me every five minutes wondering where you are and threatening to send out a search party."

"Yeah, right," responded Quill.

CHAPTER SIX

After Punk hopped out, Quill did as she was told and drove straight home.

Crow was in the yard pulling Baby Boy and Niswi around on an old yellow plastic sled. Each of her children, dressed in snow pants and thick down jackets, looked like they had gained twenty pounds. Crow held a rope that was tied to the sled and he was swinging it around in a circle before letting go. Niswi wrapped her arms around Baby Boy as they flew across the yard on the sled until it banged into a snow pile, or a shrub. If it headed toward a tree, Niswi tipped them out to avoid hitting the tree.

The innocent joy on her family's faces wrenched Quill's heart. Everyone in her small part of the world was safe, unaware of the dangers close by.

Niswi called, "Come on, Mom! Ride with me, ride with me."

"Get on," said Crow, standing Baby Boy up on his feet. "Let me spin you around."

Quill got on with Niswi. While she didn't weigh more than 110 pounds, she was more weight than either of the kids, and when Crow spun them around, she held tightly to Niswi as they went flying across the yard when he let go of the rope. Niswi squealed with excitement. Quill, the adrenaline of the day spun out of her body and replaced by the thrill of the moment, tried to gauge how to steer the round plastic disc away from the largest pine tree in the yard. She stuck out a foot into the snow and kicked, sending them uphill on the driveway, where they came to a stop in a snow rut.

"Again, again," said Niswi.

"Nah. You and your brother go, I'm gonna take a shower then put food on the table. Your dad's been playing all afternoon. One of us has to work." She hugged Niswi and gave Crow a kiss on the lips. Playfully she pushed Niswi into a snow pile, then picked up Baby Boy and put him on the sled. "Tell your daddy to give you a ride," she said, and headed into the house.

Quill and Crow sat at the dining room table playing the card game cribbage. Supper was finished and Niswi was in her room for the night. Crow rocked Baby Boy to sleep. Ever since language camp they had tried to play a nightly game in which they counted in Ojibwe to help them learn the language. Crow was twelve pegs ahead of Quill on the board with the crib, the spare hand belonging to him. Quill had a hand of sixteen and if Crow didn't hit fifteen or get a "go," giving him a free peg on the board, she was set to win the game.

"Patrick called today while you were out running. Ashi-naanan nizh." He laid a seven on her eight card and moved two pegs ahead.

"What'd he say? Niizhtana ashi-naanan." She laid a jack.

Crow studied his cards. "They haven't heard of anyone making a report or of a woman missing. Might have been a couple out there having a domestic. Nisimidana." He laid down a five.

"Wasn't a domestic."

"They don't have anything else to go on at this point. He said he would let me know if he heard anything. And that maybe you women should run on the main roads. Or maybe even the track over at the high school."

"Maybe they oughtta do more patrolling." Quill looked at the cards in her hand. No ace. No way to make thirty-one and peg out. "Damnit. Go."

"Nisimidana ashi-bezhig." He laid an ace down and moved his peg forward again.

Quill dropped her cards. "You win. Even if I count my cards you win. Seriously, if it was a domestic it would have been posted on Facebook by now. Too good of a story for the community not to gossip about. That scream gave me the creeps, Crow. You hear about all the missing and murdered women, kinda freaks you out. And I need to train for Boston. Running in circles on a high school track isn't going to cut it."

Crow gathered the deck of cards and cribbage board and put the game set on top of the fridge. "Come on, let's go to bed."

Quill followed him into their room. Crow picked up Baby Boy and softly put him in his crib. He gently patted the boy's back to keep him asleep. "We're going to have to get him a regular bed. Look, his feet almost touch the end of the crib."

"Go into Duluth and see what they have at Walmart. Or maybe Barbie has an extra bed she'd loan us."

Both pulled off their clothes and crawled under the sheets and the dark blue star quilt. Crow pulled Quill into his arms. "I mean it. I don't want you out there running alone."

"I know. Punk and Gaylyn went with me today. Be quiet. Kiss me."

When Quill woke up the next morning Baby Boy was running a yellow toy dump truck around the living room. Crow had gotten Niswi off to school and was sitting at the table drinking a cup of coffee, scrolling through his phone. "I'm heading over to the vehicle maintenance building. A catalytic converter was stolen off one of the trucks. Damn drug addicts. This might take me all day. I'll either have to run into Duluth for parts or order from the Cities."

Quill poured herself a cup of coffee. Added cream from the fridge. "I'm going to drive over to Leech Lake and see if Giigoonh Jones has any new beadwork for sale. Baby Boy and I will have an adventure."

Quill saw a cloud cross Crow's face.

Before he could say anything, she said, "I'll call Punk or Gaylyn and see if they'll ride with?"

Crow got up and put on his winter coat and a stocking cap. "Don't spend all our hard-earned money on Giigoonh's beadwork. Every time we see that woman selling at a powwow, I'm out at least a hundred bucks."

"She makes the best beaded earrings around. And besides, I'm just looking."

"That's what you always say." He kissed Quill. "Be safe. Watch out for ice on the road."

"Always."

Quill downed her coffee and quickly got dressed. She put warmer clothes on the boy than his dad had dressed him in. "Come on, sweet boy, we're gonna go for a ride." She texted Punk and Gaylyn to see if either of them or both wanted to ride along. Gaylyn responded right away that she needed to work her housekeeping shift at the casino hotel in the afternoon, starting at two. Quill assured her they would be back before then.

Gaylyn asked, "ETA?"

"Shortly."

Quill called Punk when she didn't get a response to her text. When Punk finally answered, it was clear from her groggy tone she was just waking up. When Quill asked her about riding with them to Leech Lake, Punk giggled. "Nah, girl, I got better things to do this A.M."

"I bet," Quill responded. "Sounds like you got someone in that bed with you. Tell him to get up and get to work. That is, if he has a job. Get your butt out of bed and ride with us. I'll be there in less than five minutes."

Punk groaned. Quill heard a muffled "Gotta get up" before the phone clicked off.

Quill put Cheerios, water, an apple, and gummy fruit snacks into a bag. Living in northern Minnesota meant you never left home for a drive in the winter without extra food, blankets, and good winter boots.

Quill remembered Thanksgiving a few years back. Baby Boy was an infant. They loaded up the car to go visit one of Crow's brothers down in Hinckley. When they left their home, the sun was shining and there were still blades of green grass showing through on the dried fall lawn. Halfway to Hinckley a snowstorm moved in from the west. Within a half a mile they were in a whiteout. Crow slowed the car to twenty-seven mph, hoping no semi would come barreling up behind them. Or if it did, that the truck driver would see their taillights in time to swerve into the next lane.

He crept along Interstate 35 as both he and Quill leaned forward in the front seat as if the twelve more inches would give them greater visibility through the blowing snow. Luckily a gust of wind cleared the road ahead in time for them to see the green exit sign to Hinckley. Once they were off the freeway, driving through the small town, the houses created a barrier to the wind and snow, so they were able to find his brother's house safely.

They ate turkey with all the trimmings. Told groan-worthy jokes about Pilgrims and Indians. His brother and sister-in-law insisted on taking pictures of everyone together. By early evening the storm blew over, and on the night ride home a crescent moon and Orion shone brightly overhead.

But today the weather was clear, and the report online said it would be sunny all day. Quill grabbed her phone and the plastic bag of food. Filled a travel mug with the rest of the coffee. She helped Baby Boy out to the car and into his car seat. Picked up Punk, who was dressed all in black with a bright green scarf around her neck and matching bright green mittens.

"Whoa. What's up with the mittens?"

"My grandma made 'em for me. Don't hate on my mitts."

"Psssh, girl, those mittens would wake the dead."

Punk took one off and swatted Quill on the arm. "Leave me and my grandma's mittens alone."

Next stop was to pick up Gaylyn, who was waiting outside on her front steps, breathing out cold winter mist with each breath. Quill barely stopped the car when Gaylyn ran over and hopped in.

"Warmth," she said as she held her bare hands up into the warmth of the front seat.

Quill glanced back at her. "There's an extra pair of mittens in the glove box. Can you get 'em for her, Punk?"

Punk did. Gaylyn sat back, put her seatbelt on, then rubbed her hands together for additional warmth.

As Quill zipped down the highway, twenty miles over the speed limit, she skillfully scanned the road ahead for ice and the side ditches for suicidal deer. She talked about running and said, as she looked at Gaylyn in the rearview mirror, "You almost scared me being so ferocious about that pickup truck."

Gaylyn responded with a "Hmmph."

They talked about the asshole who had been driving. Punk gossiped about a mutual friend who slept with her sister's "man" and got p.g. How the guy tried to say that a long time ago all Indian men married two wives. The un-p.g. sister kicked him out. And the p.g. sister quit the relationship but stayed p.g. and had the kid on her own. She and the kid were living with the un-p.g. sister now. Gaylyn said she knew that sister. Quill admitted she'd followed the drama on Facebook.

"I'd have to kill Crow."

"Girl, you got nothin' to worry about. That guy's so in love with you he can't see straight," Punk said.

"Better stay that way." Quill laughed.

"Look. There goes one of those pickups with no plates in front." Punk pointed at a pickup driving the opposite way.

Gaylyn quickly turned around in her seat to try and read the rear plates. "His rear plates are mudded over. We should find their camp, sneak in at night, and wash the mud off all the plates."

"Oh yeah, that would be a real adventure," said Quill.

Baby Boy started to chant, "Hungry muffin. Hungry muffin."

"My kid's been so quiet I almost forgot I brought him. Hand Baby Boy some of those gummy snacks, would you, Punk?"

Punk rummaged around the food bag and handed the fruit snacks across the backseat. "Does this kid have a real name?"

"I don't remember. He's been Baby Boy for so long," Quill joked.

"OMG. He'll be in seventh grade and the teacher will say, 'What's your name?' and he'll say 'Baby Boy.' "

They all laughed.

At a sign that read WELCOME TO THE LEECH LAKE BAND OF OJIBWE, Quill said, "Look, here's the turnoff to Giigoonh's. Drove all this way, hope she's home."

Quill turned off the highway onto a well-maintained gravel side road. They passed a few HUD houses that sat back off the road. The farther they went the thicker the forest got. "Lookit, there's the carved walleye statue she has marking her driveway," Quill said as they pulled in. Giigoonh's yard had toys strewn around—abandoned Hot Wheels, assorted bikes with one tire or no handlebars. At the tree line were abandoned cars, their dead headlights looking longingly toward the house. A brand-new shiny SUV was parked by the front steps. "She must be home. You fend off any rez dogs while I get what's-his-name out of his car seat."

Gaylyn muttered under her breath, "Sure, leave the deadly job to me."

Giigoonh wore black elastic-waist pants and a very thin, well-worn nurse's uniform top as a blouse. On her feet were bright yellow Crocs, sans socks in the cold winter air. She stood, holding her front door open, as the trio walked up to her house. "Come on in. What brings the Red Pine riffraff over this way? Let me put on a fresh pot of coffee."

Giigoonh lived in an old-style HUD house. You walked in the front door right into the living room and straight ahead to the kitchen. The room was toasty warm and filled with the smell of freshly brewed coffee. There were dreamcatchers hung on each wall along with Southwest Indian prints in cheap fake-gold-trimmed frames. A star quilt in varying shades of dark orange and yellow hung across the back of the couch that faced the biggest TV screen Quill had ever seen.

"Sit down, sit down," Giigoonh said as she pointed to wooden chairs around the kitchen table. The table was strewn with odd teacup saucers that held various shades of tiny beads. Beading needles, beading thread, and beadwork in different stages of being finished sat next to or on the china that held their color of beads. "Let me turn on Disney Channel for the boy." She fiddled with her oversized TV until Mickey Mouse showed his ears. "There you go, kid." Without ceremony she picked him up and sat him on her couch.

Back in the kitchen area, she poured three cups of steaming

coffee and edged them between the saucers of beads in front of each woman. "Good to see you. What brings you this way?"

"We were wondering what new beadwork you have for sale," answered Quill.

Giigoonh waved her hand over the table. "This is it. Got beaded lighters. Been working on these big medallions. Great big chubby guys need great big medallions on their great big chests." Laughter around the table. "Hair clips, barrettes. Started making these birch-bark bracelets with copper wire and beads. Lot of work."

The women sat around the table and visited. Quill and Gaylyn would reach out and finger various pieces of bead-work while they talked. Looking at the back clips of the hair barrettes. Punk repeated the same gossip from the car ride over, this time to new ears. Coffee cups were refilled. Talk shifted to the pipeline that was going through and the influx of pipeline workers. Giigoonh said, "I'm an old lady. Went to bingo at the casino last Tuesday and a cute kid, redhead, bearded guy, looked to be in his thirties, called me 'Sweet pea,' all in a syrupy southern drawl, and invited me to his motel room. I said, 'Do I look like a spring flower?' and I dabbed random squares on the bingo cards he was playing. He got all mad and stormed off."

When the laughter quieted down and more coffee was being sipped, Quill brought out the tiny purple-beaded stud she kept in her pocket. "Are you still making these?" she asked Giigoonh, holding it out in the palm of her hand.

"Enyanh." Giigoonh shook her head yes. Then took the earring from Quill. "I made this." She rolled the tiny beaded stud between her thumb and pointer finger the same way Quill had. "For sure." She looked at Quill. "You only have the one?"

"Yeah, I found it in the woods when I was out running on the hunting road. It's beautiful. As soon as I saw it, I said, 'Giigoonh made this.'"

"These are Czech cut-glass beads. Called true cut. Expensive little buggers. Haven't made very many of these. I could only afford a few hanks in different colors. I made red ones, purple ones, and yellow. And such a small-size bead I need to put on my coal miner's helmet to bead."

"What's that?"

Giigoonh reached down into a basket on the floor at her feet. "Glasses, a light, and magnifier all rolled into one. Put it on like I'm going into a cave and I can bead like a crazy woman. Tell me again where you found this?"

"Out running. It's beautiful. I bet the owner misses it."

"I only sold three sets at a hundred fifty bucks a pair. Tiny Czech beads jack up the price. Not many buyers for this quality of work."

"Whew. Bet she wants it back."

"Yeah, not cheap. It's delicate work." She put the magnifier back into the basket at her feet. She stared out her dining room window. The women sat quietly as they watched Giigoonh sort through the memories in her mind.

Turning her head back to the table she said, "Ah! The girl's name was Mabel. Who names their kid Mabel these days? That's an old lady's name. Heck, when I was a kid the old ladies were named Mabel. What the heck was her last name?" She looked again out her window. A sparrow flew by. Snow dropped from a pine bough at the edge of her yard. Quill took a sip of the strong but tepid coffee from her cup with a Jackpot Junction logo on it. She looked over at Punk's cup, a red metal camping cup with white flecks all over it.

Giigoonh snapped her fingers. "Beaulieu. That's who bought the purple ones. I only had one purple pair beaded at the time. Mabel Beaulieu. Beautiful girl. Long black hair past her butt. She didn't need to put all that eyebrow makeup on that some young women wear these days." She looked pointedly at Punk. "Perfect eyebrows. Mabel Beaulieu. Who goes and names their kid Mabel? Couldn't forget a name like that. Guess there's a Beaulieu running around out there who did, huh?"

"Where is she from? I can try to track her down and get her earring back to her." Quill reached over and picked up the earring from the table in front of Giigoonh. Put it back in the crease of her jacket pocket. Tucked it in safe.

"Hmmmm. Seem to recall she said she was staying in Duluth. But she was from Fort Frances. No, not Fort Frances. Rainy River? Fort McKay? Sorry. It was a reserve up north that starts with 'Fort.' But she was staying in Duluth."

"She say where?"

"No. But I got the impression she was new out of treatment. She said the earrings were to celebrate her new life on the Red Road of Sobriety. You know that shiny look folks have once they get off the alcohol and drugs. She was filled with excitement about a sober life."

"Maybe she was at the halfway house in Duluth. I can check there."

"You girls want more coffee?" Giigoonh pushed her chair back from the table.

"No. No, thank you. We should head back home. The kid should sleep on the drive all the way home. Take his nap in the car."

"I wanna get these." Punk picked up a matching set of yellow barrettes from one of the saucers.

"Those don't have the backs yet." Giigoonh got up and walked out of the room. Came back with a handful of finished barrettes and set them down in front of Punk, who picked out some yellow ones. "I only have three pairs of those tiny stud earrings left." She laid the earrings on the table in front of Quill.

Quill picked up each pair and gently rolled them around between the tips of her fingers. One set was a purple replica of the single one Quill kept in her pocket. Quill placed the pair on the table. "I'll take these."

Giigoonh ran the women's credit cards on a small white card reader she stuck into her smartphone, then handed the women their purchases. Quill stuffed hers in her pocket and Punk's went into her saddlebag-size purse. Quill got Baby Boy pried from the TV and into his coat. Waves and quick hugs were exchanged at the door.

Twenty miles down the road, Punk stated, "We came all the way over here, and I bought barrettes I don't need. And you bought a pair of hundred-fifty-dollar earrings? What the heck?"

Quill stared at the road in front of her.

"Come on, what's up?"

"Remember I told you about the scream?"

"So?"

"When Crow and I went back out there the next day, I found this earring."

"And you didn't turn it in to the cops? Every cop show warns you not to mess with the evidence."

"I didn't know it was evidence until after I picked it up and put it in my pocket. Crow doesn't even know I have it."

"Well, it's got your DNA all over it now. If she's dead they'll haul you in. I'll have to get the Innocence Project involved to clear your name."

"Shuddup!"

Punk laughed. "Serious."

"We don't need DNA. Giigoonh knows she made it and who she sold it to. We can go into Duluth and ask around. See if we can find this Mabel Beaulieu."

"Oh my god. Remind me again why I'm your friend? All you do is drag me into trouble. And then Crow yells at me. Thinks I'm the instigator. Heck, I'm just a follower at heart. He thinks because I have a mohawk and a few piercings everything is my fault."

"A few? And Crow yells at you? He never yells at me."

"'Cause he's scared to death you'd punch him. Or leave him. You all Miss Perfect Indian."

"Hey, look behind us. Is that the same truck we passed when we were going to Giigoonh's?" Gaylyn asked, her head turned around to look behind them.

Quill looked in the rearview mirror and saw a maroon pickup truck, oversized tires, with tinted windows that made it impossible to see the driver or passenger if there was one. And no front license plate. The vehicle was on the road about two car lengths behind them. "How long has it been back there?" asked Quill.

"I saw it at the crossroad back a bit. When it pulled out it sped up and I thought it was going to pass us, but it slowed down and stayed behind."

"I'll see if he passes," Quill said as she lifted her foot off the accelerator. The truck behind them appeared to back off, keeping the same distance between the two vehicles. Quill looked at the road ahead and saw four cars headed in their direction, which made it impossible for the truck behind them to pass safely on the two-lane highway.

"This is creeping me out," said Punk, as she turned to look behind them. "Is that the same truck that threw gravel at us back when we were running?"

"Nah, there's so many trucks on the road these days. It's hard to tell one from the other," said Quill.

"Well, just speed up. Get us home as fast as you can."

Quill pushed the gas pedal, watched the speedometer needle creep up to eighty, then ninety mph. The truck stayed behind them.

"Should I text Crow? What's the point of having a husband if you can't keep him on speed dial for emergencies?"

Quill looked in her mirrors again. "We're fine. It's broad daylight with other cars on the road."

On the side of the road up ahead she could see the green road sign that read APAKWANAGEMAG RESERVATION in white lettering with RED PINE RESERVATION in English underneath the Ojibwe.

As she whipped past the sign, a tribal cop car, lights flashing, zipped out from a crossroad where he had been hiding among some pine trees. As she braked to slow down and pull over to the side of the road, the truck behind her slowed too. Driving the speed limit, the truck passed them. A white hand emerged at the top of the passenger-side window, which was slightly rolled down, and waved as it went by.

Gaylyn said, "Leave me the fuck alone." Under her breath to the passing truck.

Quill rolled down her car window as the tribal cop approached. She pulled her license and insurance card out from her jeans' back pocket.

Quill didn't recognize the cop. He had a military haircut and sharp edges to his body that said maybe all he ever did in his spare time was work out.

He bent down and looked at the women without removing his sunglasses. Quill briefly wondered to herself, sarcastically, if the snow glare bothered his eyes. He tilted his head to look beyond Quill to where Punk sat. He stood back up and stared down the road ahead of them. Quill held her license and insurance card at the window for him to take.

The cop leaned back down. "You were twenty miles over the speed limit."

Punk leaned toward the driver's side of the car. "We thought those idiots in the maroon truck were chasing us. They're the ones you should have stopped. We were just trying to get safely home. Thank god you pulled us over."

The cop and Punk were talking over Quill as she leaned back in her seat and watched the exchange.

"They were chasing you?"

"I don't know. Maybe. They been following us for like ten miles. Quill would slow down, they'd slow down. Finally, she just sped up to get us home as fast as possible."

"Where do you live?"

"In the village." Punk pointed up the road.

"You get a license plate?" He stood back up and looked down the road again.

Punk leaned on the steering wheel to get closer to the driver's window. "It was covered with mud. And their windows are tinted so dark you can't see who's in there. Didn't you hear about the woman who was attacked out in the woods around here? That could have been us."

Quill looked hard at Punk. She could swear Punk was flirting with the cop. Or then again, maybe she was just working hard to get the cop's attention off Quill's speeding.

"Can I see your ID?" he asked Punk, leaning back down.

She reached across Quill to shake the cop's hand. "Punk Fairbanks. I wasn't driving though. No ID on me."

He stood up, looked up the road. "Well, I'll give you girls a warning this time. Considering the circumstances. Take care. And if they show back up, call the tribal station, don't try to outrun them."

"All right. Chi-miigwech," gushed Punk.

Quill watched him in her rearview mirror as he walked back to his cruiser.

"He's kinda cute, don't you think?" Punk asked.

Quill responded, turning the key in the ignition, "If you go for the robo-cop type. 'Give you girls a warning,' my ass." She signaled and pulled out onto the road. She could see in her rearview mirror the cop driving back into his hiding spot. She scoffed again. " 'Girls.' "

Two miles down the road the dark pickup pulled out from a side road and again dropped two car lengths behind them. Quill and Punk looked at each other, fear in their eyes. Gaylyn muttered, "Asshole."

"I'm going to drive to the casino, and if we don't lose them there, I'll drive to the tribal police station, okay?" Quill said.

"I can't be late for work," said Gaylyn.

Punk nodded. She twisted around in the seat so both she and Gaylyn could watch the truck behind them.

At the casino, Quill drove around the hotel lot to drop Gaylyn off at the service door. She then drove to a corner of the building where, partially hidden, they could watch the gamblers' parking lot. At the same time, the women saw the truck pull into a parking spot. Quill drove slowly down the next row and watched for whoever was in the truck to get out. It was two men, too bundled up in winter gear for her to get a good look at their features.

As the men entered the casino doors, Quill slammed on the brakes and opened the car door.

"What are you doing?" Punk asked.

"Getting the license plate."

"Are you crazy? Someone will see you." Punk looked frantically around the parking lot.

"Get real. All anyone cares about is their next big win." Quill jumped out of the car, leaving it running and the door open.

She ran to the maroon truck and swiped the dirt off the back license plate with her mittened hand. Punk yelled, "Quill, they're coming back!"

Quill spun around to dash back to the car.

"Hey!" one of the men yelled. Both men walked as fast as the snow and ice on the pavement would allow them to move. Quill, less cautious, ran and jumped in the car. She threw it into drive and sped off. In her rearview mirror she saw the two men, standing at the end of the parking aisle, staring after her.

At Punk's urging, Quill circled the casino, where they sat in the employee parking lot for a long nervous ten minutes. Punk scolded Quill. "What the hell were you thinking? You got your kid in the car."

"I got part of the plate—NW—then a P or an R. That mud was plastered on. My heart's pounding out of my chest. Did you get a look at them?"

"Nah. Too bundled up. Cops aren't going to be able to track a plate off of just two letters. You're crazy, you know that right?"

"Leave me alone." Quill pulled out of the parking spot and drove out on the opposite side of the casino.

CHAPTER SEVEN

It was prime rib and all-you-can-eat crab leg night at the casino buffet, and tribal members got a 20 percent discount. It was the one evening a month Crow and Quill dined out at the casino for their "Indian Date Night." Even though Quill was leery of returning to the casino because she was worried the two men might still be there, she still helped Crow load the kids into her Saturn. Knowing he was already worried about the woman in the woods, Quill didn't tell him about the truck that had followed them back to the reservation. She asked about his day and listened to him talk about mufflers and alternators while they dropped Baby Boy off at Barbie's and drove the ten miles to the casino. They stood in a long line of dark-haired, dark-skinned Indians, many with kids in tow. Clumps of white-haired white men and women, some in wheelchairs, some leaning on walkers, some with oxygen tanks strapped over their shoulders, were interspersed among the gamblers and family groups along the line.

At the slot machines next to the buffet line, a loud group of middle-aged white men hooted and hollered as wheels spun, lights glittered. They didn't seem to care whether they were winning or losing. They took turns feeding the machines. They laughed loudly, slapped one another on the back or punched one another on the shoulder, their laughter and roughhousing punctuated by loud swear words.

Niswi moved behind her dad and hid her head underneath his jacket. There was a tug on Quill's heart as she realized her young daughter was already learning not to trust certain men. It broke her heart that Niswi felt compelled to seek the safety of her dad in the presence of a group of grown men. At the same time, Quill was grateful that Crow was the man he was, the safety net of their small family.

One of the men saw Quill looking their way and winked. She turned her back to him. She shivered and quickly looked back toward the guy when it occurred to her that he might be one of the men who was in the truck chasing them. The guy winked at her again. Quill couldn't tell if he was from the truck or not. She moved closer to Crow, her back to the casino floor. Relieved when they finally reached the front of the line and were able to enter the buffet.

As Crow went to the buffet to get his plate of food, Quill asked Niswi about school. When Crow returned, she went and got a plate for herself and helped Niswi get hers. On the way back to their table, she stopped and chatted with a few people, working her way around to asking if they knew a Mabel Beaulieu. They all said no between mouthfuls of food.

One woman mentioned the recovery halfway house in Duluth. Quill responded with "Yeah, we thought about that.

Might be the best bet for finding Mabel if she was in treatment. We'll check it out."

Niswi got impatient with the grown-up talk, tugged her mom's arm, and said, "Come on, Mom."

Back in the booth, plates piled high with crab legs, Quill told Crow about driving over to Leech Lake. She didn't share the reason for the visit other than to look at beadwork. For some reason she didn't quite understand herself, Quill felt an attachment to the woman whose earring it was. Whether it was realistic or not, she felt that if she didn't talk about it, in the same way that no one ever talked about Jimmy Sky, somehow keeping the earring secret and in her pocket kept Mabel Beaulieu safe. At least in her mind Mabel was still out there, waiting to be found.

While they ate, they talked, laughed, and greeted friends who walked by their table. After multiple plates of prime rib and crab legs, with stomachs full, the family left the buffet. Crow held Niswi's hand in his left and his right arm was across Quill's shoulder as they walked toward the glass sliding exit doors of the casino.

Twenty feet ahead, one of the security guards at the door stopped two men who were also leaving. They were the same caliber of men as the one who'd winked at Quill earlier. She wished she was closer to determine whether one of them was the same guy or not. One man had an arm wrapped around the waist of a long-haired Indian woman. Another guy's hand appeared to be holding her up under the armpit of the black satin jacket she wore with the tribal insignia on it. She stumbled as they propelled her forward to get past the security guard, who continued to hold his hand up in the stop position.

As Crow and Quill got closer, she heard the guard sharply say, "Hey."

"What's up, chief?" one of the men said. "Trying to get my girlfriend outta here. Had a bit too much to drink in the bar."

"Bullshit."

"Whatdya mean?" The guys tried to steer the mostly limp woman around the guard.

"What's her name?"

"Wouldn't you like to know?"

"What's her name, asshole?"

"Fuck you." The two men looked ready to fight.

"That's my cousin." And with that the security guard tasered one guy, who dropped to his knees, hands instinctively reaching for the wires on his chest. The woman dropped out of their arms to the ground. The other man took a swing at the guard as three more guards joined the fracas.

Crow pushed Niswi behind him and told her and Quill to go sit down inside the buffet before pulling his phone out to call the tribal cops.

Niswi followed her dad's instructions, but Quill broke away and ran to the woman lying on the floor. She grabbed her by the sleeves of her jacket and pulled her from the center of the brawl. Crow rushed to help. Quill felt the woman's neck for a pulse. The woman's skin was cold and clammy. The edges of her lips were tinted blue. But there was a faint beat. "Get Narcan!" she yelled at Crow, who rushed to the hotel desk a few feet away then hurried, opening the Narcan on his way back.

Quill had taken a health management class with Punk and Gaylyn in preparation for the longer marathons. Because opioid addiction was on the rise on the reservation and in neighboring communities, part of the training included an afternoon of learning the signs of opioid overdose and the administration of Narcan. She grabbed the syringe from Crow, squeezed the woman's thigh, and injected it. The hotel clerk rushed over with a complete first-aid kit. She asked, "CPR?" as she held out a mouth shield.

Crow, who was part of the tribe's volunteer fire department, dropped to the carpet, put the shield over the woman's mouth, and put his hand behind her neck, lifting while pinching her nose, and began breathing into her.

Quill, kneeling beside him, looked toward the front door. Tribal police, including Patrick, arrived. One man from the brawl was in handcuffs and being escorted to the waiting squad cars that were pulled up at the sliding doors. The man who'd been tasered was sitting on the floor, his back against the security podium. Quill could see ambulance lights turning in to the circular drive.

When the EMTs entered the doorway pulling a gurney, she hollered, "Over here." They rushed over. Quill stood and looked around the casino until she spotted Niswi at the buffet window that looked out on the casino floor. She waved an "All's okay" wave. Niswi gave a timid wave back.

Police pulled the tasered man up and walked him out to a squad car. A crowd of Indian elders gathered at the end of the slot machines. They whispered to one another behind hands held to their mouths. This was more excitement than getting bingo at Coverall. Crow explained to the EMTs what had transpired and gave them the syringe Quill had used and told them the dosage of Narcan. They put an oxygen mask on the woman and gave her a second shot of Narcan after placing her on the gurney.

The EMTs asked for the woman's name. Crow motioned for the security guard who'd said he was the woman's cousin to come over. Patrick stepped in closer. Quill and Crow stood, arms around each other's waists, and listened to the exchange between the security guard and Patrick.

"Her name's Julie Jackson. You know her, Patrick. That guy's not her boyfriend. Her boyfriend, Migizi, is home with their kid. I saw her come in earlier with her girlfriend, Lisa, if I remember her name right."

"Do you see her? Lisa? Is she around here now?" Patrick asked.

The EMTs started to wheel the gurney out to the ambulance.

"Where you taking her?" the security guard called after them. "I gotta call her partner and her ma."

"St. Mary's," one of the guys hollered over his shoulder.

Patrick asked again, "Do you see the girl Lisa?"

"No."

"She from around here?"

"Cloquet maybe. I have seen her around."

"Take me upstairs to the security cameras. Maybe we can find her."

Quill watched them walk off. She looked around and realized she and Crow were the only ones still standing where all the excitement had occurred. The elders were back at bingo. There was a new line at the buffet. People were seated at the slot machines—wheels spinning, lights flashing. Crow went back into the buffet and walked out with Niswi. The sliding exit doors were closed, and security stood in clumps of two or three talking under their breath about what had happened.

Quill took a deep breath. Put her hand into her jacket

pocket and felt the nubs of the earrings stuck in there. When Crow and Niswi reached her, she put her arms over Niswi's shoulders and walked with her husband and daughter out to the car. Here on the rez, shit happened, and you just kept going.

CHAPTER EIGHT

At home, Quill sat at the kitchen table searching for Mabel Beaulieu on the internet. Anxiousness coursed through her body while Baby Boy snored a baby snore, fast asleep on the couch, where Crow was also sleeping, his arm thrown across his small son. She found a page with a profile picture of a beautiful young woman dressed in a dark blue jingle dress. It was the sacred healing dress of the Ojibwe people, dreamt into existence by a father during the deadly Spanish flu pandemic of 1918. Every Ojibwe jingle-dress dancer, every pow-wow dancer, knows the story of the father who dreamt the dress, asked his wife to make it, and then, when it was put on their very sick daughter to dance in, she was healed.

The young woman also wore a kookum scarf tied over her head and under her chin. Quill knew stories of how in the early 1900s the kookum scarf was a staple accessory for Native women to cover their ears when it was cold, or worn to keep their hair back when leaning over big kettles of boiling maple sap in the spring or when cutting up deer meat on the kitchen table.

More recently, Native women, whose hair was forcibly shorn during the boarding school era, learned to put bobby pins in their shortened hair to create curls. These women tied the kookum scarves under their chins in the style of Hollywood starlets from an earlier time but jingle-dress dancers from Canada had since begun to modernize the scarf.

Quill learned from Mabel's profile pictures and status posts that her family was from Fort St. Patrick in northern Ontario but the family moved to Thunder Bay when she was little. She called herself an urban NDN who was a traditional powwow dancer. She was, or had been, taking business classes at the tribal college. Didn't have a boyfriend or children. One of her last posts was a selfie with two young Indian women. *Sobriety—we got this* was written across the photo. All three with big grins, clear eyes, and hope. Their whole lives ahead of them.

Next Quill searched for Julie Jackson on social media. Found her right away. Lots of profile pictures of her and her newborn. And as many pictures of the baby with her partner. No wild party pictures or baby-daddy drama on her page at all. Both parents beamed with pride, and in the pictures that included them both, they looked happy. Nothing sinister there. Nothing that indicated a party girl willing to head off with a group of men she would have just met.

Contrary to media stories about the missing and murdered women being homeless or street workers or drug addicts, Quill knew from talk around the various communities that all the women were someone's mother, sister, daughter, auntie.

Folks talked in hushed tones about women taken—just taken, most never seen again.

Quill typed "trafficking in northern minnesota" into the search engine and found a recent article in a local newspaper that described a sting operation at a "local casino" where five men were arrested and charged with a "commercial sex crime." Three of the men were pipeline workers who, according to the article, were subsequently fired. The corporation issued a statement saying it had "zero tolerance for such illegal and exploitative actions."

Quill pushed away from the table. Stuffed her arms into a down jacket, pulled a stocking cap down on her head, and threw a scarf around her neck. She kissed Crow on the forehead. "I'm gonna run to the casino and get a midnight snack from a vending machine or the Snack Shack."

He groaned. "Geez. Be careful. And bring me a chocolate bar." And immediately fell back asleep.

The casino was the only place open late at night within a thirty-mile radius of the reservation. It wasn't unheard of for folks from the village to drive there for a soda or a candy bar at all hours of the night. But Quill was more interested in checking out trucks in the parking lot and men at the machines who might be engaged in "exploitative actions" than in getting a candy bar.

She had a knot in her stomach as she pulled out of the driveway and decided to take a quick swing by Punk's to see if she wanted to ride along. Punk's house was dark, and there was an unfamiliar four-door sedan parked out front. Punk didn't own a car, so the presence of this one confirmed Quill's suspicions that Punk was seeing someone. Quill, from force of habit, next drove by Gaylyn's. Through the thin curtain over the living room window, Quill could see into the house, where a dim light was on over the kitchen stove. "Dingy" was the word that came into Quill's mind.

At the casino she drove up and down, viewing the parked cars. Lots of farm pickups bearing Minnesota or Wisconsin plates. A few from Ontario and Iowa. She found two with mudded-over license plates; one was dark-colored, parked next to one that might be black. It was hard to make out the exact colors in the parking lot lights. Quill scanned the lot. Just as she was getting ready to jump out, scrape the mud off and look at the plates, another car, its headlights blinding her in the rearview mirror, pulled up behind her and gave a short tap on the horn, indicating she should move on.

Quill pulled ahead into a parking spot two lanes over. Inside the casino, the bright lights and *ching-ching-ching* of the machines greeted her. She pulled off her gloves and got a free cup of hot coffee from the beverage stand. The cup warmed her cold hands and the steam warmed her face as she lifted it to take a sip.

She walked the carpeted aisles of the slots. Lonely people stared glassy-eyed into the machines—the ones that ate pennies, the ones that sucked in dollar bills or chomped on quarters, eating up mortgages, car payments, and children's school clothes—and smoke swirled up from ashtrays where unsmoked cigarettes sat; gamblers' right hands hit buttons, pulled levers. The ever-present spinning of numbers held their attention, oblivious to Quill walking behind them.

She walked past the 21 tables. A group of men, stubble on their faces, stared expressionless at the cards laid on the table in front of them. Quill struggled to tell one white guy from another. Any one of them might have been the same ones who were in the casino earlier. So far, they were the only men who looked like they might be pipeline workers.

Quill had hoped to find the truck that had followed them. Maybe even figure out which men drove the truck. It was all too impossible to tell. Mission failed and over, she stopped in the gift shop and got two candy bars on her way out, making it a point to walk by the two pickup trucks she'd seen earlier. She figured that since the men went to the trouble to cover their plates, they would notice if she wiped them clean. Instead, in the dust of one truck she drew a four-petaled flower. On the next one she wrote, WASH ME.

The next morning Quill got ready to head to Duluth. She bundled up Baby Boy and got him seated in the car while she wiped a dusting of snow off her car windows. Crow had left early, and his empty candy wrapper remained on the coffee table, near the couch where he had slept all night. A note on the kitchen table said a driver had veered off the road when he hit a deer early in the morning and he needed a tow truck to get his car out of a ditch.

Punk had been messaging all morning, without saying anything except *hey, text me* or *you busy*. She didn't answer Quill's questions about whose car was parked in her driveway overnight. When Quill swung by her house to pick her up, there was no answer to her knock on the door, whereas Gaylyn ran out before Quill pulled all the way into her driveway.

It was a short drive to Duluth and Gaylyn insisted Quill

give her a blow-by-blow description of the fight at the casino. She said that by the time she heard about it way on the other side of the casino hotel and got to the scene of the crime everything had been handled. She asked if Quill knew Julie. Quill asked if Gaylyn knew Julie. They both said no; maybe they knew who she was but not really.

As Quill drove into the city, wide ditches on either side of the road were filled with snow. Farther back from the road were stands of birch and poplar trees interspersed with pine trees. Around a curve, Lake Superior came into view. The inland freshwater ocean stretched out ahead of them. The shipping industry was evident in the harbor. There was a canal with a drawbridge that large international cargo ships passed through even in the dead of winter. A two-thousand-ton Coast Guard cutter rammed through the three-foot-thick ice to keep a water trail open for them. On the freeway side were the businesses that thrive in industrial areas. Corrugated-steel buildings with big doors at the loading dock for trucks to back up to. There were dash-in, dash-out restaurants to feed the port workers. Gas stations. Storage units.

The women continued to talk. While everyone on the rez seemed to always know everyone, there was the rare occasion when people slipped in unnoticed. The tribal college brought a new round of folks from around the neighboring reservations each school year. The casino hired folks from the Cities. And the treatment center that focused on traditional teachings for recovery brought in large groups of Native people from around the upper Midwest and from Canada.

As Quill described Julie, Gaylyn thought she remembered her from high school, and she was sure she knew her boyfriend, Migizi. "He's a solid enough kinda guy, if I remember right."

"Thank god it was her cousin standing there on security. And he had a taser. I half expected to see electricity go into the guy's body. I guess that only happens in the movies." Quill exited off the freeway onto a main street that led up into the very steep and hilly downtown district of Duluth. In her rearview mirror, she could see steam lifting off the water of Lake Superior, its shore frozen with ice.

"Maybe it was the same assholes who sprayed us with gravel," Gaylyn added quietly.

"Or the ones who followed us to the casino yesterday."

"We should be looking for them. Our focus is always on the women who are missing. How come no one ever goes after these men?"

Quill thought for a bit, then said, "We've all heard the stories of the man camps out in the Dakota and Canadian oil fields and the increase in missing women. Apparently, these camps are lawless. Men with no families. And they're protected by the oil companies' own security forces. The guys themselves make good money. You should have seen them in the casino last night while we were standing in line to get into the buffet. They had money to burn at the slot machines. Laughing and joking, not caring how much money they spent." Quill pulled the car into a parking spot on what seemed to be the steepest hill in Duluth. She turned her front wheels toward the curb and put on the emergency brake. "Come on. Let's go see if Mabel Beaulieu lived here at the halfway house."

A carved wooden eagle hung on short chains over the door.

A small sign taped over a doorbell read, FOR THE SECURITY OF OUR RESIDENTS, PLEASE RING DOORBELL. Quill pushed the button. Gaylyn blew warm air from her mouth onto her hands. Finally, she picked up Baby Boy and held him for more warmth.

"Can I help you?" asked a tinny voice that came over the intercom.

"We'd like to talk to a counselor or whoever is in charge?" Quill looked at Gaylyn and shrugged.

"Do you have an appointment?"

"No. Can we talk to a counselor?"

"Children aren't allowed in here unless their parent is a resident and we have prior releases signed by the county. The kid will have to wait in the car."

Surprised, Quill looked up and there was the round dark orb of a camera pointing down at them.

"I'll sit with him," said Gaylyn, already heading back to the car with Baby Boy.

"Here." Quill tossed her the car keys. "Turn it on so you all don't freeze to death."

When the door buzzed, Quill stepped in. It was a rehabbed old house that now carried the aura of an institution. The floors were slick linoleum. Easy to clean. The walls were painted hospital yellow or green. City code sheets papered the wall of the entryway. Straight ahead was an industrial kitchen.

"Turn to your right and come into the reception room," a voice from nowhere directed her. Quill looked up for a camera, then followed the plastic carpet runner to the right. A young Indian woman, whom Quill didn't recognize, sat behind a big metal desk. "Can I get you to sign in?" She handed her a clipboard. "Have a seat and Becky will be out here in a sec."

Quill signed in, then moved to sit in a dark green fake-leather chair with metal armrests. She could hear muted voices coming from behind closed doors in the old house. Quill looked at an old print of an Indian on horseback with a tipi in the background. Here they were about as far north in Ojibwe country along the Great Lakes as one could get, and the picture chosen to represent Indians was of a Plains warrior.

At that moment a big wooden door that covered half the wall behind the receptionist slid open and a line of Native folks emerged. The ones from the rez who recognized Quill nodded. Some looked with blatant curiosity, clearly wondering if she was a new resident. But one look up and down at the woman sitting in the reception chair, a woman who wore quality winter boots and an expensive down jacket, her hair neatly styled (albeit in braids), convinced the residents this was not a new client.

The last person to come out of the room was a tall Scandinavian blonde. Her full chest filled out the snug-fitting wool sweater she wore over a blouse with cuffs and collar peeking out at the neckline and sleeve ends. She looked at Quill. She turned and carried on a hurried, hushed conversation with the receptionist before turning to her. "Come on, we can talk back here." And, without waiting for Quill, she strode back into the room she had moments earlier exited.

As Quill entered the meeting room, she noticed one woman, with the dark hair and skin that said she was not of the Scandinavian type, busily picking up literature and returning coffee cups to a wheeled cart on the far side of the room.

"How can I help you?" the blond woman asked, without introducing herself. Her overall manner suggested Quill was a waste of her time. She quickly sat down in a green chair and motioned to another in a circle of about twenty.

"I'm looking for Mabel Beaulieu," Quill said. "A mutual friend told us she might be staying here."

A flicker of recognition went across the woman's face, but she said, "We're a halfway house. We can't give out information to just anyone that walks in. There are confidentiality laws. How do you know this Mabel Beaulieu?"

Quill said, "She's a distant cousin of mine. Down from Canada. I heard she was here and wanted to say hi."

The woman looked at Quill. She gave her head a tiny shake no before saying, "Sorry, we can't even say if we have a client here by that name or not. Sorry for your wasted trip." She rose from the chair.

"Are you the director?" Quill asked.

"I'm the head counselor here."

"And you are? I'm Quill." She stood and extended her hand out in an offer to shake hands.

"Becky Swenson," the blonde finally offered. Her hand barely grazed Quill's palm. She gestured to the doorway. "I'll walk you out."

Quill had no choice but to leave as Becky Swenson walked her all the way to the entrance. The woman opened the door for Quill and shut it behind her.

Quill stood on the sidewalk and looked back at the door. She looked up at the security camera and then over to her car. The engine was running, and she could hear country music coming out of the car's radio.

"What happened?" asked Gaylyn as she rolled down the car window.

"Got me," Quill answered as she went around the car and got in behind the wheel. Inside the car was toasty warm. "She wouldn't talk to me. But it sure seemed like she recognized the name. She threw out the word 'confidentiality.' "

"Oh, right."

They both turned at the sound of footsteps walking down the sidewalk. "That woman was cleaning the group room I was just in. There must be a second exit."

The woman wore a thick leather jacket. No gloves. No hat. Quill felt cold looking at her.

As the woman got closer, without breaking stride, she said directly to the open passenger window on Gaylyn's side of the car, "I'm going to walk to the Mayan Brew coffee shop at the bottom of the hill." And she kept walking.

Quill quickly put the car in drive and hit the turn signal to let any drivers on the road know she was pulling out of the parking spot. Gaylyn leaned over into the backseat and barely got Baby Boy buckled back up in his car seat before Quill started driving.

Straight downhill. "There it is," Gaylyn said as she twisted back around. She pointed at the Mayan Brew sign. Quill was already pulling into a parking spot. She threw the car into park, twisted the front wheels toward the curb, and hopped out. "Come on."

The trio walked into the coffee shop. The energy around them was so electric, people turned and looked. Others leaned a little away from them as they walked past. Gaylyn spotted the woman from the halfway house and tilted her head in that direction for Quill to follow her.

The woman sat at a corner table in the back of the coffee

shop. Out of sight of anyone who might walk by the storefront window. The two women pulled out chairs at the table. Quill sat Baby Boy on a chair next to her. Gaylyn took coffee orders and went up to the counter and ordered. The woman fussed and asked Quill about Baby Boy as they waited for Gaylyn to come back with the drinks.

"Here, I got him a small hot chocolate," Gaylyn said as she returned. "Might be too hot for him to drink right away. And a cookie. Here's your mochas." She sat down on the empty chair. They both looked at the woman who'd led them down the hill and into the coffee shop.

"How do you guys know Mabel?" the woman asked.

"We don't," answered Quill.

"Then why are you looking for her? Her cousins came to visit her in treatment, and I would remember you being with them."

Gaylyn left the lying to Quill. "She bought earrings from a Leech Lake friend of ours at the art gallery about a month ago. Mabel never went back to pick up the barrettes she ordered. We are trying to track her down to let her know the rest of her beadwork is done."

"Mabel went to work at a motel down at the waterfront a couple nights ago and never came back after her shift."

Quill gave Gaylyn a look.

"Yeah. Everyone at the halfway house is worried. The residents, I should say. The staff blow it off as a client who went back to using. Mabel wasn't going to use again. She wasn't."

"So, she's been gone how long?"

"Two nights."

Quill calculated backward. That would fit with when she

heard the scream in the woods just the other day. "What has the staff done to find her?"

"Nothing that I can tell. They called her workplace when she didn't return the next evening. They said she worked her shift and that was the last they saw of her."

"Did she leave with anyone? Have a boyfriend?"

"No. She was working and waiting until spring session to start at the tribal college. She was already enrolled, just waiting for classes to start. Her cousins came down last weekend to visit."

"And she wasn't using?"

"Not at all. Went to all the aftercare programs. Went to meetings three times a week. We were going to go to ceremony not this weekend but next."

"Ceremony?"

"Sweat lodge. One of the counselors from the treatment center runs a women's sweat lodge around full-moon time."

They sat in silence. Drank their coffee. Gaylyn took Baby Boy to the restroom with her.

Quill broke the silence. "So, no one has called the cops? Called her in as missing?"

"Nope. The program assumes she's using. The whole approach of 'You can only help those who help themselves; you can lead a horse to water, but you can't make them drink.' That's the tough-love attitude of the staff. Wouldn't want anyone to be codependent around here," she said sarcastically. "The treatment staff is all Native folks, but here at the halfway house the staff are all white except for the receptionist and the tech. Guess they get most of their funding from the county."

"Can you call the cops? Tell them she's missing?"

Gaylyn returned from the restroom with Baby Boy and stood listening to the women's conversation.

"They'd know it was me. If I get caught breaking confidentiality I'm out on my ass. It's damn cold out here this time of the year."

Gaylyn lifted Baby Boy up on a chair and sat down herself. "This is a little bigger than not picking up beadwork, aye, Quill?" Gaylyn had put two and two together. Mabel missing and the scream in the woods.

"Look, we'll ask around," Quill said to the woman. "That's all we were doing was asking around. Is there a way to reach you if we hear anything?"

The woman scribbled the name Suzy and a phone number on a napkin. "That's the house number. You have to say who you are. I tell all my family to say their name is Alice. That way, any of them can call at any time. If I'm not in a meeting or group they'll come get me right away. If I am, leave a number for me to call you back."

Quill tore the napkin in half and put the piece of paper with Suzy's name and number into the same pocket where the beaded earring sat. Then she scribbled her own name and number on the other half of the napkin. "Miigwech. If we hear anything, one of us will call. If you hear anything, here's my number."

The two women stood to leave. Pulled their coats back on. Quill gathered up the empty coffee cups and returned them to the service tray while Gaylyn got the kid back into his winter gear. They said their thanks and waved as they exited.

Gaylyn put Baby Boy in his car seat, and once she'd buckled her own seatbelt on in the front seat, she leaned her head against the passenger window. "Well, shit," she said.

Quill asked, "What?"

"I see Suzy and how well she's doing in treatment. Just wish some others would think to get some help."

"Takes a long time for some folks to see the bottom. I decided long ago to avoid the bottom rather than go looking for it."

"Wish my dad . . ." Gaylyn's voice filled with shame.

"Your dad what?"

"It's all fucked up, man. So fucked up . . ."

Quill sat in silence. Waited her out.

"Wish he thought like that. Wish he'd get into treatment."

"What's going on?"

"He's on meth."

"Your dad? He's an old man," Quill blurted out. "Sorry, but he's old. I thought folks grew up and didn't do that kind of crap."

"Yeah, well, some folks never grow up, I guess. I just want him to get help."

CHAPTER NINE

The air in the car was heavy as Quill let that news sink in. She put the key in the ignition without turning on the car. Leaned her chin on her arms, crossed on the steering wheel. Gaylyn kept her head against the passenger window. Her breath created frost on the glass, where she then drew tiny stick figures. Finally, Quill moved and fiddled with the heat controls.

"We need some heat," she said.

"Let's go, chicken bumps. Let's go, chicken bumps," Baby Boy said.

"Your kid is cold," said Gaylyn, looking briefly away from the window.

"All right, Baby Boy. Turning up the heat." To Gaylyn she said: "Can you throw that blanket over his legs, please?"

Gaylyn did as asked. The blanket was immediately kicked off as he continued his chant, keeping rhythm with his legs.

"Oh god, the sugar kicked in." Quill pulled out of the parking spot and drove to the next intersection, where she was stopped by a light that turned red. She looked at Gaylyn for the length of the light.

"What?" Gaylyn felt the stare.

"You could pass for Julie's cousin."

The light changed and she drove another block before again catching a red light. "Hospitals are much more lenient about letting family in. Especially for us Indians. If you tell them at the front desk you're a cousin or an auntie, they let you right in. I remember when Crow's uncle died. There were twenty people in that room. Half the room were his old drinking buddies. Everyone was a cousin that day."

"And your point is?" Gaylyn's quiet voice asked.

"How about we go to the hospital and see if Julie Jackson is still there? You can be her cousin. And I can be your cousin. And maybe if she's there we can ask her questions about what happened last night? Knowing what happened to her might give us some answers as to what happened to Mabel. Maybe it was the same guys, you know? Maybe we can find out if it was the same guys that followed us."

"All right. Even though that's a lot of maybes. How could that woman at the treatment center not give you any answers?" asked Gaylyn. "How can they not care? How can they care more about their confidentiality laws than a human life?"

"We don't exist to them. A line item on the business sheet. Or a problem to society. She can't imagine that Mabel was serious about her sobriety. To so many people we're nothing but a bunch of drunks—all the while they collect their paychecks 'serving' us," Quill answered, making a swift turn to slide through a yellow light. "They said they were taking her to St. Mary's. When we get there, we'll stop at the burger joint that is right in the lobby, get the kid a small order of fries. That should keep him quiet for a bit."

After getting Baby Boy a fast-food fix, Quill and Gaylyn parked at the hospital and walked to the security desk. They showed their IDs, and each got a paper stick-on badge and Julie's room number. The security guard pointed to the elevators to his right. "Fourth floor. To your left."

In the elevator Gaylyn said, "You talk to her. You're the one who was with her last night."

They found room 4320. Quill did a soft rap on the door, pushing it open and quietly saying, "Hello?"

The woman sitting upright on the bed with an IV in her arm was Julie, much more awake than the last time Quill saw her. A young man with long dark braids that hung down over the red LAND BACK T-shirt he was wearing sat in a rocking chair. He held an infant that appeared to be about eight months old. Its black hair stood straight up like porcupine quills. The baby slurped hungrily at the bottle of formula he held.

Quill spoke to Julie from the doorway. "Hey. I gave you a Narcan shot last night. I wanted to make sure you're okay?" She pointed at Gaylyn. "We said Gaylyn is your cousin in order to get up here and visit you."

"Come on in."

"This is my kid." She sat Baby Boy down in an empty chair with his fries.

Quill and Gaylyn stood near and waited for Julie to speak.

"Oh, I remember you," Julie said, looking at Gaylyn. "You were a foot taller than any of us back in junior high. I remember we teased you. Teased you a lot. Called you Sketti. Asked you how the air was up there." Julie looked down at her hands as she remembered the poor treatment she and her classmates gave Gaylyn back in school. She nervously rubbed the cotton nubs on the hospital blanket that covered her legs. "I'm sorry," she said, finally looking Gaylyn in the eye.

Gaylyn shrugged.

"She's a runner now. Those long legs make it hard for the rest of us to keep up with her," Quill said. "I see you have the celebrity suite view from here?" She looked out the window onto Lake Superior.

Julie gave a faint smile. "Guess so. You're the one that gave me the shot of Narcan? Maybe *you* can tell *me* what happened."

"What do you mean?"

"The city cops came and asked me a bunch of questions this morning. Then Patrick and another tribal cop, his sidekick, just left. Bet they were going down the elevator while you were coming up. Last thing I remember, this white guy sat down next to me at the penny slots and started talking to me. Tried to hit on me. One guy was talking to Lisa, who was sitting on the stool next to me. I told him I was married and had a baby. Next thing I knew I was riding in an ambulance, IVs stuck in my arm."

"Dang."

"Yeah. Migizi came last night with Baby Girl. We're just waiting for the doctor to sign the discharge papers and then we're gonna go home. The cops said there were two guys taking me out of the casino and that my cousin tasered one of them." She gave a short laugh. "Didn't even know my cousin liked me enough to stand up for me. His mom and my mom are always fighting."

"Family's family," Migizi said.

"I saw you fall down when the guy got tasered. We were coming out of the buffet. They took the two guys out in cuffs," Quill said.

"They're from the pipeline. I remember them saying they were from Tennessee, at least Bob, the guy talking to me. They all had three- and four-letter names—Jim, Bob, Lyle. Migizi says he's never gonna let me go to the casino by myself again."

"It's the only time in eight months she finally trusted me to watch the baby by myself," Migizi interjected. "She and Lisa were going out for a couple hours for Lisa's birthday. The doctors found a date rape drug in her system. Can't remember the name of it." He switched the baby, now sound asleep, into the crook of his left arm.

"We both quit drinking and smoking pot the day I found out I was pregnant with her. And I've never done hard drugs. Ever."

"They must have dropped something in her soda," Migizi said.

"Do you know where Lisa is?" Julie asked, looking at Gaylyn.

"I don't know Lisa," Gaylyn said. Quill shook her head no also.

"She's from Grand Portage. Last name is also Jackson. Met her at the tribal college. She doesn't drink either. We were playing penny slots."

"Did you ask Patrick about her?"

"He didn't answer me. Do you remember what he said, Migizi?"

"Nah, kinda talked around the issue."

Before they could finish the conversation, the room filled with nurses with papers for Julie to sign and a cart with her nonhospital clothes and possessions. Quill, Baby Boy in her arms, and Gaylyn backed out of the room, signaling goodbye. Quill stopped at the doorway, handed her son to Gaylyn, and went back into the room. She wrote her phone number on a piece of paper. "Call me, text me," she said before she turned and left the room.

They were silent going down in the elevator. And silent while they walked through the hospital corridors. "Let's head back to the rez," said Quill quietly.

Baby Boy sang, "Red ball, blue ball, ring around the rosy."

Back at Quill's house, she heated up the leftover deer stew. She made a pot of strong coffee, and while she waited for it to brew she texted Crow. He texted back that he'd gotten one guy out of a ditch but now he was off to tow a second guy out. She made a grilled cheese sandwich for the kid. Put bowls of stew in front of Gaylyn along with French bread made by a European chef who traveled once to the rez and never left.

"These guys are going to kill us."

Quill, her mouth full, looked up at Gaylyn, surprised at the vehemence in her voice.

"And they're going to get away with it."

Quill continued to slowly chew her food.

"Maybe not kill *us*. But who knows what would have happened to Julie if her cousin hadn't been at the door? She might have been another scream not heard out there in the woods. And where is Lisa?" Gaylyn's voice raised. "Does anyone know where Lisa is?"

Quill didn't know how to respond. Gaylyn asked loudly,

again, "I'm asking you: Does anyone know where Lisa is?!" Baby Boy stared at Gaylyn, plastic fork halfway to his mouth. Gaylyn dropped her fork. "Fuck, I don't even know *who* Lisa is." She pushed away from the table and stomped to the bathroom.

Quill told Baby Boy to go ahead and eat, everything was okay. They heard water running in the bathroom and the toilet flush. When Gaylyn returned to the kitchen, her face was damp and her hair slicked back with water. She sat down and went back to eating her stew.

"Let's talk this through," Quill said, breaking the silence. "I heard a scream in the woods. And found an earring we now know belongs to Mabel Beaulieu. Who went missing two days ago from the Duluth treatment program, according to her housemate. What would have been the next morning, I heard the scream out in the woods. Julie Jackson would be missing if her cousin hadn't tasered the asshole who drugged her. And we don't know Lisa or where she is. And a pickup truck followed us back from Leech Lake yesterday. What a mess." She reached in her pocket to make sure the earring was still there. "Nobody but us knows about Mabel. What the fuck. Nobody."

"What do you mean, nobody?" asked Gaylyn.

"Well, I have the earring. We went to Giigoonh and that's how we found out it was Mabel Beaulieu's earring. We're the only ones who know she is missing. Except the girl in the coffee shop. The one who doesn't want to get kicked out of the warm halfway house in the dead of winter. I haven't told Patrick, or Crow, that I have the earring. We're the only ones that know it was in the woods and belonged to Mabel. And now my DNA is all over it. Cops can't use it to prove anything."

Both women sat in silence. Staring at the food growing cold in front of them, and then out the window at snow clumped on the evergreen branches.

"I bought the matching pair from Giigoonh," Quill said. "They're identical. I could give that one to Patrick. Tell him I didn't realize it was vital evidence. Didn't know what to do. But after what happened with Julie, I decided I should say something."

"Why can't you give him the one you found in the woods?"

"I'm attached to it, okay? Holding it gives me a connection to her. It's a way to keep her safe, at least in my mind."

"Oh, geezus. And how many lies did you tell today? How many new cousins I get today?"

"Come on. It's not that bad."

"Nah, not that bad. But you do need to talk to Patrick. Give him all the info." Gaylyn started to sound really irritated again. "I want to know what the hell is happening. Mabel is missing. Lisa is missing."

"Okay. Okay. I'm going to go talk to Patrick." Quill took a bite of stew. It was cold. Chewed what was in her mouth but pushed the rest of the food away. "Maybe I better tell Crow what we've done before I talk to Patrick."

"'We'? Don't include me in your misadventures." Gaylyn raised her eyebrows.

"And I haven't told him about the truck following us either. He's going to be upset that I kept that from him too."

"Duh."

Quill squinted her eyes. "Why are you siding with him? I don't think I ever heard my mom ask my dad when she wanted to do something. She just did it. And I don't ever remember my dad questioning her about what she was doing or why."

"But was she ever doing something illegal? Like keeping evidence from the police and not telling her husband about it? What about that? Huh? Was someone, or somebodies, chasing her down the highway? And she didn't tell him?"

"Oh, all right. I'll tell him, I'll tell him." She punched a bunch of keys on her phone. "There. I just texted him and said we need to talk."

They both laughed. Baby Boy slapped his hands on his food tray.

CHAPTER TEN

Quill knew Crow worried about her safety, but she needed to train. Besides, outsiders to the rez almost never found their way back to the road that ran around the village. Crow said he would be back "around four." There was plenty of time for a quick run, and what Crow didn't know wouldn't hurt him was how Quill justified it in her mind. And not letting him know all her plans would keep the peace in her marriage.

Quill asked Gaylyn to sit with Baby Boy while she went out for a run. Wouldn't be more than twenty minutes. Gaylyn agreed and sat on the couch with the TV turned to a true-crime show.

Quill quickly changed into her running gear and took off. She ran up the snow-and-gravel-packed driveway. Her breath made puffs of clouds in the cold air. Her neighbor across the way pulled out of his driveway. He grinned and waved as she headed down the road in the opposite direction.

The village was a collection of HUD government-built houses set back off the unpaved road in the middle of a pine forest. There were yards with sparse grass and in others the house sat right inside a cleared tree line. The gravel road ran in a square with the elder housing and the old community center in the middle. There was no grocery store, post office, or other shops. Just HUD houses set in the middle of a pine forest.

All the dogs from each of the houses knew her. The untrained guard-dog types barked, but when she yelled at them in her deepest voice they ran back to their yards. There was a little white puffball, a miniature husky. It would run with her for the length of the roadway past his owner's house, then turn back and run home when Quill turned the corner to head past the old church and cemetery.

Even though it was a Catholic cemetery, scattered among granite headstones were the small, body-length, Traditional burial houses sitting over a good number of graves. Some people in the community practiced the new religions right alongside the old ones, *just in case,* her grandma was fond of saying.

It wasn't the long run she needed to clear her mind or push her body as hard as she wanted to, but it got the blood flowing and reminded her muscles of the job they needed to be prepared to do.

When she got back to her house, Gaylyn wrapped up in winter gear and said she would walk home; it wasn't that far, and she really needed the fresh air. Quill watched her leave up the driveway until all she could see were Gaylyn's legs below the branches of the pine trees that bordered the road.

Quill did household chores, fed Niswi a snack of home-made quesadillas when she got home from school, then thawed out a pound of ground buffalo and made a quick spaghetti sauce so that she wouldn't have to deal with supper while she was trying to talk to Crow.

She was folding clothes in the bedroom when she heard Crow come in the door. Cold winter air drifted into the bedroom and across her bare feet. She heard Niswi push back her chair from the table where she had been studying. Two pairs of feet ran to Crow. Niswi giggled as her dad play-wrestled with her. Quill could hear mock body slams onto the couch. Baby Boy kept saying, "Me too, me too." Quill thought, *This is why the couch sinks to the floor whenever anyone sits on it.*

The sounds in the living room died down when Crow instructed his daughter to get back to her homework. He passed the open bedroom door on his way to the bathroom. He held up grease-stained hands, signaling he needed to wash up before coming in to talk to her. Moments later he came back, hands and face scrubbed clean. He sat on the edge of the bed. "You want help?"

"No, I'm almost done. Let me put these away real quick. I'll fold the rest later." She put handfuls of clothing into the drawers of the dresser, then sat down on the edge of the bed. She clasped her hands in her lap to try to hide her nerves. "Niswi doing homework?"

"Yeah."

"And the boy?"

"Running trucks around the living room."

"Heard anything about what happened at the casino last night?"

"I talked to Patrick. A guy who claimed to be an attorney

from the pipeline came over and got the two guys released. Patrick said he's not even sure the IDs the men showed him are who they really are. All from Tennessee. The hospital found opioids in Julie's system but there's no proof they drugged her."

"No proof?"

"Nothing caught on camera. The lawyer hinted that she must have been using on her own."

"No way. I talked to her. And her partner. Both swear they haven't had a beer or smoked a joint since she got pregnant with the baby."

Crow twisted his body to get a better look at Quill's face.

"Don't look at me like that. I just stopped by the hospital today to see how she's doing. And I believe them. And Lisa?"

"The security cameras show her being led out the casino doors by the event center. Two guys on either side of her. They couldn't see their faces. You know how those guys were carrying Julie out? One guy was carrying Lisa out in the same way, arm under hers, kinda propelling her out the door. The parking lot cameras show they lifted her into a truck with no front license plate and the back one is all muddy. Windows tinted so dark you can't see into the cab of the truck."

"Could be the one that threw gravel at us when we were getting ready to go run."

"What?" he asked sharply, cupping her chin in his hand to have her look up at him.

"We were out running." Quill realized she'd opened her big mouth too soon. Shaking her head out of his hand she quickly added, "It was me, Punk, Gaylyn. When we were stretching, warming up by the road near the trail that runs back into the woods, a big-ass truck, dark-colored, with no front plate and a smeared back plate, pulled up by where we were. Dark-tinted windows. When the window was rolled down we saw a white guy with a light brown beard, not too long, and he was wearing a hat and those reflector-type sunglasses. He fishtailed the back end of his truck and screamed at us to 'go back to the rez.'"

Crow's face darkened.

"There were three of us, Crow. Gaylyn was ready to kill. But he drove off. We did our run, and all is fine."

They sat in silence for a minute. Quill wondered how to tell him about the ride home yesterday. She could tell he was trying hard to keep his emotions in check. Finally, Quill said, "Something else."

"What?" Crow sounded exasperated.

"Yesterday when we were coming home from Leech Lake a big dark pickup truck with tinted windows followed us."

Crow stood up. "What the fuck?"

"It followed us right until we crossed onto the reservation. I got pulled over for speeding. Think it was the new cop. All militaryish. And the truck zipped on past." She finished by telling him about driving to the casino rather than have the truck follow her home. Crow was pacing the bedroom floor. He ran his hand over the top of his head, a gesture he often made when frustrated.

Quill waited for him to speak. Instead, he sat back down on the bed. Put his arm around her and pulled her close. Quill could smell engine oil on his shirt.

Finally, he asked, "Anything else I need to know?"

"Well . . ."

He loosened his hold and looked into her eyes.

"Remember when we went out in the woods the other day? To look at where the scream came from?"

"Yeah."

"I found this." And she held out the earring.

Crow took it. The tiny thing was dwarfed in his palm. "And? There must be more to this story for you to text me and want a 'talk.'"

Quill took the earring back. Rolled it around in her hand. "Um. We know who it belongs to."

"What?" Crow's face tightened. "How?"

Quill stuffed the earring deep into her pocket. She told him about recognizing the beadwork as Giigoonh's. Driving over to Leech Lake. About Giigoonh remembering who bought the beadwork. How the women went to the halfway house in Duluth. How they went to the hospital.

Crow was livid. The bed creaked as he stood up. He stormed out of the bedroom. Quill sat for a good minute. She heard him slam the door on his way out of the house. She got up and finished folding the clothes. Put them away.

On the way to the kitchen to finish making supper, she looked out the front window. The days were getting shorter as winter progressed. Crow had a large mechanic's work light plugged into an orange extension cord and was leaning under the hood of Betty Boop. Niswi was still sitting at the table when Quill passed her. She asked, "What did you do to Dad?"

"What do you mean, what did I do to Dad? I didn't do anything."

"He stormed out of here all mad. He never gets mad."

"Never, never, never," chanted Baby Boy as he pushed small trucks full force under the couch.

"Give me a break." Quill opened a cupboard door and pulled out a cooking kettle. "Do your homework. That's all you gotta worry about." Quill filled the big kettle with water and put it on the stove to boil. "Didn't do a damn thing to your dad. Why blame me for your dad's attitude?"

"'Cause you're always crabby," Niswi said under her breath.

"I heard that!" Quill stood in front of the stove, watching the water, waiting for it to boil, a big handful of long pasta in one hand. Eventually the water boiled, the pasta cooked. The meat sauce was simmered.

"Niswi, set the table, then call your dad in to eat." Niswi did as she was told.

Crow came in. Silent. He went to the bathroom and again washed the grease off his hands and face. Sat down without speaking. Even Baby Boy sensed the tension in the air and kept his chatter to a soft mutter under his breath as he slurped long noodles into his mouth.

After eating, Crow sat on the couch with the kids and watched a horror movie. Quill bit her tongue. Didn't suggest that maybe it wasn't an appropriate movie before bedtime. Baby Boy was on the lap of his dad, who had an arm around Niswi. Quill sat in the kitchen and scrolled social media.

Quill couldn't get her mind off Mabel and Lisa. Or the big truck with the dark-tinted windows. Her body was fueled with anxiety and her mind raced. If two women weren't missing on the rez she would go for a nighttime run. A week ago, she could have done exactly that. Crow might tackle her to the ground if she went out there in her running gear now. Or take the kids and move back with his ma. She needed a hobby. There were women on the reservation who did beadwork. They made earrings and big medallions. Quill didn't have the patience for the tiny little beads. And while her mother loved making birch-bark baskets, Quill hated the chalky smoothness of birch bark on her fingertips.

There were men and women in the village who worked with birch bark all winter long. They would harvest the birch bark in the spring when the wild roses bloomed, in the season when the sliced birch bark would pop right off the trees. What they didn't turn into baskets over the summer, between fishing or gardening or powwows to go to, they would save to work on in the winter. Then they would sit in the warmth of their homes and make decorative baskets and winnowing trays for wild-rice season or spirit dish plates for ceremony.

There were women who learned the ancient craft of birch-bark biting. They created intricate images on paper-thin layers of birch bark by folding and refolding a layer of bark, then biting it with their eyeteeth. When it was unfolded, images of dragonflies or butterflies, bear, and deer would appear. Quill tried it once at language camp but couldn't figure out how her teeth could "see" the bark in her mouth clearly enough to create a believable picture. Some Ojibwe woman she was.

Both women and men were sewing ribbon skirts and shirts. Row upon row of satin ribbon decorated the hemlines of skirts. The best designers appliquéd clan symbols over the ribbons, or Ojibwe floral designs copied from old-style beaded leggings and vests. Everyone was creating beauty. Quill had made her own jingle dress. And Niswi's. She'd made Crow's grass dance regalia for the powwow season. But she didn't go all out. Some women made their family members three or four jingle dresses. Made their menfolk two or three changes of dance regalia. Crow's mother always asked when she was going to make a new grass-dance outfit for Crow. Hinting that maybe, just maybe, Quill wasn't a good enough wife for her son.

Quill didn't have the skill or patience for craft work. She did go hunting with Crow. Sometimes she worked on the cars and trucks with him. They went ricing each fall. Crow would pole the canoe through the wild-rice field on the lake and Quill would pull the rice over and use cedar knockers to tap the grain into the bottom of the canoe. This year had been a good year. They'd harvested enough for the year and stored it in burlap bags in the shed out back, and Crow had sold a few pounds at the last powwow of the season.

There were times she rode shotgun when he went to pick up parts or she helped him tow a vehicle out of the ditch. She also liked running. She needed to move. Not sit still. That was why the casino held no lure for her. Sitting in front of a machine hour after hour would drive her crazy.

Same with bingo. Once, before she met Crow, when Quill complained about never meeting anyone, Punk told her to try bingo. "All Indians play bingo" was what she'd said. Quill bought four cards. At the old community center, she sat next to a guy she didn't recognize who she thought looked interesting. Tried to strike up a conversation. The guy responded with "Shh. Shh. What was that number?" Fed up, Quill pushed her cards over in front of him and left the building.

That was when she discovered running. Discovered she was good at it. Loved it, in fact. A group of women in the Twin Cities, eighty miles south, advertised that they were going to hold a triathlon. A campaign to get Native women moving, be active and healthy. Quill talked Punk and Gaylyn, a teenager

back then, into going down to the triathlon with her. They
didn't train at all. They wore cut-off jeans and old T-shirts.
They wore the same tennis shoes they wore ricing or to the
powwows all summer. A ragtag threesome team.

They ran the 5K, and biked the 10K around one of the city
lakes along with 120 other Native women. The third event required them to canoe, with a partner, across the lake and
back. The three of them made it across and back in record
time. Near shore, they purposefully tipped the boat and swam
it to shore. The water cooled their bodies. They pulled the
canoe up on the sandy shore. Winded. They lay laughing, the
late morning sun beating down on them. They complained
about how sore their leg muscles and stiff their arms would be
tomorrow. They laughed good-naturedly at their "rez" outfits
and compared them to the logo-bearing running suits of the
"city-NDNs" who changed into actual bathing suits for the
canoe part of the triathlon.

They washed themselves off one more time in the lake before collecting their ribbons for finishing the triathlon and
getting in Quill's car for the drive home. In true Indian style
there were no winners. Everyone who finished won. They
laughed all the way home. And that was when Quill gave up
her quest for a hobby and began her running career.

Quill heard Crow shepherding Niswi into bed. He carried
Baby Boy to the bedroom. Quill could hear him rock their
youngest to sleep, singing a lullaby to him in Ojibwe. Heard
Crow lay him in the crib. Only then did he return to Quill and
say softly, "Let's talk. You want coffee?" he asked.

"Half a cup."

Crow set hers in front of her. "I heated it up for you," he

said and sat down across from her. He still didn't make eye contact. The anger from earlier was gone. When he did look directly at her, his eyes were filled with sadness. "Quill, we have kids. Two of 'em. I can't bear the thought of living without them. Or you. My mind went crazy when I thought of you driving all over with Baby Boy, tracking down missing women. My mind can't go there."

"Punk and Gay—"

Crow cut her off. "I don't care if there were ten women with you. Obviously, there are guys picking up Native women. Not only picking up but picking off Native women. You think the three of you are big enough to fight off a group of them?"

"We can run."

"Don't joke with me."

"Sorry." Quill took a sip of coffee. She looked deeply into the cup, stifling a nervous giggle that threatened to erupt.

"You need to stop being so impulsive. We've been hearing these horror stories of four thousand, maybe five thousand women missing across Canada. Missing down here. The stories of what has happened to women and children"—he emphasized *children*—"in the man camps over the Dakotas. And they are here now." He jabbed two fingers onto the table when he said the word *now*. "Those same men are here now." He jabbed the table again. "I don't want anyone in my family to go missing. To end up dead in a ditch or river. No. Not on my watch."

"I don't plan on it."

"No one plans on it, Quill. Jesus Christ, I'm serious. My mind imagined all kinds of disasters. What if the car broke down? Or you hit ice and slid in the ditch? You took the kid with you, for god's sake. Anything can happen on these roads up here. You know that. And these predators are cruising around looking for an opportunity. At the casino last night, Patrick said these assholes saw an opportunity and took it."

"Do they know where Lisa is?"

"No. Patrick doesn't know. Did that guy take her out in the woods, rape her, and dump her off? Kill her? Take her back to the camp and pass her around? He doesn't know. Said the attorney for the oil company all but laughed and said, 'Boys will be boys.' Treated Patrick as if being a tribal cop wasn't being a real cop. Pissed him off."

"Ah, man." Quill shook her head in disgust.

"You have to talk to Patrick tomorrow. Tell him what you told me. No sense doing it tonight. Too late. They wouldn't be able to do anything now anyways."

"How about after Niswi is in school? Maybe you can drop Baby Boy off at Barbie's in the morning. That way I won't be dragging him around with me."

"And about your training."

"What about it?"

"I don't want you running out there by yourself."

"I already agreed to that. I've been going with Punk and Gaylyn."

"Why can't you run around the village here, or the school track, until this thing gets straightened out? The three of you."

"Okay. The village. I hate that school track. Can't always be the three of us. Gaylyn has to work at the casino, and Punk—who knows what Punk does? She does her artwork and that's off and on when she has to go to galleries and art shows. And if she gets a boyfriend, she tends to disappear. We're two miles off the main road. No one even knows we're back here except the other Indians. And I was smart enough to go to the casino, not have that truck follow me here. Besides, Old Man Jack across the road calls you or Patrick every time an unknown vehicle drives past his house. Who needs security cameras when we have him and all the senior women at the elders housing? They know who boogits before the person who boogits knows they're going to." She made a farting sound with her lips.

Crow gave a small grin.

"You can even track me on your phone." She enabled the location sharing on her phone. "There. Now you can always check and find out right where I'm at."

"How do I find you?" Crow fiddled with his own phone.

Quill took it from him and flicked through his screen. Showed him how to locate the "Find my" button, then selected her name and zoomed in on her. It showed her phone next to his. "There, see? You'll always know right where I am."

"You'll talk to Patrick tomorrow?"

"Yep."

"I love you." He grabbed her hand.

"I love you too. And I would never let anything happen to these kids. Someone would have to kill me first."

"That's not a comforting thought. I want you to be safe too, okay?" He gently massaged her hand. "Come on, let's go to bed."

In the bedroom they undressed in the dark so as not to

wake the baby. After making love, quietly, again so as not to wake the boy in the crib, Crow fell asleep holding Quill tightly.

Quill lay in his arms wide awake. Her eyes eventually adjusted to the darkness and she looked at her husband's face. Some of his black hair escaped his long braid. Like many Indian men, he couldn't grow a beard or mustache if his life depended on it. He had broad shoulders with muscles from taking tires off vehicles, turning engine nuts and bolts. Guy muscles.

They had met shortly after the triathlon in the Cities. "Met" wasn't the right word. They had both grown up on the rez. Went to the same high school, although he was two years ahead of her. Her family knew his family in the way people on the rez did. His family were hunters, wild ricers, backyard mechanics. Her mom did traditional crafts and traveled around the state demonstrating how to make birch-bark baskets. She even won a couple art awards for the things she did. Quill's dad always worked for the state highway construction crew. A quiet man. A steady worker and provider.

The summer of the triathlon Quill went with Punk to the yearly Ojibwe language camp. She stood on the shoreline, orange life jacket on over her T-shirt, wearing cut-off jeans, while she waited for Punk and their turn at a round in the canoe races. Quill still had no idea who yelled "You need a partner, take her!" The next thing she knew she was pushed and pulled by the elbow to a canoe and told to hop in. Crow was sitting in the rear of the canoe, ready to go. As soon as she sat down, there was a countdown of "Naanan, niiwin, niswi, niizh, bezhig." Crow dipped the oar into the water, and they were off.

They fell into immediate sync with paddling. The canoe skimmed out over the water ahead of everyone else. Solidly in the lead, they rounded the buoy and headed back to shore. A couple canoes collided and were still sorting out how to head in the direction of the buoy. One canoe tipped right at the shoreline. The drenched pair were laughing and accusing each other of causing the tip-over. Quill dared a quick glance over her shoulder and saw three canoes right on their tail. "Faster!" she hollered to Crow.

The crowd onshore was shouting, cheering on the team they wanted to win. Punk—who back then wore only half her head shaved and it was dyed blond—jumped up and down. Quill couldn't hear what she was yelling over the rest of the crowd, so she shut them out and matched Crow stroke for stroke. Because race rules required each team to get the entire length of the canoe out of water to be considered at the finish line, within five feet of the shoreline, Crow jumped out and pulled the canoe, with her in it, up onto the sand. They were immediately surrounded by folks congratulating them on winning.

Crow hugged her, lifted her off the ground, and spun her around. Punk hugged her and whispered, "Snag him quick, girl." Quill started to say no and playfully push Punk away but Crow reached out to spin her around again. When he set her back on the ground, he kept his arm around her and they smiled at each other. Fourteen years and two kids later, they held the record for the number of canoe races won at language camp. There were a couple years in there when Quill was too pregnant to race or with a baby too small she wouldn't leave him or her in anyone else's arms.

Quill watched Crow sleep soundly beside her. She knew exactly the weight of their love. Their level of commitment to their marriage. The strength of the bond. Their relationship was the exception, not the rule, on the rez. They came from a people who had survived wars against their people. They were surrounded by families who were broken apart by forced incarceration at federal boarding schools. Adult children who were raised by parents who hadn't had parents but who were raised by grandparents or foster parents.

She and Crow were raised by people who because of the hurts they themselves had endured loved their children fiercely but distantly, even when in the same room with them. It was why she and Crow hugged their kids and said "I love you" at every leaving. Why they said it often, even in public, even when the elders and other young couples laughed at them. Teased them, told them to "get a room."

Quill stayed in bed as long as she could, held tightly in Crow's arms. Her thoughts raced over the events of the last couple days. Sleep avoided her. When she felt his breathing become slow and steady, she eased out of his arms and off the bed. She pulled on his big T-shirt and felt around in the dark for her panties on the floor. She crept barefoot out of the room. The clock on the kitchen stove said 1:30 in white digital glare.

She stood in the dark in front of the living room window. A beat-up white car, an unfamiliar rez car, drove slowly by. She texted Punk and Gaylyn and asked if they wanted to do a run around the village roads in the morning.

She got an affirmative response from Gaylyn. Punk said, *I have a date,* and refused to answer any more questions. Run time was set for nine A.M.

Someone else can't sleep, Quill thought as she watched the beat-up white car pass the house again, this time going in the opposite direction.

Quill went back to bed. Crawled in carefully so as not to wake Crow with her feet, which were cold from standing barefoot in the living room.

CHAPTER ELEVEN

In the morning, Quill left before Crow and the kids awoke. She put a note on the kitchen counter asking Crow to take Baby Boy to Barbie's and get Niswi off to school. She said, *Going running with P & G. Will get to Patrick later this a.m.*

She pulled into Punk's yard alongside the same sedan that had been parked there the other day. She jumped out of the car and knocked on the door. Then pounded on the door. A disheveled Punk finally answered. The door cracked a good two inches. "Jeez, woman. I gotta sleep. I'll call you later." And she shut the door.

Gaylyn, on the other hand, was waiting on the front steps for Quill. "Just park. We can run from here," she said, jogging in place, vapor rising from her mouth.

The two women ran the village road. When they passed Punk's the visitor's car was gone and Punk came running out wearing a hunter's orange tracksuit.

"Thought you said you couldn't join us?" Quill said without slowing down.

"Had to kick him out. Told him I needed my exercise if I was going to keep up with him."

"OMG. TMI," Quill said sardonically.

"And who's 'him'?" Gaylyn asked.

"Probably just a one-night stand. No need for names this early in the game." And Punk ran ahead of the other two women.

When they got back to Gaylyn's after their run, Quill said, "Whyn't you come over for coffee? Punk here can tell us about her love life and we can come up with a plan to find who took Lisa." Everyone piled into her car.

Sitting in Quill's kitchen, Punk finally, after a lot of smiles, sighs, and giggles, spilled her guts about the man she was "in lust with." "It's the new cop. The one who pulled you over for speeding," she gushed.

Gaylyn rolled her eyes but didn't say anything.

Quill nodded. She should have known, she thought, as she remembered how Punk behaved that day. During their long friendship, Punk had had a long history of falling in love. Her relationships tended to last about six months before she threw them out or they left because she was "just too much." "So how did this happen?" Quill asked.

"I went to bingo at the casino a couple weeks ago. Ran into him. Asked him what a hunk like him was doing there in the middle of nowhere. He said, 'Looking for you.' " Punk looked at the other two women with a big smile. "How could I refuse? Bingo! One thing led to the other."

When they were talked out, laughed out, the women gathered their winter gear and bundled up for the ride to their respective homes.

"You guys got a minute?" Quill asked. "I gotta swing by the station and put some gas in."

Both women joined her in the car. Quill drove to the gas station on the main road, pulled her gloves back on, and jumped out to put gas in the tank. Gaylyn and Punk headed into the station to get coffee and snacks.

As Quill pumped gas, she surveyed the vehicles passing on the road. She thought about how she and her friends, and Crow, would not have worried in the past if she went out for a drive or run, but the abduction of women was taking a toll on everyone's trust issues—maybe not of one another, but of the environment in which they were currently living.

Quill vigilantly scanned the road and passing cars. Her heartbeat increased when three pickups pulled into the station. They parked diagonally at the front of the station. Two had southern state license plates and the third was from North Dakota. None had a flower or WASH ME written in dust on the tailgate. Men in work clothes exited the trucks and entered the store without looking back at her.

Quill frowned. It seemed her friends were taking a long time coming out of the station. Were they? Or was she just superconscious now that the trucks had pulled in?

At the same time the pump signaled her tank was full, Gaylyn and Punk came walking out, each with steaming cups of coffee. Gaylyn carried two, one in each mittened hand. She handed one to Quill before getting into the backseat.

The windows fogged over with the steam of the coffee in the cold air. Quill cranked on the defrost. "You guys okay in there?"

"Yeah, why?" asked Punk.

"Those three pickups." Quill nodded her head in that direction, turning on the ignition and putting the car in gear.

"Ah, a group of men came in talking about how cold it is up here in the north. I grabbed our coffee and left," answered Gaylyn.

"I was worried they might try to mess with you."

"I'd love to see one of them try to fuck with me," Gaylyn said, breathing a new layer of fog onto the back window.

"Chill. Who's going to go with me to talk to the cops?" The front window was cleared of fog enough for Quill to see to drive.

"You going right to Patrick's?" asked Gaylyn.

"I guess. I'll drop you at your house and then I'll drive to the cop shop."

"I gotta work today. Can you drop me off at the casino instead?"

"Sure."

"Good thing you have Punk with you," said Gaylyn. "No one should talk to the cops by themselves. Even if they're innocent. You gotta watch more cop shows and learn this stuff."

"Good to have one that's sleeping with the enemy, at least."

Punk fiddled with the radio until she found a rock station. The women drank their coffee in silence and scanned the highway as Quill drove. When they passed a roadkill deer with two of its legs sticking straight up in the air, Punk said, "It's thoughtful of them to crawl to the edge of the road to die. Get out of the way of all the traffic."

All three laughed and then fell into silence as they sipped coffee. Lost in their own thoughts, each woman watched the snow in the ditches slide by. No one said anything until Quill pulled into the casino lot. It was late morning and already, or still, filled with cars.

"Drop me in back by the service door?" Gaylyn asked. "Let me know what happens. And if you go running later." Gaylyn hopped out of the car and gave a half wave without looking back.

"You know, I worry about that girl," Punk said.

"Why?"

"I'd hate to get into a fight with her. She seems all quiet and calm but every once in a while, that anger pops out. Almost as if she is waiting for an excuse to kill."

"You ever go to her house?"

"Nah."

"There must be difficulties with her parents. She never talks about them. I went to the door a couple times to pick her up. Never invited me in. Looks a mess in there from the doorway. I get the impression that maybe there's domestics that happen. She's got a couple older brothers. Both left the rez a long time ago; one is in the service, one in prison. She has a younger sister."

"I never ask about her business. You're lucky. Being an only child. Maybe why you picked a guy who just spoils you."

"Gimme a break."

Quill pulled into a parking spot alongside three tan cop cars at the tribal police headquarters. One of the newer buildings on the reservation, it sat off the paved road between the casino and the gravel road that led to the village. It was a lonely-looking all-new brick one-story structure with brand-new smooth sidewalks and plenty of glass, at least on its front.

The far side had tall narrow windows, skinnier than the

human body turned sideways, to prevent escape from the holding cells in that part of the building. The other half of the building held the tribe's social service agencies. The ever-present pine trees of the reservation wrapped around. The tops swayed in the slight breeze that also caused the American and tribal flags to flutter in the air. "All right. Skoden," Punk said, hopping out of the car. "Don't say anything to Patrick about me and his new sidekick."

Quill rolled her eyes.

Everything inside the headquarters was shiny new. A polished floor. Walls so fresh they smelled of new paint. Inside, the tribe's flag hung beside the American stars and stripes. Twenty-one eagle feathers were tied to a wooden staff, along with multicolored ribbons. It was the veterans' eagle staff that was carried into the powwow arena for each grand entry. An officer, dressed in his police uniform, sat stiffly behind a glass partition. Quill didn't recognize him. While it seemed everyone knew everyone on the reservation, people from different reservations often moved where the jobs were.

Quill walked up to the window. "I need to talk to Patrick."

"And you are? About what?"

"Quill. He knows who I am. Tell him it's about the woman screaming in the woods that Crow talked to him about. It might also be related to the abductions at the casino."

The officer turned on his chair and pushed buttons on a black phone that sat on the desk next to him. He lowered his voice when he spoke into the mouthpiece. Quill couldn't understand what he said. Punk was looking at a painting on one of the walls by a local artist. Quill had heard or maybe read on social media that the tribe allocated a certain amount of money in its budget to buy art from local artists. Something about healing and building pride in the community. Creating beauty all around the rez.

"He'll be right out."

Quill nodded and walked back to Punk. "Pretty good artwork, aye?" Quill reached into her pocket and pulled out the earrings she'd bought from Giigoonh. She removed one from the card it was attached to and stuck it in her pocket. The other she kept on the card and stuck it in her pocket also. She made sure the earring from the woods was still tucked into the crease in the pocket of her jacket.

"Yeah," said Punk.

"Quill?" A male voice behind them. They both turned to see Patrick standing there. All five-foot-nine of him, dressed in the dark blue tribal cop outfit with gun on one hip, handcuffs and taser on the other. Over one shirt pocket was the American flag, over the other a gold badge. He smiled when he saw Quill and held his hand out to shake hers and then Punk's.

"Hey, Patrick."

"Crow said you were going to stop by. Let's go back to my office." He sounded all formal, as if he hadn't known Quill her entire life. As if his mother and her mother didn't go out and gather birch bark together. As if he had never caught her and her dad out shining deer a few years back. He gave her dad a lecture about using a floodlamp attached to the roof of his pickup truck. The bright light used to stop the deer in their tracks. Gave meaning to the phrase "deer in the headlights." Let them off with a warning. As if he and Crow hadn't played on the same basketball team all through high school. As if he and Crow didn't still play as a team, and win, the horseshoe tournament each year at language camp.

The women followed him into a conference room. A six-foot table with a microphone and phone on one end dominated the room. Office chairs on wheels sat around the table. There was a whiteboard on one wall and a projector on a wheeled cart on the opposite end of the room. A wall of windows looked out on pine trees.

This is the view we all have here on the rez. Every window of every home looks out at pines, Quill thought as she sat in a chair Patrick pointed at. Punk sat down beside her and slowly spun her chair all the way around before resting her elbows on the table in front of her. Both stuffed gloves into pockets, unwrapped scarves from around their necks, and undid winter coats.

Patrick looked at them with raised eyebrows. "I'm gonna ask the new guy to sit in on this." He punched a button on the phone. "Cliff, can you come in here a second?" And he clicked the button. He fiddled with more buttons on the phone. "And I'm going to record this. For the record. Make sure we have it all down."

Quill and Punk looked at each other. At that moment, the door opened, and the cop who had pulled her over for speeding entered the room. He carried himself with the straight back and squared shoulders of a soldier. He ignored the two women, pointedly not making eye contact with Punk; he looked only at Patrick and didn't move until Patrick pointed at a chair next to him, indicating where he should sit. "Cliff, this is Quill. She's married to Crow. He's the one who came in to the station the other day. This is Punk. Do you have a last name, Punk?" He didn't wait for her to answer. And Punk turned to stare out the window. "Everyone around here is known by their nicknames," he said in an aside to Cliff.

"Sometimes it isn't until they die and we need to bury 'em that we find out their real names. So, Quill, what is it you came here to tell us?"

He clicked buttons on the machine beside him and spoke into it, giving the day, date, and time. His full name and Cliff's full name. He said he was interviewing Quill about the scuffle his men investigated in the woods on the hunting road. "Go ahead," he said, looking at Quill.

Quill looked at him. At Cliff. And started talking. When she got to the part of the story where she and Crow drove out to the hunting road, past where the tribal cops had gone, her voice took on an accusatory tone as she said the cops didn't go down the road far enough. She told how she and Crow went far enough to find the point of struggle. To the spot across from the trail where Quill was running when she heard the scream. Probably the exact spot the scream came from.

She reached into her pocket and brought out the new earring, an exact match for the original one tucked securely into the corner of her jacket pocket, the earring she found in the woods. "This earring was in the snow out there. I picked it up. I wasn't thinking. I'm sure it has my DNA all over it now."

And she continued with her story. Their story. The women's story. Of recognizing the earring as Giigoonh's work. Going to Leech Lake. Getting the name Mabel Beaulieu. Going to Duluth. Talking to the woman Becky from the halfway house, who wouldn't give them any information. Talking to the woman Suzy, who gave them new information. She emphasized how Suzy and other residents were worried, but didn't want to speak up, did not want to get kicked out of the halfway house during the winter. Going up to the hospital to visit Julie. Ending with "Do you know where Lisa is?"

"You know you can't mess with a crime scene, right? Take evidence?"

"We didn't mess with the crime scene. Crow was careful. And he wouldn't let me walk anywhere. He told me, 'This might be a crime scene.'"

"But you took the earring. Kept the earring." Patrick reached and picked up the earring.

"I saw this shiny thing in the snow, and I picked it up. I didn't know it was evidence right away."

Punk gave her leg a slight kick under the table.

"Well, when you realized it was evidence you should have come right in."

"I know. That's what Crow said. That's why we're here."

"Anything else?" Patrick looked at Punk. "You got anything to add?" She didn't say anything until Cliff turned and looked directly at her. Then she relayed how they, with Quill driving, were chased by a black pickup with tinted windows on their way back from Leech Lake. How they drove to the casino lot where the truck parked and two men got out.

When Patrick asked if they would be able to identify the men, both women responded that no, the men were covered in winter gear, so they couldn't see them clearly. Punk left out the part about Quill speeding. She left out the part about Cliff stopping them. She left out the part about sleeping with Cliff. She did say that she heard that the woman Lisa, from the casino, who was still missing, was put into a dark pickup truck with tinted windows.

Patrick added some notes to the paper in front of him. He stood up. "Wait here." And exited the room.

Cliff looked at them one by one, then swiveled his chair around and looked out at the pines.

Punk stared out the window also. Quill wasn't used to Punk being so quiet; it made her nervous. To fill the quiet she asked Cliff, "Where you from?"

"Turtle Mountain."

"What brought you here?"

"Being a cop."

"You were in the military?"

"Yeah."

"Why here? No one in their right mind moves to our quiet little rez."

He swiveled and looked at Punk, whose eyes lit up before she turned her chair in the opposite direction. He likewise gave a slight grin then went back to staring at the pines.

Patrick walked back in. Sheets of paper in his hand. "This is a transcript of what you reported. Can you read it over and make any corrections, additions? Sign and date if it's good."

Quill read through the pages. Handed each one to Punk when she was done with it. When Punk gave her back the last page, Quill held out a hand to Patrick for a pen. She signed and dated. "That's all?" she asked.

"That's it. Thank you," Patrick said.

Cliff stood. Reached across the table to shake Quill's hand, then Punk's. "See you around," he said. Quill thought Punk blushed as he held her hand a bit longer than needed.

Back in the car, Quill held out her hand to Punk while saying, "See you around."

"Shuddup."

"Well, thank god that's over," Quill said, and checked to see if there were any messages from Crow. She felt a tiny bit of relief when she saw he hadn't texted at all. "Let's go for a longer run. Crow made me promise to not run the wooded trails around here, but we can drive to Duluth and take a quick jog through one of the parks up there."

"Sure."

"On the way, I want to drive through the casino parking lot and look for that pickup with the tinted windows."

"Why go looking for trouble?"

"I'm not. I wrote in the dust of a couple of the trucks. Don't look at me like that. I just put a flower on one and WASH ME on the other. Like some little kid would do. With all this ice and snow, I doubt they're the kind of guys to get their trucks washed every week. Figured that would be an easier way to mark them than trying to clean the plates and get the number right then. If we see them now we can scrape off the dirt and give the numbers to Patrick. It's broad daylight. Nothing's gonna happen. We'll just look." Quill was already driving toward the casino.

"I'll text Gaylyn and see when she gets off. If we're going to the casino, maybe she'll want to come to Duluth to run with us." Punk was already texting. Her phone lit up almost instantly. "She says she won't get off till after dark. We should go without her. You keep slipping right past the truth on stuff, you know."

"What do you mean?"

" 'Didn't know it was evidence.' Are you for real?" Punk raised a pierced eyebrow. "And now running on a city trail instead of one around here. Not sure it's any safer in Duluth. I'm sure those pipeline workers know about the city of Duluth. And there's all the stories about women being trafficked out of the harbor too."

"Me skipping around the truth? What about you and your cop boyfriend pretending you never met?"

Punk smacked her on the arm. "Leave me and my love life outta this."

Quill didn't respond. When they reached the casino she drove slowly through the parking lot. Up and down the vehicle-filled rows. There were plenty of pickups. Some were clearly old-man farmers' trucks. Worn. Rusted. Threadbare tires. Some were this year's model, jacked up on oversized tires. Some sported neighboring reservation license plates, while most had regular Minnesota plates. The black pickup with tinted windows was nowhere in sight. None of the pickups had messages on their dusty tailgates.

Not seeing the truck she wanted to see, Quill pulled out of the casino lot, at which point Punk said under her breath, "Thank god. Lord knows what kind of trouble you would've dragged me into if we saw one of them trucks."

Quill didn't respond, just headed back north on the freeway into Duluth to one of the wooded city parks with running trails. In the parking lot, shielded by open car doors, the women quickly changed into running gear while cussing at the cold weather and throwing the clothes they took off onto the backseat. Fifteen minutes into the run, Quill's phone rang. She slowed and looked at the screen. It was Crow. She steadied her breathing. "Hey, babe, I'm out with Punk. What's up?"

"What are you doing in Duluth?"

"Nothing much. Just out running around with Punk." Punk slapped her on the arm.

"Well, after your talk, Patrick put out a reservation-wide call for volunteers. He wants as many people as possible to be at Cemetery Road in an hour. Says we'll line up at the road and walk in, see if we find any more evidence of the woman who is missing."

Quill motioned for Punk to stop running. She turned around and started back the way they entered the park. "Okay, Crow, we're heading home now."

She hung up and relayed the information about the search party to Punk. They picked up their pace to the car. Quickly changed back into their regular clothes.

Headed back to the reservation, Quill said, "What do you see in that new guy?"

"Who?"

"The new cop."

"Do I look like his type?" Punk raised her pierced eyebrow and brushed a hand through her mohawk.

Quill laughed. "He seems kinda cold to me. Unfriendly."

"He's a cop. He's gotta be all macho and 'professional.'" Punk put air quotes around *professional*. "Maybe he thinks you're doing hard drugs. And you'll be his first big bust here on the rez."

They both laughed. "Can you text Crow and tell him we'll meet him on Cemetery Road? We need warmer clothes if we're going to be out tramping in the woods. I can drop you off and then come back and pick you up. Text Gaylyn and see what she wants to do."

"I already did. She said she's leaving work early and will meet us there."

They rode in silence until it was time to turn off the freeway onto the highway leading to the reservation. "Are we going to find her in the woods?" Punk asked quietly.

"I hope not. I want to believe she's alive and I'll be able to get her earring back to her."

"Me too."

Back at home, Quill put on three layers of shirts. Long johns under leggings. Sweatpants over those. Good thick socks in Sorel boots. A down jacket. Winter gloves. A stocking cap. She hated when her ears got cold. She put a call in to Barbie, asked if it was okay if the school bus dropped Niswi off there. Barbie told her that Crow was way ahead of her; he'd already called her. And the school. Nothing to worry about. She'd feed the kids supper too. All set.

Quill circled back around the village roads and picked up Punk. "Geez, we both gained ten pounds in twenty minutes. If we fall over in the woods, they'll have to roll us back out to the road."

There was a line of cars on Cemetery Road when they got there. Folks stood in small groups. Everyone wore layers of winter gear. Many cars sat with engines running, people sitting in them to keep warm. Quill parked across from Betty Boop, going as far off the shoulder of the road as she dared. Punk climbed out into the snow in the ditch, then up onto the roadway. She brushed snow off her legs as she came up out of the ditch.

They found Crow, who was wearing fluorescent-orange hunting gear, standing with a group of tribal officers. Cliff carried a bullhorn. Patrick nodded to him. Cliff put the bullhorn to his mouth and called everyone to gather round. Car engines shut off. Car doors slammed. Soon fifty or more people were crowded around. Quill noticed a small group of white guys wearing duckbill hats. She nudged Gaylyn and Punk and slid her eyes in the direction of the men. They scanned the road for the black pickup truck but didn't see it. The men appeared to have driven out in an old beat-up sedan. "They look like local farmers," Quill said.

They stood in the cold and listened to Patrick explain how they were going to line up, half on this side of the hunting road, half on the other. No one under eighteen would be allowed on the search. There was grumbling by a couple of groups of teens, who retreated to parked cars. The adults remaining were instructed to walk into the woods, arm's length apart. In a straight line. They were to look for anything that didn't belong in the woods. Another cop handed out rolls of colored tape. They were instructed to mark anything that looked out of place. To use their phones to take a picture and document it if they saw anything suspicious. Anything at all.

"We'll go in as far as we can get before it gets too dark. Then we're going to carefully backtrack out. Depending on what we find, or don't find, we'll come back out and go back again tomorrow at sunrise." Patrick had taken over the bullhorn but handed it back to Cliff.

"Line up."

Quill stood with Crow on one side; Punk and Gaylyn stood on the other side.

"Let's go," hollered Cliff into the bullhorn, and the entire line of volunteers moved forward collectively.

Quill could hear conversations happening up and down the line. People were joking even within the seriousness of the job. She shared with Crow her conversation with Patrick. He in turn shared that Patrick had made a call to the halfway house and confirmed that the staff had not seen or heard from Mabel since the day Quill heard the scream in the woods.

After talking with the treatment staff, rather than waste

more time, Patrick had decided to search immediately on the off chance that Mabel was in the woods, possibly hurt and needing assistance.

It seemed as if every year, especially during hunting season, someone would get lost or shot, and a search crew would need to be called out. More frequently, and recently, what was occurring was overdoses in the woods. Young folks, and sometimes the not so young, would go off down a hunting road to shoot up drugs, and invariably someone would overdose. Or, disoriented from the drugs, they would wander off deeper into the woods, off the road, their phones left back in whatever vehicle they drove out in. At that point, Patrick would need to call in a search team, usually an eclectic group from the village of whomever was available. Even though it was going on two days since Quill had heard the woman's scream, Patrick was hoping for a live recovery. Or at least a sign that she was still alive.

As happens in a forest, it gets dark sooner than in wide-open spaces. By the time the searchers reached the three-and-a-half-mile mark, those with flashlights or headlamps worn over their stocking caps turned them on. Dusk was rapidly approaching. Cliff's voice, calling out over the bullhorn, stopped them all. He instructed them to turn and walk to the hunting road. They would all walk back out on the road.

Back on the main road, a French chef set up a coffee stand. He had arrived as a tourist, intending to visit the reservation for just one day, but never left. He served croissants and hot coffee to the volunteers from the back of his SUV. People stood around in groups, stamping their feet to warm up. Holding the hot cups of coffee in their cold hands. The only significant find was a small torn piece of cloth found near the edge of the hunting road, where Quill knew a struggle had taken place. It was surmised that it came from an individual's shirt.

There were plastic bags found farther off the road that in all probability blew in with the wind. Everything was bagged and tagged in case it might be from the vehicle that had driven back into the woods. There were rabbit and deer tracks. Bear tracks. No human tracks were found off to either side of the hunting road.

Patrick, Cliff, and a handful of officers huddled around a squad car. Steam from their breaths in the cold air created a halo above them. They broke apart and Cliff held the bullhorn to his mouth. "We want to thank everyone for coming out this afternoon. The elders will have Indian tacos for everyone at the community center in about half an hour." The crowd quickly started to disperse.

"Wait. Wait. Hold on a sec," Cliff added. "We want you all back out here at seven A.M. We'll walk in on the hunting road and spread out from there. We'll go another mile into the woods and then meet at the main road. At this point we don't expect we'll find anything more, but on the off chance that we do, we'll take a look. Again, miigwech, wiisinin, go eat." Before he finished his last sentence folks were already heading back to the warmth of their cars.

"Want me to grab the kids, or will you?" Quill asked Crow.

"I'll go get them. See you at the center." He gave her a quick kiss with ice-cold lips.

"Thank god we didn't find a dead body." Gaylyn slammed the car door shut behind her. She decided to catch a ride back with them instead of with the casino worker who brought her to the search.

"Don't say that. Gives me the creeps," said Punk.

"Then where is she?" asked Gaylyn. "And does anyone know anything about where this Lisa chick is?"

Both women in the front seat said no.

The next morning's search was as fruitless as the previous afternoon's. Gaylyn pestered Quill to find out from the cops if they knew anything about Lisa and her whereabouts. Punk volunteered to talk to the new cop and find out what he knew, if anything. Quill watched as Punk walked up to Cliff and carried on a conversation. Something about their body language, or at least Cliff's, told Quill that Cliff wasn't happy with Punk's questioning. When Punk came back, she reported that Patrick was still tracking down leads on the guy who'd been seen taking Lisa from the casino. Patrick was also talking to the attorney for the camps as well as security over that way. They were denying any involvement of pipeline men in Lisa's disappearance.

"What's with Cliff? He didn't look too happy with being questioned," Quill asked.

Punk laughed. "Nothin'. He's new. I think he's just trying to make a good impression. Wants to keep our 'relationship' "— she made air quotes with her fingers—"quiet until he's more settled here."

Gaylyn said, "I don't like him."

Punk rolled her eyes.

Quill talked them into going for a run after changing out of the winter layers they'd worn to the morning search. They ran through the village numerous times. They waved at folks looking out their front windows. A handful of little kids joined them for a few yards before falling back, laughing. The next time around the loop those same kids were lying in wait in the ditch with a pile of snowballs they pelted the women with. It was all in good fun. The women jogged backward for a spell, volleying snowballs back at the kids.

When they passed the elder housing, one of the women stood in the doorway, sweater pulled around her chest to ward off the cold. She hollered, "Did they find her?" The women shook their heads no and kept going.

Back at Quill's house they changed into regular clothes and sat around the kitchen table eating leftover ham-and-bean soup Quill heated up for them. Crow texted saying he was on a run to help someone with a flat tire.

Over soup, Quill convinced the two women to ride with her to the casino parking lot and look for the black truck. To try again to get the rest of the license plate number. Both women said she was crazy, but when she got on her winter coat and boots and said she was going with or without them, they both piled into her old Saturn.

Quill drove them up and down the rows of cars in the parking lot. There were a couple big trucks with out-of-state plates, no front license plates. They looked like the trucks that belonged to pipeline workers. The black truck with tinted windows was not one of them.

Quill pulled into an empty parking spot and debated with Punk and Gaylyn about what their next steps should be. She wanted to drive west and check out motel parking lots, to which Punk screamed "Hell no!" She was all for letting the tribal police handle the matter.

Gaylyn fantasized out loud about ways to get back at the pipeline workers: everything from slashing tires to putting sugar in their gas tanks. Eventually the talk ran out and all three women sat in the car with the heater blasting while Quill and Punk scrolled through their social media pages. Alert pings sounded on both phones, breaking the silence in the car. Fingers scrolled like crazy trying to keep up with the messages pouring in.

Child abducted outside Walmart in Duluth—White van grabs child outside Walmart—Child missing after being pulled into van.

CHAPTER TWELVE

"Where is Baby Boy?" Quill asked the air in the car. "Where the fuck is Baby Boy?"

"Chill, he's with Barbie. Remember?" Punk was reading messages as fast as they popped up on her screen. A worried scowl crossed her face. "Damn. Did you see this?" She handed her phone to Quill.

It was a picture snapped of the crowd gathered outside Walmart. Barbie was clearly in the picture, a group of brown-skinned, dark-haired kids gathered around her. Niswi was front and center. Baby Boy was not in the picture. But the picture was cropped. There still might be people on Barbie's right side that were off camera.

Quill jumped to life. She threw the car into reverse, then drive, and sped out of the casino lot.

With one hand on the steering wheel she used her thumb on the other hand to frantically scroll through her phone. Unsuccessful in finding anything she asked Punk, "What are they saying?"

"Nothing new. They don't say who was pulled into the van. A child."

Quill was shaking until she told herself, *Knock it off, get your shit together.* Icy resolve took over. She hit her phone with her middle finger and threw it at Punk. "Call Crow."

Punk dialed. When Crow answered she tried to hand the phone to Quill, who shoved her arm back at her. "You talk to him."

Punk relayed the news that was coming across Facebook. She told him Barbie was in one of the pictures but not Baby Boy. That Quill was driving them to Walmart right now.

"He's going to call Barbie."

Quill looked at her. Started to laugh. Her high-pitched laugh, bordering on hysteria, made the other two women uncomfortable. "Never entered my mind that I could have called her." The Walmart sign hung over the trees on the road ahead of them. It was the fastest trip to the store they had ever taken. Ahead they could see the flashing lights of cop cars blocking the entrances and exits to the megastore.

The store was in a new development area on the edge of the city. Not many buildings were close by. A couple warehouses. Then Quill spied an auto-glass company a few buildings down from the Walmart. She slammed on the brakes and slowed to the speed limit as she drove past the cop cars. She could see a crowd gathered outside the front door of the large retail store. Cops were walking among them. Quill could not see Barbie, but she was more intent on getting into the auto-glass parking lot. Once there, she didn't bother to park legally, but simply braked hard and jumped out of the car. She ran across the auto-glass parking lot and the adjacent building lots toward

Walmart. Punk and Gaylyn were on her heels. There was no police presence to stop them from entering the Walmart parking lot from the side.

As she neared the crowd, Quill slowed to a fast walk. Even in her anxious state, she knew enough that running toward a crowd being patrolled by police was not in her best interest. She walked into the crowd from the side, toward the back, and worked her way to the front, where Barbie had been standing in the picture on Facebook. Punk and Gaylyn snaked in behind her. Barbie and her kids were no longer there.

Panic burst through Quill's chest again. She gasped for air. She turned to look at Punk and Gaylyn with terror in her eyes.

"Come on. They went into the store to get out of the cold. Come on." Gaylyn's tone was quiet and sensible. Quill and Punk followed her into the store.

Gaylyn said, "I'll stay with Quill. Punk, you walk that way and look for them. Holler if you see them. We'll go this way. We'll go all the way around. Meet in back by electronics." And she steered Quill in the opposite direction from Punk. "Barbie wouldn't let anything happen to the kids."

"Not about Barbie. It's about these idiots who are out here looking for women or kids to exploit." They were rapidly scanning up and down every aisle.

They hadn't walked five aisles when they heard a *Lliillliillii* coming from the direction Punk had walked in. They turned and ran toward the sound, an ancient call Native women often use to signify victory.

There at the pizza place at the front of the store sat Barbie and the kids. There were two female police officers with them, along with three male cops. Quill scanned all the kids. Baby Boy sat on Niswi's lap. Quill ran toward them and got strong-armed by a cop who tried to stop her. Baby Boy squirmed off his sister's lap and was on his way to her. He grabbed her leg. "Mommy!" he yelled.

The cop dropped the arm he'd restrained Quill with. "You're his mom?" he asked. Without waiting for a reply, he motioned for her to take a seat.

"These are his aunties." Quill beckoned to Gaylyn and Punk, who quickly sat around the table the cop directed Quill and Baby Boy to. Niswi came and joined them. She crawled up on her mom's leg opposite Baby Boy and put her arms around Quill's neck. Barbie looked at Quill, gave a slight shake of her head, signaling that everything was okay. Quill counted the kids still around her. All Barbie's kids were accounted for.

A pizza worker brought out large cheese-and-pepperoni pizzas and set one in front of each group of people. One for Barbie and her troop. One for Quill's family. Another server brought out pitchers of soda pop.

Quill watched her children eat pizza while she eavesdropped on the interrogation of Barbie. Her son had gone into the men's bathroom. Barbie was in the women's bathroom with the girls and Baby Boy, who was too young to send off with the older boys. She was in a stall with her youngest daughter when she heard a little girl's voice say, "I don't know you."

A woman responded, but in a voice too low for Barbie to hear.

"No," the same girl said.

Barbie quickly unlatched the stall door, with her daughter still sitting on the toilet. When she stuck her head out, she saw a white woman. White. A bit overweight. Puffy down coat—blue, dark blue. A stocking cap. She was pulling a young Indian girl, maybe ten or eleven years old, out of the restroom. The girl? She wasn't a child Barbie had seen around before. Native. Wearing jeans, tennis shoes. Long dark hair. Her oldest daughter, Barbie Junior, was holding Baby Boy up to the sink, his hands all soap bubble with the water running over them. "I told Bee Junior to get Niswi into the bathroom stall where her sister and Baby Boy were and lock the door. By the time I pulled the bathroom door open, the woman and the young girl were gone. I yelled at my kids to stay in the bathroom, and I ran through the store looking for the woman. I got scared and ran back and got my kids and my boys from the men's room. By the time we got to the front doors, everyone was saying a white van stole the kid."

"We're under siege. This shit hasn't stopped in over five hundred years," Punk said under her breath.

"Whose kid is it?" asked Gaylyn.

"They don't know yet," answered Punk.

One of the male cops asked the boys if they saw or heard anything. No one had. The female cop sat down near Quill and Niswi. She offered Niswi a piece of pizza. The cop munched on a slice. Poured soda into a cup and took a drink. Offered a cup to Niswi. "Did you know the young girl in the bathroom?" she asked Niswi.

Niswi, mouth full of pizza, shook her head no.

"Did you know the woman she left with?"

Another headshake no.

"How many times have you asked her this?" said Quill.

"We need to make sure. Witnesses will often give us different answers to the same question."

"Shouldn't you be out trying to find her?" Gaylyn's voice was sharp.

"They're looking."

"Do you know who her parents are?"

The female cop ignored the question. She munched on a piece of pizza.

Oh my god, she's trying to bond with my kid over pizza, thought Quill. A different female cop was busy questioning Bee Junior, who was also shaking her head no. Another headshake no. And another.

Quill's phone pinged. It was Crow. He wanted to know where in the store she was; the tracker wasn't giving him her exact spot. He'd found her car, engine still running, in the auto-glass parking lot. Quill texted back, *Pizza place, inside Walmart.*

At the sight of his dad, Baby Boy jumped off Quill's lap and ran to him. Niswi settled fully on her mom's lap. Crow sat down. He slid Quill's car keys across to her, his eyes questioning. Quill gave a slight shrug. His eyes asked Barbie if she was okay. Her eyes answered yes. Whole conversations took place without the cops seeing or hearing.

Finally, the two families were allowed to leave with the caveat that they might be called back in for questioning. The parents were instructed not to ask their children any leading questions but to be open to listening if the children wanted to talk. And to relay any pertinent details they might remember immediately.

Outside the store, Baby Boy wanted to ride home with his dad. Crow hugged his sister, who apologized over and over, tears brimming in her deep brown eyes. Crow assured her it wasn't her fault. Barbie turned and hugged Quill, murmuring apologies to her too. All Quill could see, in her mind's eye, was Bee Junior, herself eleven years old, holding Baby Boy up to the sink. Either one could have been an easy target. She hugged Barbie back and assured her all was okay.

Back in the car, Niswi crawled into the front seat between Quill and Punk. Punk looked worriedly at Quill. Quill kept what little conversation that happened in the car light. She laughed and shared with Niswi about the kids pelting them with snowballs on their run. Niswi, a big smile on her face, told how her auntie took them all sledding in the snow. After Quill dropped Punk and Gaylyn at their respective homes, she went straight home.

Crow and Baby Boy were waiting for them. Crow held Quill a long time, wrapped her in his arms and held her tight. Finally, he leaned her back, looked in her eyes. And pulled her tightly back into his arms.

Niswi giggled, already engrossed in a video game.

Quill pulled back from Crow's arms and asked Niswi, "What are you giggling about?"

"The kids at school would say, 'Get a room.'" She giggled again. She went back to playing the video game. Baby Boy sat beside her, his fake game controller moving rapidly in the air before him. Quill, still in Crow's arms, said, "She's trying to shut out what happened. Do you think we should try and talk to them?"

"Let them be kids. If they need to talk, I think they'll let us know."

Crow unwrapped his arms from around her and said he needed to check the oil in his truck. Did she want to come out and have him check hers too? Parental code for they should go outside to talk without the kids around.

With both their heads stuck under the hood of his truck while Crow checked the fluid levels, Crow told her he'd found out that the young girl missing was a Lone Eagle originally from one of the Lower Sioux communities downstate. She lived in Duluth with her grandma. She'd gone to Walmart with teenage cousins, who were in the electronics department looking at phones when she left them to use the bathroom.

Quill and Crow threw questions back and forth at each other. Was it her family that took her? A custody thing? Since the Indian Child Welfare Act was passed by Congress in 1978, Indian kids were most often placed with grandparents if the grandparents were alive and considered by the courts to be suitable guardians. It wasn't unheard of that a mom or dad, with limited visitation, would miss their child so much they would take their child for an approved visit, but their hearts couldn't handle bringing them back when they were supposed to. And there were times when a noncustodial parent would pick a child up at school, or the local burger joint, and take off with them. The cops would be called. If a child was believed to be in immediate danger, an Amber Alert was issued. Most often the child would be returned one or two days later, unharmed.

There were a couple cases Quill remembered hearing about

where children were hurt badly, even killed. In most of those instances there was a history of domestic abuse. Sometimes one parent was determined to not let the other parent have the child. Those stories reverberated throughout Indian country.

Given the long history of governmental interference in Indian families, most parents treasured their children to the point of caretaking them well into adulthood. Which then presented a whole set of different problems. Grown men who never left home. Women who married but moved their new husband into their mother's home. Quill looked across the truck engine at Crow.

She had chosen wisely when she married Crow. He was calm and steady. A good worker. Not a drinker. Didn't do drugs. Valued family and wanted children. He didn't confine her. Welcomed her company when she helped him with his auto mechanics, or when they went hunting together. She felt safe with him. Felt that she herself and their children were safe with him. And together, they built a home and a good life right here, in this stand of trees. Both were still close to their families but building and nurturing their own family.

Crow looked up at her, looking at him. "Patrick said there didn't seem to be an issue with the family. But of course, they're checking it all out. This happened twice over in Bemidji this past fall. At the shopping mall. Same scenario. A white van. But it ended up an attempted abduction. Both times, the kids screamed bloody murder and the van took off without them."

"Twice? Geez. Why are we always the targets, Crow?"

He looked at her. Wiped oil from the dipstick with a greasy rag. Put the stick back. "The oil is good. You know the answer, Quill. We've been targets since the chimook arrived here. First war. Then boarding schools. Then foster homes. And Indian women have been targets all the way back to Pocahontas and Sacajawea. Teenage girls taken and used. Women taken and used."

"Makes me sick. We don't exist. Or if we do exist, we're expendable. How many U.S. presidents said 'The only good Indian is a dead Indian'?"

"And how many times did John Wayne say it in a movie? In real life and in the movies, we're erased or eliminated. Lemme check the oil in your car," Crow said. They backed away from the truck as he put the hood down. Quill pulled her stocking cap down farther over her ears, stamped her feet, and curled her fingers into the warmth of her palms inside her gloves.

"What's the windchill?" she asked.

"Not too bad, maybe minus seven. The temps are supposed to drop next couple days. You can hear the trees talking in the cold." He lifted the hood of her old Saturn. Pulled out the oil stick.

"And they never found the folks in the white van in Bemidji?"

"Guess not. But both kids who escaped said it was a man and a woman. White. Your oil is okay." Still leaning under the hood over the car engine, he pulled out a different stick. "You might be low on brake fluid. I'll check tomorrow. Too cold right now. I could use a cup of hot coffee. Hungry too." He shut the hood of the car. Wiped his hands on a grease rag he pulled from his back pocket.

They trudged back inside. Quill turned on the oven and they both stood in front of it until they warmed up. Niswi was watching a movie while Baby Boy was back to pushing cars and trucks under the couch.

Crow and Quill worked together to make the evening meal. Crow thawed out ground deer meat in the microwave to make a pot of chili and Quill baked cornbread with hot chilis in it. They streamed an adventure movie online after eating and watched it together, all of them huddled on the couch.

Occasionally Crow's phone would ping. So would Quill's. Patrick was keeping Crow updated on the search for the girl. Punk, Gaylyn, and Quill updated one another back and forth. Crazy rumors were flying throughout the community via texts and social media. All posted with vibrant emojis. The girl was taken by her dad. The girl was kidnapped by her mom. It was a white couple who were holding her as a sex slave. It was a white couple who were going to sell the child to the man camps. The child was already on one of the ships in the Duluth harbor on her way to Russia or Italy or Portugal. Each different story depended on who was doing the posting.

There was a plan for a rally the next day in downtown Duluth led by a group of local women who organized under the hashtag #mmiw. Because the national news now reported that there were more than five thousand Native women missing or murdered, almost everyone in Indian country knew what #mmiw stood for—missing or murdered Indian women. The organizers asked women to wear red ribbon skirts because that was the one color the spirits could see.

The organizers asked women to bring their hand drums and sing songs to call the women home, or to call the women's spirits back home. They cautioned walkers to dress warmly; the windchill was predicted to keep dropping overnight. The march would start at ten A.M. in the Walmart parking lot, and they would march to the shipping harbor, where large international ships passed through the canal. It was known that numerous Native women, for as long as ships had passed through the shipyard, had disappeared on ships that moved through the harbor, never again seen by their families.

When Quill checked social media, people were starting to mention the attempted abduction of Julie and the successful abduction of Lisa. Word also spread like wildfire about the search for the missing woman in the woods on the reservation.

Once the movie was over, Quill sent Niswi to bed while Crow rocked Baby Boy to sleep. When Quill went to get ready to go to sleep herself, Baby Boy was sound asleep in the middle of their bed tucked into the crook of Crow's arm. Crow looked at her, a soft grin on his face. He whispered, "I couldn't let him go to sleep by himself way over there." He looked at the crib not five feet from the end of their bed.

Quill smiled back and nodded. Got undressed and crawled into bed. She reached an arm over Baby Boy and put a hand on her husband's chest. Crow fell asleep before she did. Her hand rose and fell with each breath he took and released. Baby Boy was warm under her arm, his sweet brown face turned toward his dad. A piece of cornbread was stuck in his shiny black hair. Quill softly pulled it out and dropped it on the nightstand.

Her mind raced over all that had occurred in the past week. Today, when she hadn't known where Baby Boy was—how she jumped out of the car and left the car running, keys in the ignition. Her only thought to get to her baby. The dread that had filled each of them as they walked through the snow in the woods. Hoping to find Mabel. Hoping to not find Mabel. Knowing the cold and snow would make it next to impossible for it to be a live recovery if she was out there.

Quill felt warm tears slide down her cheeks before she finally drifted off to sleep.

She jumped awake when she felt a soft tap on her shoulder. She rolled over and there stood Niswi in the soft light coming through the bedroom window from the moon and stars outside. Tears streamed down her face in the faint light. "Oh, baby, come here." Quill pulled her up on the bed and into her arms. "Shhh, shhh, baby, it's okay. It's okay," she murmured over and over while she brushed Niswi's hair back off her forehead, tucked errant strands back behind her ear. Wiped her tears with the palm of her hand, all the while continuing to murmur, "It's okay, baby. Mama's here. Mama's right here."

Crow rolled over and quietly asked, "Everything okay?"

"Yeah," Quill answered, then went right back to comforting Niswi. "Shhh, baby, it's okay." Eventually, Niswi's sobs turned to soft hiccups and then to soft breaths while she fell asleep in her mom's arms.

Quill reached out and found her phone on the nightstand. It was 3:30 A.M. She saw she had unanswered texts from Punk. She put the phone back down. She didn't bother to read them as she lay there and remembered being told that this hour of the night was when the spirits were the most active. She had one baby at her back. Another in her arms. *How the hell did we survive this long?* she asked herself. *How did our ancestors survive the broken hearts of children gone? Parents murdered? We have lived with losing loved ones for century after century. And we still have babies and keep loving. This love will break my heart. I would have died today if Baby Boy were stolen away. I hope the family—that little girl's family, her grandmother—is okay. Those poor girls who took her to Walmart with them. They must be driving themselves crazy with guilt for letting her go to the bathroom by herself.*

Quill's mind raced, reliving the moment she saw the photo on Facebook. Baby Boy not there. Her heart began to physically hurt. The familiar anxiety, her companion since Jimmy Sky jumped off the railroad bridge in front of her when she was nine, coursed through her body. Her body wanted to get up and run. Run fast and hard. Run away. Run and keep running. Escape the overwhelming emotions.

Yet the adult Quill, the mom Quill, didn't dare let go of Niswi, for fear of waking her up. Niswi would wake and find her gone and start to cry all over again. Quill took deep breaths. Someone had once given her advice to take deep breaths, then shape her tongue into a straw and push the air out through the straw to a slow count of six. She breathed—in and out.

Despite how hard she and Crow tried to build a home of safety, to shield their children from the traumas so familiar to so many around them—alcohol, drugs, broken homes, violence—shit happened.

Her mind spun off on a nervous tangent. *Should I take her to the march? Have her see that lots of people care and are searching for the girl? Or would that traumatize her more? Shit! What's the best thing to do?* She thought of herself and Punk and Gaylyn running, running. No matter how fast she ran, the anxiety still crept in. Gaylyn seemed to be getting angrier every day. Why? Maybe that was her way of handling the anxiousness they all felt. Or maybe there were other difficulties related to her dad and life at home. And Punk and all her bravado, with the colored mohawks and self-mutilation with numerous piercings. Quill remembered Punk telling her how she would cut herself during hard spells as a teenager. Quill wondered if the piercings were a different, more socially acceptable form of cutting. But what the hell did she know? When every time the fear rose in her body and tightened her chest, her own response was to take off running. Exactly what she did when Jimmy Sky jumped.

But she knew there were resources that didn't exist back then, or that her parents didn't know about when she herself was a kid. She knew folks today who went to treatment for alcohol and drugs. Maybe they went to the same therapists as white people who went to therapy.

In that hour of the morning, when the elders say the spirits are walking, when they say the spirits are most active, Quill determined that when she woke, she would do what white people do. She would go online and find a therapist for her daughter, for her child who'd witnessed the trauma of another child being taken against her will. Enough of this "Shit happens on the rez and you just keep going."

And maybe Barbie would watch them so she and her friends could go to the march. Even if none of them owned a red ribbon skirt. Her last thought before sleep eased into her mind. *The spirits know my intention, with or without a red skirt.*

CHAPTER THIRTEEN

Quill didn't own a ribbon skirt, let alone a red one, so the next morning she threw on a red sweatshirt over a couple layers of shirts and thought, *Folks will have to live with me in long underwear and jeans.* She rushed the kids through their bowls of cereal while she called Barbie and asked her to again watch Baby Boy.

Crow came out of the bedroom. Overnight, errant black strands had escaped his long braid and crossed his forehead. He wore a white T-shirt with holes in it and a baggy pair of gray sweatpants.

"God, I need a cup of coffee."

Quill reached up into the cupboard. From a shelf filled with mismatched cups, all of which sported a Native geometric design or a tribal organization trademark or easily recognizable Native American motif—lots of bears and eagles and eagle feathers—she pulled a cup out for him. The red one she picked had a flute-playing Kokopelli dancing around on it. "I'm going to drop Baby Boy at your sister's. Niswi will get on the school bus in a bit. Then I'll pick up Punk and Gaylyn and go to the march in Duluth. Should be back about one."

"I wanna go," Niswi said.

"Not this time, kiddo. Too damn cold for kids out there today."

Crow pulled his wife into his arms.

Quill gently pushed Crow back. "I gotta run. This march starts at ten."

"Indian time. It's eight A.M. You got lots of time," Crow said. He pulled out a chair at the table next to Niswi, sat down, and poured himself a bowl of Cheerios. "Did you know that there are mothers who make real pancakes? Or eggs and toast for their families at breakfast?"

"Good thing the kids get a second breakfast at school then, eh?" Quill jabbed back as she pulled on her winter boots. She picked up Baby Boy off his chair and stuffed him into a snow-suit, winter boots, and a stocking cap. She tied a wool scarf around his neck and put mittens on his hands. Once dressed for the winter cold he was almost as wide as he was tall. "Yikes. You're gonna have to waddle out to the car. You're too big for me to carry. Love yous. See you later." And she was out the door.

At Barbie's she stood inside the front door and talked in a low voice with Barbie. Neither wanted to disturb the children with their worries. Quill assured Barbie she wasn't angry with her, that it certainly wasn't her fault there were crazy people in the world. She reassured her that she had done the best she could to keep their children safe.

Both said they hoped the Lone Eagle girl would be safely

found and that thank god their own children were safe. Both said they would die if anything happened to either of their kids. Quill didn't consider herself a hugger, but she hugged Barbie, thanked her for watching Baby Boy, and went back out to her car.

In the few minutes that she chatted with Barbie, the car had turned cold, and Quill's warm breath fogged up the windshield. She cranked the heat as high as it would go. She reached under the front seat and pulled out an ice scraper to clear the windshield enough for her to see to drive. With the heater throwing off enough warm air to keep more condensation from forming on the inside of the windshield, Quill took off to pick up Punk and Gaylyn.

Quill knocked on Punk's door. She rarely visited, as it had become habit over the years for the women to gather at her own home.

"Come on in," hollered Punk.

Quill opened the door and walked up the short flight of stairs into the living room, where an easy chair sat in front of a new large-screen TV. A muted basketball game played on-screen. Punk sat on the couch with her leg propped on a pillow. Her leg was encased in a stiff brace with Velcro straps around her thigh, knee, and calf.

"What the heck?" exclaimed Quill. "What happened?"

"I guess I twisted a muscle or pulled a tendon yesterday. Nothing to worry about. The clinic doc said it should be okay in a week or two." When she saw the look of concern on Quill's face, she quickly added, "It looks worse than it is. It's not broken or anything."

"Oh my god, Punk. Why didn't you call, text me?"

"I been trying to text and call you all day." Punk looked close to tears.

"I'm sorry." Quill pulled her phone out of her pocket and looked at the string of texts that had come in from Punk. She had been so preoccupied with getting up and out the door she hadn't checked her phone all morning. "I haven't even looked at my phone today."

Punk took a deep breath, then put a big smile on her face. "Cliff took me to the clinic and has been waiting on me hand and foot since I got back."

"You sure you don't need anything?" Quill looked around the room. "Smells good in here. What's cooking?"

"Stew. Cliff started it before he went to work. He's always starving when he gets home." She pointed to a half-empty bowl of stew on the coffee table in front of her and a stack of saltine crackers.

"So he's moved in, has he?" Quill looked around the room again. A vase of fresh flowers sat in the middle of the table. Pretty. The rest of the house looked the same as the last time she'd visited, although the easy chair was closer to the big-screen TV and three pairs of men's shoes sat on a rug by the entry door.

"Yeah." Punk turned her face away from Quill. When she looked back, she wore a bright and smiley expression. A little forced, maybe from the pain of her leg, but happy neverthe-less.

"Things okay though? How bad does your leg hurt?"

"Little bit. And, yeah, getting used to shacking up. You must know how that goes. Guys are a little high maintenance at times."

Both women laughed.

"I thought you were going to the rally with us. I got worried when you didn't come out right away." She looked around the room again, and back at Punk's leg up on a cushion. "I'm still hoping to be in shape for one of the marathons next year. You still my partner?"

A look of sadness crossed Punk's face. Quickly replaced by a half smile. "Of course. We been planning this for too long. This is just a minor setback. I'll be back out there with you before you know it."

Quill looked around the house again. It was totally spotless. And now that she noticed it, it smelled of cleaning products. "Wish my house looked this good."

Punk looked around, almost as if she didn't recognize the place. "You've got kids."

"Yeah. They wreak havoc with beauty and order. I better get going, I gotta pick up Gaylyn." Quill zipped her jacket back up and pulled her stocking cap down tighter on her head.

"I'll be back out soon. Don't worry," Punk said.

Quill stopped with her hand on the doorknob. "You need anything, you let me know, okay? Anything. I gotcha."

"Thanks, Quill. Catch you later." Punk waved at her from the couch. "Go on, get ready for Boston." Punk gave her a big grin and shooed her hands toward the door. "I'll be up and running before you know it."

Quill left. She stood outside and willed away the uneasiness she felt before hopping in the car to get Gaylyn.

Gaylyn opened the front door and asked, "Where's Punk?"

"She's got her leg in a brace. Said she twisted a muscle or tendon yesterday."

"Is she okay?" Gaylyn asked.

"No!"

"That's crazy. We haven't been training that hard."

"Guess you never know what can happen, huh?"

They both went silent until Quill noticed Gaylyn's ribbon skirt. The long blue calico skirt was thrown over her shoulder. Three rows of ribbon—yellow, red, and blue—circled close to the hem of the skirt.

"You brought a skirt?" Quill asked.

"Yeah. I'm not gonna get skirt-shamed by a bunch of Mide ladies," she said.

Quill side-eyed Gaylyn. "Geez, go ahead and make me look bad."

"You didn't bring a skirt? Oooh, kwe. What if those old ladies from the lodge say you can't walk?" teased Gaylyn.

"I don't own a skirt. I'm wearing a red sweatshirt. That should count for something."

"You better get to sewing then. I made mine at a class they offered at elders housing. You could go. They're still doing it on Wednesday nights."

"Hmm." Quill pulled onto the county highway that would take them into Duluth, past the casino. Gaylyn groaned when Quill insisted on making a quick run through the casino parking lot to check for the black pickup truck. She gave an exaggerated sigh of relief when it wasn't in sight and Quill pulled back onto the freeway and headed to Duluth.

The parking lot of Walmart was filled with cars. A large group of Indians was gathered in the southwest corner. From the highway, the crowd resembled a flock of red cardinals instead of the usual pale Thayer's gulls usually seen scavenging in the parking lot rather than feeding on the fish of Lake Superior.

Quill parked. The women prepared themselves mentally to step out into the cold. They sat and listened to one full song on the radio before Gaylyn said, "Skoden." And they piled out, their breath creating clouds around their faces in the frigid winter air. Gaylyn pulled her skirt on over her jeans. Quill stamped her feet in the cold while she waited for her. They wrapped scarves tighter around their necks, pulled their stocking caps down over their ears, adjusted their mittens so they covered their wrists, and walked to the edge of the gathered crowd.

An elder woman was giving a long-winded prayer in the Ojibwe language. She wore a long black wool coat with floral and woodland appliqués adorning the hem and lapels. A red ribbon skirt peeked out at the bottom of the coat. On her feet were beaded mukluks, the kind the Canadian tribes are famous for. Beaded with an ornate blueberry-and-green-leaf design. Quill guessed they were smoke-tanned caribou hide. On the elder's head was the beaded top hat so many of the traditional women wore.

She prayed to the four directions. She asked the manidoog to walk with them. She asked the manidoog to go out and find the young girl taken the day before. She asked the manidoog to guide the police who were looking for her. She asked the manidoog to help the police find Lisa, from Grand Portage. *Lliillliillii* rang up from the crowd. The elder prayed on. She asked the manidoog for guidance for the searchers to find all the missing women. To heal the hearts of the families. To heal the minds and hearts of the traffickers. She asked the manidoog to protect the walkers. She prayed on and on.

Quill stamped her feet to keep warm. Tucked her mittened hands up close to her armpits. Gaylyn, who Quill was sure was dressed in fewer layers than she was, stood calmly, hands in her jacket pockets, listening intently to the prayer.

Finally, the elder said, "Miigwech, Daga bi-wiidokawishi-naang wii mino bimaadiziyaang." Throughout the crowd, one could hear "Miigwech" and "Aho" murmured by the women gathered, and the sharp women's warrior cry of *Lliill-liillii* filled the air. Several of the women raised their right arms, their fists closed in solidarity.

The elder introduced Raven Lone Eagle's grandma to the crowd. She was placed in a chair in a pickup truck facing the crowd. Wrapped in blankets. The teenagers who were responsible for taking their young cousin to Walmart huddled around the tailgate of the pickup. They cried and hugged one another; unresolved guilt floated in the air around them.

A woman up front started singing a song in Ojibwe. She held a hand drum with a red handprint on its face. Women joined her in singing, each holding her own hand drum.

A group of younger women, all dressed in red ribbon skirts and red sweatshirts or winter coats, helped the Elder of Long Prayers into the bed of a pickup truck. They sat her on a powwow chair facing the crowd and wrapped her in wool blankets with Native designs. Several hand-drum singers climbed up on the tailgate, also facing the crowd. They kept singing. When the pickup truck moved forward, a group of males acting as security walked alongside the truck as did the crowd of cardinal-colored women. Quill and Gaylyn started walking. Soon they were engulfed in the middle of the crowd.

"At least we have frybread-friendly bodies for a wind-break," Gaylyn said.

Quill nudged Gaylyn with her elbow. "Oooh, look, there's Punk's new honey. He's standing security by the elder and singers."

Gaylyn answered, "Are you talking about the new cop? I see him up there on the left. Got a whole bunch of women sidling up next to him."

Quill said, "Story of Punk's life maybe. Just once I hope for her sake he's a decent guy."

"Hmmph."

The women finally reached the Duluth Aerial Lift Bridge in Canal Park harbor, a tourist attraction during the summer season for thousands who walk out on the promenade and watch the humongous cargo ships pass through the canal. Ships from all over the world carry wheat, salt, iron ore, and taconite out of the harbor. They bring in products from around the world.

Most of the women at the walk were well aware that for years Native women were a "product" trafficked out of the harbor. After several speakers, a middle-aged woman took her place at the podium. She talked about how a family member trafficked her to the ship crews for two summers before she overdosed, trying to numb her pain with opioids. The near-death experience got her into treatment where the twelve-step program and traditional teachings brought her back to herself and the community.

The woman ended her speech by begging the crowd, "Bring our women home. Cherish our women and children. We are the sacred keepers of the future generations."

The *Lliillliillii* warrior trill rang through the crowd. A group of women hoisted signs that read, WHERE IS LISA?; BRING LISA HOME; NO MORE STOLEN SISTERS; and #MMIW GRAND PORTAGE ELDERS AND WOMEN.

The elder stood in the back of the pickup. She kept the wool blankets wrapped around her shoulders. Quill squinted her eyes to shut out the pickup truck and the metal structures of the Aerial Lift Bridge behind the elder. In her mind's eye, the elder resembled a Curtis photograph of a Native woman from the turn of the century. The elder was handed the microphone. She thanked everyone for coming out on such a bitterly cold day. She asked them to watch their children and to protect each woman. She closed with a prayer, another long prayer, for the safe return of the Lone Eagle child. "And we have warm coffee and donuts up here for everyone. Come warm up."

The two women moved forward with the crowd. Up by the pickup truck, coffee urns, with the tribal casino logo taped on them, were set out on a six-foot table. Sugar, diabetic sugar substitutes, and fake powdered coffee creamer sat next to environmentally friendly paper cups. Women stood in groups under outdoor propane heaters, the orange-red heat pouring down on them while the steam from their hot coffee drifted upward.

"Look, there's Suzy, the woman from the coffee shop." Quill nodded her head toward a group of women huddled under one of the propane heaters. Gaylyn looked in that direction.

Suzy sensed them looking at her. She looked directly at them before she turned her back to them.

"She must be with the women from the halfway house," said Gaylyn.

"Doesn't want them to know we know her," added Quill.

There were more women than the heaters could accommodate, so the two women huddled near one in the hopes the women under it would soon move on. But the women near the heaters seemed to be in no hurry to leave the warmth penetrating down. Quill drank her coffee and wondered how soon they could appropriately leave the march. She was freezing. She also noticed the side-eyes women gave her while looking at her legs in jeans. She glanced around the crowd. All the women wore a skirt except for her.

"I guess I'm the shame of the Nation," she said, taking a sip of her lukewarm coffee. She had dumped in two sugar packets, calculating that the fake cream along with real sugar would give her enough calories to ward off the cold. It wasn't working.

A deep voice asked, "What's the shame of the Nation?"

Quill looked up from her coffee and saw that Cliff had joined them. He wore his tribal police winter uniform. A whole lot of wool. And thick black leather gloves. His cheeks, brown as they were, looked red from the cold.

"Quill is getting the look of shame from the lodge women 'cause she's not in a skirt," answered Gaylyn. Her mittened hands held a cup of hot coffee in front of her face as if the rising steam would keep her warm enough.

Cliff, hands clasped, trying to keep both hands warm in his gloves, looked around. "Yep, lotta red out here today."

"What are you doing here?" asked Quill.

"The organizers wanted us to come along for security. Be on the lookout for any potential troublemakers."

"Or maybe they thought the white van would return to the

scene of the crime the way it happens on all the cop shows?" said Gaylyn.

"Any news about the Lone Eagle girl or Mabel? Or Lisa?" asked Quill.

"Nah."

"I stopped by Punk's." She looked at Cliff to gauge his reaction as she said, "Her leg's in a brace?"

He looked at Quill. "Twisted her tendon or something. I took her in to emergency last night."

"How'd that happen?" Gaylyn asked sharply.

He just stared at her, then looked back out at the crowd.

Quill, who was getting used to Gaylyn's anger, interjected, "How are we supposed to get back to our cars? I forgot to find out that tiny detail."

"I can get you a ride back. Follow me. There are cars shuttling folks back and forth."

As they approached the pickup where the elder sat with a couple cars idling beside it, a flurry of activity occurred. One man beckoned for Cliff to get over there.

Gaylyn, under her breath, asked, "What the hell is happening now?" She walked away from Quill until she stood near the circle of men, most of whom were off-duty tribal cops, and the women who had organized the march. Gaylyn, quiet as she was, had the ability to appear invisible. No one paid her any attention as she moved silently in among the small crowd of men and women who leaned in to hear the important news.

Quill heard exclamations of "No!" repeated over and over from the small crowd near the pickup truck. Wails arose in the air from the teenage cousins. One of them fell to the ground and was lifted by the women near her and laid on the tailgate of the truck. A group of women and teens huddled around her.

The women who were still drinking coffee under the propane heaters sensed the change in the atmosphere. They walked briskly to the pickup, quickly ditching their half-empty coffee cups in the trash containers set around the site. Soon a sizable crowd surrounded the truck once again.

A Channel 5 news van, which had left right after the crowd was invited to partake of coffee and donuts, returned and pulled up next to the curb a block away. Brakes screeched and car doors slammed. The news crew, with cameras and mics at the ready, ran toward the women and handful of men gathered around the pickup truck.

Gaylyn came back to Quill as quietly as she had left. "They found the Lone Eagle girl. She's dead."

Quill sucked in a deep breath. She peppered Gaylyn with questions. "How? Why? Where?" and, finally, "Ah, shit."

Gaylyn shrugged and said, "They're going to make an announcement." Right then, one of the hand drummers up front started singing the mourning version of the Ojibwe traveling song. Slowly, quietly, more women's voices joined in.

The drumbeat reverberated within Quill. Tears, ice cold, slid down her cheeks. She used the backs of her mittens to wipe them away.

"Well, what the fuck," Gaylyn repeated over and over as she stood immobile. Her face a quiet mask.

At the end of the song, the Elder of Long Prayers stood in the back of the pickup truck. Mic in hand. Her voice broke when she delivered the news. "We have received word that our little sister, Raven Lone Eagle, was found this morning. All the way over on the Minnesota–North Dakota border. Her family has requested privacy. Keep them in your prayers."

"How?" a voice shouted out from the crowd.

Someone else yelled, "Did they kill her?"

The Elder of Long Prayers held a hand up for silence. The crowd quieted to a soft murmur of outrage and concern. The elder held out her hand for the teenage cousins to pull themselves up into the back of the pickup with Grandma Lone Eagle and the girl who had crumpled to the ground. Cliff closed the tailgate and hit the side of the truck, signaling for it to drive off. It slowly moved forward, then picked up speed as it left Canal Park, the heads of all the women in the bed of the truck huddled together in sorrow.

Cliff walked back toward the women. "Damn" was all he said.

Quill broke the silence. "What happened?"

"Don't know much right now. They found her body by the side of the road close to the Montana border."

"Was she killed?"

"I don't know. They didn't say."

They stood in silence. Even from a distance they could hear soft murmurs from different groups of women. Huddled together, their voices sounding soft and scared.

Cliff broke the silence. "Come on. We can get one of these cars to take us back to the parking lot." He walked with them over to the line of waiting sedans. He tapped on the window and opened the back door. "Hop in." He got in the passenger seat.

The temperature change from outside to the toasty warmth of the car made the women shiver. "Sucks, huh, man?" said the driver to no one in particular. Quill recognized him as one of the security guards who had jumped into the fight when the oil workers tried to carry a drugged Julie out the casino door.

"For sure," answered Cliff. The women murmured agreement. Quill and Gaylyn looked out their respective passenger windows.

"So, who called? How did you guys hear that they found her?" Quill asked.

"It came over our scanners," answered the driver.

"One of the cousins overheard the scanner and then we had to tell the grandmother and the cousins who are here. Nip any rumors in the bud," said Cliff.

"Oh, there will be rumors," said Gaylyn.

CHAPTER FOURTEEN

Quill and Gaylyn rode in silence back to the rez. Quill always marveled that no matter what time of night or day it was, the casino parking lot was invariably full. Unconsciously she scanned the lot for vehicles without license plates. Gaylyn noticed and said, "No. Just get us home."

Quill continued to drive slowly but didn't enter the casino lot. Nothing stood out among the heavy-duty pickup trucks, family-sized SUVs, and run-down farmer's cars with winter road salt caked on the sides of the doors and rear wheel hub.

At the village, Quill pulled into the gravel driveway and stopped a few feet short of the front doorsteps of Gaylyn's home. She glanced at her watch. "I gotta pick up Baby Boy and get home. See you tomorrow."

The door to the house, which had been white at one time in its life, was now yellowed with age and loose on its hinges. Quill saw a makeshift curtain move slightly on the back bedroom window and then immediately drop shut. Gaylyn quickly jumped out. "Thanks," she said.

As she pulled out of the driveway, Quill stopped to wait as a yellow school bus blocked her exit. The bus on the road moved past the driveway. It went north and Quill turned south to Barbie's.

As Quill stepped inside the door at Barbie's she was greeted with warmth and the smell of baked cookies. Baby Boy ran and hugged his mom's legs as soon as he saw her. Barbie ruffled his hair. "He's been a good boy all day. Helped me make chocolate cookies. Might be a little sugared up. How was the march?"

"Cold." Quill lowered her voice, Baby Boy still wrapped around her legs. "Did you hear the news?"

Barbie put a hand to her ample chest. "Broke my heart. Honest to god, broke my heart. It is horrible to say but thank god it wasn't one of our kids. You know?"

"I know," said Quill. She rubbed Baby Boy's hair back from his forehead and looked down at his smiling face. She used her thumb to wipe a smear of chocolate off his cheek. "I gotta get this kid home and fix supper. Thanks for watching him."

"I was afraid you might never trust me with them again."

"Wasn't your fault, Barbie. And they're all safe. They're all safe," she repeated as if to assure herself as well as Barbie.

Barbie was a couple years older than Crow, so Quill didn't know her growing up. Had only come to know her after marriage and having the kids. A stay-at-home mom, Barbie was their go-to babysitter, not just for her family but for many of the families on the rez. Warmhearted and with a stable home life, she was a role model for many of the younger mothers around, who called her up for advice with newborns or kids going through teenage angst.

Barbie reached out and squeezed Quill in a tight hug. "You keep an eye out when you're running. Scary people out there." Quill gave her a quick squeeze back. "I will. Thanks." She turned to Baby Boy. "Come on, kiddo, get your gear on and let's get you home to Dad."

In the car Quill's phone dinged and dinged. With snow on the road and Baby Boy in the back, she didn't dare check her messages.

She took a quick pass by the casino parking lot. Did a quick eye search for the black pickup truck. Not in sight. As she passed the tribal station on the way home, a beat-up white four-door swerved by her. Quill caught a glimpse of a woman she didn't recognize. She was sure it was the same car that had driven down the road the other night. Someone driving through the rez who didn't know the roads, over the speed limit, was a dangerous situation. Never knew when a kid, dog, or deer would run out or there might be an unexpected curve in the road up ahead. At least it wasn't a dark pickup with tinted windows. Quill gave her head a shake to clear the anxiety that arose with the thought of the truck.

As soon as she parked in the driveway at her own home, she grabbed her phone off the passenger seat. Seven messages from Punk. Three were emojis with hearts for eyes. The fourth was a heart engulfed in fire. The next three were *where are you?— talk to me, talk to me—got news about Lone Eagle.*

Quill typed, *Cool it. Gotta make supper. Later.*

"Come on, Baby Boy. Your Auntie Punk has fallen off the deep end. Go grab your daddy by his legs and distract him while I cook, okay?"

Baby Boy ran to the house. By the time Quill got inside,

Crow had taken off the little boy's winter gear. He was holding him, asking him how his day was. Baby Boy was telling him how his cousin hid cookies under the pillow in his bedroom. "Midnight snack!" Baby Boy said to Crow, his chubby hands on both his dad's cheeks, as he looked seriously into his face. Crow laughed.

Quill took that opportunity to walk into the kitchen and pull leftovers out of the fridge. As she went about the everyday routine of getting food ready to feed her family, overwhelming sadness crept into her being. Grief for the death of Raven Lone Eagle. *Who in the hell takes an innocent child and then leaves them on the side of the road?* She felt anger on the verge of rage that pipeline workers were invading her rez. Making her woods and roads unsafe places for her to be, to live her life. Building a pipeline that would surely break and contaminate the water around them for generations. Abducting women, which left the community always on the edge of fear. There were generations of women raped and children stolen. Thousands of Jimmy Skys who couldn't live with the pain, either their own or that of the generations before. It all came at you so fast, one could barely adjust, integrate, come to terms with one disaster before the next thing slammed into you. With that thought she slammed plates and soup bowls down on the table. In the middle, she set a bowl of potato chips.

"Chips!" squealed Niswi. Since Quill had started seriously training for the marathons, she'd made a rule of no junk food—chips, ice cream, cookies, cake, donuts, frybread—in the house.

Quill said sharply, "You don't need to scream."

"Quill," Crow warned.

"Don't 'Quill' me. Get over here and eat. Come on before it gets cold."

They were quiet as they ate. Crow broke the silence by saying, "Niswi, did you hear about the girl who was taken from Walmart?"

Niswi shook her head no.

"Her name was Raven Lone Eagle. They found her today. Way over on the North Dakota–Minnesota border," Crow said.

Niswi asked softly, "Is she okay?"

"No, baby girl, she's not."

Niswi looked quickly at Quill. Fear in her eyes.

"Come here, my girl," said Quill. She pushed her chair back from the table. Niswi ran to Quill's lap and buried her face in her shoulder.

Crow continued, "This is scary. For all of us. Her family is struggling right now too."

"Do they know who took her?" asked Niswi.

"No. We don't know. We don't want you to go wandering off by yourself." He threw a stern look at Quill. "Best to stay in groups. If your mom or I won't be home, we'll leave a message at the school and you'll get off the bus over at your cousins', okay? And if your auntie takes you to the store or somewhere, you all stay in a group, okay?"

Niswi nodded. That night Crow played a quiet game of "push the trucks around" with Baby Boy. Niswi followed her mom around as she picked up the house, did the dishes, and started a meal in the crockpot for supper the next night. Worn out from a day with his cousins, Baby Boy was content to lie on the couch with a mobile device. He fell asleep halfway through a dog-that-talked movie.

Finished with kitchen duty, Quill sat down to check her phone messages. Niswi joined her with a coloring book. Neither spoke. With Niswi lost in a world of coloring fractals, Quill scrolled through social media. Her message box dinged. It was Julie.

Did you hear the news?

Thumbs-up emoji.

I couldn't go to march. Migizi had to work. I had the baby.

Too cold for a baby. Good you stayed in.

Anyone say anything about Lisa?

Punk pinged.

Quill ignored her, pinged Julie back. *Lisa was mentioned in the prayer.*

No one's heard from her at all?

No one's heard from her.

A crying emoji from Punk. *Come over!!!!!*

Can't. Niswi is scared after hearing about Lone Eagle. Won't leave my side.

Damn. Followed by a crying emoji.

Quill's phone ringing interrupted more texts from Julie. She looked at the incoming call and it was from Punk.

"What's up?"

"I get laid up and you don't even want to talk to me anymore."

"Get real. Leg okay?"

"Yeah. I'll live. Hope you're not mad at me about the guy

thing? I wanted to tell you right away, but I wasn't sure I believed it myself. We been seeing each other for a minute. Was scared it was a one-night stand. But . . . I think it's real. But that's not why I called; I wanted to tell you what I found out about Raven Lone Eagle."

"I have Niswi right by me. She's coloring."

Punk lowered her voice. "Oh. Okay. Cliff told me the poor young girl was dumped on the side of the road. They don't know if it was the people in the white van who threw her out. Quill"—Punk's voice cracked around a sob—"she was alive when they dumped her out. She might have lived if she had been found right away. The poor baby hid in the ditch, down by a culvert. She must have been scared out of her mind. People driving by wouldn't have been able to see her. No one."

"Nooo . . ." Quill recoiled. "Poor baby."

"Snowmobilers on a beer run found her. She might have been out there all day, Quill. Froze to death." Punk sobbed softly.

"So, he told you all this tonight?"

"Yeah. My twisted leg is nothing compared to what happened to that poor baby."

Both women were silent for a long minute. Punk asked, "Niswi still there?"

"Yeah."

Punk changed the subject. "He told me about growing up at Turtle Mountain. Doesn't have a girlfriend. Or a wife. Doesn't drink or smoke."

"So you slept with him? Before knowing all this?"

"Leave me alone. I'm in love."

"Listen girl, you fall in love—more like lust—all the time."

"This might be for real. He's really nice."

"Have you run a background check on him?"

"Knock it off!"

"Serious. Can't be too cautious these days."

"He's cute. Kinda chiseled cute. All-sharp-edges good-looking."

"He wasn't scared off by all your piercings and tats?"

"Nah, he just said he won't date a girl with a neck tattoo. Thank god I didn't get one when we were down at the mall. My 'unique look'—he said that's what made him curious." Punk turned quiet again before she said, "I feel so bad for that young girl. And her family."

"Me too."

"He's here. I gotta go."

"Gotcha."

Both women clicked off. Quill put her phone on silent and watched Niswi color bright pink triangles around red hexagons.

Eventually, emotionally exhausted, they all crawled into bed. Quill woke at three A.M. Crow was sound asleep on his side of the bed, under the covers. Niswi was sleeping on a makeshift bed of blankets on the floor and Baby Boy was in the crib. Quill pulled the covers over herself as she spooned around Crow, who breathed deeply but didn't wake.

Quill willed her mind to shut off, to not visualize stolen children; to not think about lost and trafficked or murdered women. About young men who dove off bridges. She felt the warmth of Crow, and the rise and fall of his chest with his breathing. The hard muscles of his back from the manual labor he did to provide for the family. She willed herself back to sleep.

She woke to an empty bed and the sound of her children

laughing. She could hear Crow as he moved around the kitchen. The sound of silverware on plates. The air smelled of bacon and fried eggs. The time on her phone said 7:45 A.M. She pulled the covers up tight under her chin and rolled the covers around her mummy-tight. *What the heck?* There were fourteen missed messages on her phone. Nine from Julie. Five from Punk. The ones from Punk were emojis of crying. *Oh god,* thought Quill.

As she scrolled through her messages, she could see the ones from Julie were time-stamped at 6:00 A.M., 6:02 A.M., 6:10 A.M., 7:00 A.M., 7:01 A.M., 7:03 A.M., 7:05 A.M., 7:07 A.M., 7:30 A.M. The partially visible, pale underlying message beginnings gave a clue. *Call me . . . Please call . . . Lisa call . . . Please . . .* The phone said it was now 8:00 A.M. Quill's stomach churned.

CHAPTER FIFTEEN

Quill called Julie. No answer. *Damn.* Probably dealing with the baby. She called Punk. Same. She imagined Punk trying to hobble to the phone with the brace on her leg. Why had they been calling all morning? She dreaded the answer but felt compelled to find out. She redialed Julie. Let it ring. She was ready to hang up on the twelfth ring when finally: "Quill? Sorry, I had to grab the baby."

"What's up?"

"Lisa called. Said she's at the gas station in Little Sweden . . ."

Before Julie finished her sentence Quill was out of bed and pulling on clothes from the night before.

". . . right on the main street."

"Where?"

"Little Sweden. Can you go get her? She sounds scared and crying. She's a mess. I can't go. I have the baby, and Migizi worked overnight. Can you go get her?" Julie repeated, then said, "She told me no when I said to call the cops. I'm worried that if a guy cop shows up she'll freak out. I told her to stay there, and I would find someone to go get her. She'd trust you. Please?"

"I was sleeping. My phone was turned off."

"I told her to wait. That you would come get her."

"Is she okay?"

"No." Silence. "But she's alive."

"Is she alone?"

"Yeah. She said she got dumped off. She doesn't remember much."

"Does she have a phone?" Quill pulled on a sweatshirt.

"No. She called from inside the station. But she's scared. She called again about a half hour ago. She was trying to hide in the bathroom but the woman who came on shift is letting her sit behind the counter with her. She's afraid those men might come back for her."

By then, Quill was putting on her winter clothes by the front door. She grabbed a blanket off the couch the kids usually wrapped themselves in.

Crow leaned on the kitchen counter. "Where you going?"

"Out."

To Julie, "I'm on my way."

Crow, louder: "Where the hell you going?"

"Out!" she hollered back at him. Quill was not emotionally ready to explain the situation to Crow. He would want answers and caution and for her to call Patrick. She was desperate to run—run out of the house and get to Lisa—to help. Once in the car, still on the phone with Julie, she said, "Julie, I'm on my way. I'm going to hang up. If Lisa calls back tell her I'm on my way. Gonna see if a couple of my friends can come help too."

"Okay. Thanks."

Quill hung up and called Punk. It went right to voicemail. *Either she can't hobble around or she's still in bed with her new cop,* Quill thought. She cranked up the heat in the car as the front window started to fog over from her warm breath. She got the windshield scraper and cleared off enough of the inside fog so she could see to drive. At the same time she called Gaylyn, picturing in her mind Gaylyn grabbing the old-fashioned handset off a landline phone.

"'lo?"

"Gaylyn, can you go with me on a ride?"

"Uh, I guess. When? Why?"

"I'll be there in a sec."

And Quill hung up.

Crow was calling and texting her. Quill ignored him. The heat from the defrost slowly cleared the rest of the windshield so she didn't have to scrunch over and peer out the small square of clear glass she had scraped free.

She tapped the horn as she pulled into the driveway. Gaylyn came running out, a piece of toast hanging out of her mouth, while she pulled mittens on her hands. "What're we doing?" she asked around a mouthful of toast as soon as she sat down in the front seat. The smell of fried potatoes hung in the cold air around her.

"You know Julie from the hospital?"

"My wannabe cousin?"

"Yeah. The girl who went missing at the same time from the casino—Lisa—she called Julie from a gas station over in Little Sweden. We're gonna go pick her up."

"Well, shit."

"I know, huh?"

"She's alive then."

"Yep."

"Well, shit . . . Did you call the cops?" Gaylyn asked.

"No. She's scared. Julie thinks she'll freak out if she sees any guys coming for her. We'll get her. Then figure out what to do. Okay?"

They drove in silence. Quill turned on a country music radio station. The only other sound was the ping of Quill's phone as Crow tried to reach her.

"Maybe you should answer that?"

"Nah. It won't serve any good purpose for you to hear us argue back and forth."

"Huh." Gaylyn went back to looking out the window at the trees going by.

It was a bit more than a half an hour drive to Little Sweden, population 391, a small Minnesota town in the middle of no-where. No one knew Little Sweden existed except the people who lived there. Or folks who spent their summers at nearby lake homes. The people who drove north from the Cities called these luxury summer homes their lake cabins. City youth spent the summer waterskiing, jet skiing, wearing small biki-nis, and jumping off square docks set beyond the drop-offs in the lake bed. When not on the water they were disrupting the quiet of the surrounding forest by riding four-wheelers on backwoods trails.

Their parents would dump ice cubes into coolers over beer and wine bottles. Pack with white-bread sandwiches made with sliced turkey, iceberg lettuce, and mayo or mustard for variety and call it a meal. Load everything on large canopied pontoons and slowly cruise the lake, drinking and pretending to fish. Midwest blond and predominantly blue-eyed, they would return home in the fall with summer tans that would fade by mid-October.

With the invasion of the oil pipeline being laid across the state, the small towns were seeing an influx of male workers from out of state coming to work the pipeline. They came without family. Without the civilizing presence and responsibility of spouses or children. They bunked in makeshift man camps or filled the local motels. They ate meals in small country diners where the main course was a hot roast beef sandwich or a meatloaf dinner. Making mega-man wages, they spent big and drank heavily. They had the spare cash to spend on illicit drugs. They tipped big, thinking it made up for trashed rooms, hangover vomit in bathrooms, and more than the occasional hallway fight.

Previously, these same businesses could rarely boast a half-full house on a winter night, unless a snowmobile ride was scheduled as a sporting event. The motels were happy to have the rooms filled all winter. Happy to hand out free coffee and artificial maple syrup on artificial pancakes each morning.

The oil workers did not patronize the community churches in the same numbers as the locals, who found themselves attending more frequently, simultaneously sitting in hard wooden pews thanking God for the influx of money into their economy while praying to keep their daughters safe.

A quiet folk, the locals tended to keep their personal business to themselves. They didn't talk to their neighbors about a daughter who arrived back home with the sun coming up, her clothes in tatters, her eyes blank and her speech slurred. When her time didn't come in the following month, they might send her to a liberal relative in the Cities who knew where a Planned Parenthood clinic was. The poorer folk—those habitually targeted as being from the "wrong side of the tracks"—watched their daughter's belly swell and kept a tighter rein, a more watchful eye over any younger siblings still at home. Families from both sides of the track watched sons and daughters get caught in the trap of opioid or meth addiction.

In communities that were generationally quiet, things got quieter while the outside noise got louder. Big pickup trucks roared through the streets. The local bars filled at night. Waitresses, adept at avoiding quiet, drunk Lutheran farmers' advances, quit, unable to handle the outright harassment by men who had no woman at home. Women walked and drove in pairs: to work, to the grocery store, to afternoon luncheons at the local grill, to Wednesday night Bible study. Fathers picked up daughters after school band practice, after basketball games, after Wednesday night confirmation studies. No more "catch a ride home with the neighbor kid." All unspoken about. All quietly done. Community trust and movement silently shifted to alert status. The taken-for-granted safety of the north woods broken forever.

CHAPTER SIXTEEN

It was this unspoken, silent uproar that Quill and Gaylyn drove into as they approached the town of Little Sweden. The town sat twenty miles south of where the pipeline crossed the Mississippi River. The local motel filled each night with oil workers. The local diner fed them dinner each night, their raucous joshing back and forth disrupting conversations of the locals, many of whom took to eating dinner at home, forgoing an evening out to catch up on the neighbors' gossip. Quill pulled into the station that fueled the oil workers' pickups and SUVs. Filled their thermoses with hot coffee and sent them out the door with a bag of chips or donuts.

As Quill put her car into park, a pickup with no license plate pulled out. Three broad-shouldered men, each sporting a week's worth of face scruff, were squeezed into the cab of the truck. Both women avoided the men's stares. Neither touched their door handles until the pickup was half a block away.

They both exited the car at the same time. Quill stuffed her phone into her jacket pocket and pulled her stocking cap down over her ears. Gaylyn pulled her mittens up to cover her wrists. They looked at each other, shrugged, and walked into the convenience store, warriors heading for battle.

Once inside, past the inch markers on the doorframe, they stood shoulder to shoulder and scanned the interior. Quill thought, *Oh my god, they might think we're casing the joint.*

Gaylyn touched her elbow to Quill's and motioned with her lips to the female cashier behind the plexiglass barrier at the register. She was blond—peroxide-streaked hair with turquoise tips. She wore a small sparkly crystal in a nose piercing and a small black hoop through her left eyebrow. Her ears were lined with more sparkly posts. Her T-shirt, snug over her ample chest, sported glittery hearts with angels flying around. There was a curlicue tattoo on her neck that Quill couldn't decipher from the doorway.

The cashier looked around the store, glanced up at the monitors that showed who was or wasn't at the pumps outside the building, then waved them over.

"You here for Lois?" she asked in a stage whisper, looking furtively around the store.

Quill and Gaylyn nodded; neither corrected the woman's use of the name Lois instead of Lisa.

"Hang on a sec." The clerk lifted the counter and exited her cashier's cage. "Follow me. I found her curled in a ball on the far side of the building. I thought I heard a cat squealing back there. She was freezing, nothing but a bra and panties on. Brought her in and let her call you. She would freak out anytime I mentioned calling the police. When the morning rush began, she started to freak out again, curled up on the floor by my feet. I snuck her back here to the storage room with a blanket I carry in my car. Poor thing." She knocked softly on a door. "Lois, your friends are here."

She lowered her whisper to the two women, repeating again, "She wouldn't let me call the cops. She got hysterical when I mentioned them. Got up, wearing next to nothing, ready to run back out the door." She turned the doorknob slowly. "She might be in shock," she whispered before she pushed the door open wide enough for them to get in.

Nothing prepared Quill and Gaylyn for what they saw. Quill experienced a flashback of Jimmy Sky right before he dove. She involuntarily stepped back. She froze like a rabbit that goes into survival mode when it senses a threat nearby. She watched Gaylyn pull all her energy into the core of her being.

Lisa was a tiny woman. Way smaller than Quill or Gaylyn. What should have been shoulder-length black hair stood out in tufts around her face and atop her head. The left side of her face was swollen, her eye shut. Her cheek and forehead black and orange and green. While most of the blanket was wrapped tightly around her, it had slipped off one shoulder and uncovered a bra strap. Her feet, sticking out from under the blanket, were bare.

Gaylyn unfroze. "I'm Gaylyn. This is Quill. She's going to go back out to the car and get fresh clothes out of her gym bag in the trunk."

Quill backed out of the storage room. The incongruity of snack food stacked to the ceiling surrounding the tiny battered woman wrapped in a blanket—it shook Quill. The image repeatedly flashed through her mind like a fluorescent bulb that flickers annoyingly.

Quill scanned the lot before exiting. Her car and one that

must have been the cashier's were the only two in the lot. She popped her trunk hood and unzipped her gym bag. She pulled out bright green running gear, a sweatshirt, and a dirty pair of socks. She grabbed her pair of running shoes, even though she didn't know if they would fit Lisa. Arms full, she clicked the key to lock the car and went back into the store.

The cashier was back up by the register. Her head moved sadly from side to side. "Glad you guys are here. I don't know what I would have done if I went around that corner and found her dead."

Quill stared at her, not knowing how to respond.

"I gave them both a hot cup of coffee. Grab one if you want."

Quill indicated she didn't need one and continued back to the storage room. Lisa hadn't moved but she was drinking the cup of coffee, both hands wrapped around the paper cup as if to draw all the heat out of it through the palms of her hands. Gaylyn sat on an empty black plastic milk crate. Her long legs put her knees up by her chest.

She held out the clothes to Gaylyn. "Here." Quill felt anxiety tightening her chest. The tension coursing through her legs said *Run, run*. Gaylyn put the coffee cup on the floor and unfolded herself from the crate and reached for the clothes. She looked into Quill's eyes and Quill knew she saw the terror there.

"I'll help her get dressed," Gaylyn said, taking the clothes out of Quill's arms. "Why don't you go out to the car and crank up the heat? We'll be out in a sec."

Quill nodded and left. She did as she was told. She sat in the car, heat blasting, eyes darting between the rearview mirror and the door mirror, watching the road behind her nervously, all doors locked. She felt in her pocket for Mabel's beaded earring. She rubbed her thumb and forefinger over the tiny beads that made the flower design. The earring, now a constant companion, had become her worry stone. Her comfort stone. Her grounding stone.

She texted Crow to let him know she was okay, that she would explain when she got home, and ignored the rest of his messages.

When Gaylyn rapped on the car window, Quill jumped with a start. She rolled down the window. Gaylyn handed the running shoes to her. "Why don't you put these on and give me your boots? These are way too big and at least your boots will stay on her feet."

Quill pushed the car seat back, quickly pulled off her boots, and handed them out the window. When Gaylyn turned to go back into the store, Quill quickly rolled the window back up. She slipped the shoes on and pulled the car seat forward and went back to watching the road behind her. She texted Julie and said, *Got her.* She didn't respond to Julie's subsequent texts. She let her phone ping.

Her heartbeat increased when a pickup pulled up to the pumps. But it was only a local farmer guy. Dressed in old-man coveralls and a wool-lined denim overcoat, popular in the sixties, he climbed painfully out of his truck and shuffled around to where his gas tank was.

Quill was watching him make his slow climb back into his truck when Gaylyn walked out toward her car with Lisa, who had a blanket wrapped around herself and a brand-new purple Vikings stocking cap on her head. She clutched the blanket tightly to her chest, the ends dragging on the dirty snow in the parking lot. Her eyes darted rapidly from side to side. Gaylyn led her to the car. Opened the door for Lisa to sit behind Quill. Baby Boy's car seat still occupied the passenger side. Quill unlocked the back door and Lisa slid in.

"I'm going to run back in and grab more coffees for all of us. Right back." Gaylyn loped back into the store.

Quill looked in the rearview mirror. Lisa wasn't there. Quill whipped around to look backward and saw the young woman curled up in a ball on the backseat. She was completely covered with the quilt she was wrapped in. Quill turned back around to look out the windshield. For maybe the first time in her adult life, she wished she smoked cigarettes. She checked her phone. Fifteen texts from Crow. Four from Punk. Six from Julie. She didn't answer any of them.

Gaylyn came back out, her hands full of coffee and a white paper sack filled with donuts. Quill reached across the front seat and opened the passenger door for her, leaving the other three doors locked. Took two cups out of Gaylyn's hands. "Lisa, here's hot coffee." She handed a cup of coffee over the seatback. Lisa's arm snaked out from the blanket. She grabbed the coffee and sat up halfway to take a tentative sip.

Gaylyn added, "And the cashier gave us donuts. Lots of donuts."

Gaylyn continued, "We're going to take her to the hospital in Duluth. Told her that's where the EMTs took Julie from the casino. Once we get her checked in and the doctors have looked her over, the cops are going to want to talk to her." Gaylyn handed packs of sugar and creamer to Quill and Lisa, then stirred two packs of sugar and three creamers into her own coffee. "Told her I would stay with her for long as she wants me to."

"Skoden," Quill said as she backed out of the parking space and headed back toward Duluth. Gaylyn had spoken more sentences this morning than Quill had ever heard from her. And when Quill froze, Gaylyn became the adult. Quill looked at Gaylyn out of the corner of her eye. Gaylyn caught her.

"What?"

"Nothin'."

Silence.

"Thanks for coming with."

Silence.

Quill, her senses on high alert, noticed things she hadn't been aware of on the drive over to Little Sweden when the focus was solely to retrieve Lisa. They drove past Minnesota forests and then by swamp prairie with orange marsh grass standing up out of frozen water. The ditches were filled with snow. In a couple spots she could see where a car had slid on ice and ended up off the road. Tow truck tires and car tracks were the only evidence left behind. On the highway were snowdrifts from the previous night's crosswinds, which had floated snow across the road. The drifts were now flat patches of white on the pavement with tire tracks creating a visible path. A llama stood in a fenced field. "What the fuck? Who the hell has a llama in this part of the country?" Quill asked no one in particular.

The air in the car carried an edge to it that the cold outside defined. All the women were aware of every vehicle on the road. Each pickup truck they met caused Lisa to duck down on the seat, quilt pulled over her head. Every time she ducked down, Quill's heart beat faster. Each duck down created a deeper scowl on Gaylyn's forehead.

When they came close to the casino, Lisa crawled onto the floor of the car. Once they turned north onto I-35W heading toward Duluth, and drove past Cloquet, Lisa crawled back up on the seat and seemed to relax a bit the farther they got from the casino and the closer they got to Duluth. She looked out the window at the snowscape.

Quill ventured to ask, "Do you know who did this to you?"

She observed Lisa's reaction in the rearview mirror. Lisa just watched the pine trees slide by outside the window.

Quill tried one more time. "Did you hear any names? Any information we might be able to give to the cops?"

Lisa's response was so quiet, Quill asked her to repeat it. Lisa answered a little louder: "I didn't know any of them."

Gaylyn turned around to look at Lisa. "Did you get any names? Can you describe them?" she asked.

Lisa shook her head no, then sank down so low Quill couldn't see her in the mirror any longer. Quill tapped Gaylyn's leg and motioned, with a hidden hand wave, for her to turn around, and her eyes told Gaylyn to let it go, to leave Lisa alone. Neither of the women spoke again, each focused on the view outside their respective windows.

As they came up over a rise in earth formed a billion years earlier, when the continent's core began to split, the city of Duluth came into sight ahead of them. On the east side of the highway was the expansive body of freshwater Lake Superior. Quill remembered learning somewhere that the lake competes with a Lake Baikal in Siberia, Russia, for the title of largest body of fresh water in the world.

In her storehouse of not-forgotten high school data she also remembered that the midcontinent rift, along with volcanic action and glacial activity, created Lake Superior and the North Shore bedrock that the city of Duluth climbed up. To the east was the harbor with the Aerial Lift Bridge and international cargo ships sitting in the water. It was hard for Quill to imagine that it was only yesterday the women had marched for the missing and murdered Indian women. Lisa's name had been printed on signs carried by the women from Grand Portage. BRING LISA HOME; NO MORE #MMIW; STOP THE PIPELINE; SHUT DOWN THE MAN CAMPS; WHERE IS OUR SISTER LISA?

Quill drove straight to St. Mary's Hospital and pulled into the driveway with big red letters overhead proclaiming EMERGENCY. Gaylyn got out and ran around the car to open the door for Lisa, who climbed out gingerly, untangling her legs from the quilt, which she then pulled tightly around her again. The emergency doors slid open as they approached, and they disappeared from sight.

On the hospital parking garage ramp Quill heard her phone ping. She parked and then checked her phone messages. A string of texts from Crow, then:

What the hell are you doing at St. Mary's?

Answer me goddamnit!

Shit. *I'm fine. Home soon. Taking a friend to the hospital.*

Quill threw her phone under the car seat, locked the car doors, and walked to the elevator in the parking lot. She got off on the main floor and walked on linoleum-tiled floors and through hospital-green hallways to the emergency department. The staff at the front desk told her the two women were in a private gyn room past the curtained partitions, and that

they were expecting her. She should look for GYN on the door.
Might want to knock softly before opening it.

Which is what Quill did, to the answer of a soft "Come in."
Lisa and Gaylyn were in a room with four solid walls, not the
standard curtained partitions she expected from previous
emergency room visits. The room was painted a pale pink
with a soft-cushioned rocking chair like one would find in the
new-mom and new-baby rooms on the birthing floor. A muted
Georgia O'Keeffe flower print adorned one wall. The décor
was clearly an attempt to put a woman's mind at rest.

Lisa sat in the rocker, still wrapped in the quilt, but under
that she wore a pale green hospital gown. The borrowed gym
clothes were folded in a neat pile on a wooden chair. Gaylyn
sat on a doctor's stool on wheels, turning back and forth, still
sipping coffee.

"They're going to examine her in a bit. They took her vitals
and drew blood. Gonna give her an IV. She's dehydrated."
Gaylyn did a half-turn twist on the rolling stool. "She's going
to call her sister to bring her a change of clothing. She doesn't
want to talk to anyone or see anyone right now. The clothes
you gave her are over there."

At the mention of clothes, Lisa looked at Quill and said,
"Thank you." Quill noticed something she hadn't before: Lisa
had a bloodied and cracked bottom lip.

Quill picked up her running gear from the chair. And her
boots from the floor.

"Sure. No problem."

"I'll stay with her," said Gaylyn. "You can go home. I'm
good here."

Quill pulled a twenty out of her jeans pocket. "Here, you

might need to eat." She stuffed the bill into Gaylyn's hand.
Quill didn't want to stay, but she didn't want to leave either.
"Call me later?" she said to Gaylyn, her hand reaching for the
doorknob behind her.

"For sure. Got it covered here."

"You need a ride home or anything, call, text me." To Lisa
she asked, "I'll let Julie know where you are? Tell her we got
you?"

Lisa nodded. "Sure. I don't wanna see her though."

"Understand." Quill paused again at the door, asked softly,
"Anything else you remember about the guys that might help
find out who did this to you?"

Lisa answered slowly, "They had white-guy names, like Bill,
Bob, John. They all looked the same." Her eyes started to
glaze over again.

Quill tried one more time. "You remember anything else?"

Lisa stared out the hospital window. "It's all kind of a blur."
She looked back at Quill, deadness in her eyes. "I don't know.
I don't know."

"It's all right. You just get better." Quill left the room and
retraced her steps back to the parking garage ramp. Outside
the elevator to the garage stood a metal trash bin. Quill
looked at the clothes in her arms. She couldn't imagine wearing them. The sight of them would always remind her of
Lisa's battered body. She dumped the running gear and boots
into the trash.

In the parking garage she found her car, pulled her phone
out from under the seat, and turned the car on. Cranked up
the heat and then sat there and tried to pull her emotions together. To slow her heartbeat. To stop the clenching muscles

in her chest. Judging from the texts on her phone, Crow was mad as hell at her. Rather than respond, Quill texted Julie.

Brought Lisa to hospital. St. Mary's. Gaylyn is staying with her. I need to go home to my family.

Great!! How is she?

Alive.

Is it bad?

Yeah.

Can we visit?

No. She doesn't want visitors. She's still in emergency. And will need to talk to cops. Gaylyn will let me know what the situation is. I'll keep you posted. Gotta get home.

CHAPTER SEVENTEEN

Dread filled Quill's being on the drive back to the rez. She replayed the earlier texts from Crow in her mind as she drove. Crow was pissed. He never swore at her. They never had big arguments. She knew he was worried about the women missing. He was worried about the kids' safety. He was worried about her and what he called her impulsiveness. She didn't want to fight with him. Crow, with his calm, easy manner, helped out everyone whenever he could. In one way they were opposites. Where she ran, he walked. Her voice rose with excitement; normally, he got quieter when upset. This time the texts read as if he were yelling at her. She hoped he would understand that she had to help, couldn't just ignore the call for help. And that there wasn't time to explain. She just had to go.

Jitters from the coffee and sugary donuts only added fuel to her anxiety. She willed herself to calm her breathing to ease the tightening of her chest, slow the beating of her heart. She turned on the car radio to a country-western station, but the noise of the music was unbearable. She switched it off and drove in silence.

When she pulled into their driveway Crow was leaning under the hood of the same pickup truck he had been tinkering on the day before. Baby Boy stood behind the steering wheel inside the cab of the truck. Her son grinned and waved at her as he pretended to drive the pickup. She waved back but went directly into the house.

She heard the pickup door open, then slam shut. Before she could get all her winter gear off, Crow and Baby Boy were in the house.

"We need to talk." The words flew out of Crow's mouth. He helped Baby Boy out of his snowsuit, gave him a tablet with a kid movie playing, and sent him into Niswi's bedroom.

Quill filled two coffee cups and set them on the table. She sat down and took a drink from her cup. Crow returned from dealing with Baby Boy. He pulled out a chair across from Quill. "Where were you?" he asked, both hands flat on the table in front of him, as if to steady himself.

"Lisa—the girl who went missing from the casino—I went to pick her up in Little Sweden."

"It didn't occur to you that maybe this is a police matter?"

"She didn't want the police."

"I don't give a crap what she wanted. Why the hell didn't you call Patrick? Why the fuck you go running off by yourself?" His hands pushed harder down on the table.

"Gaylyn was with me."

"So you and a teenager decide you know better than the cops what to do here?"

"She's not a teenager."

"Give me a break."

"Crow."

"Don't fucking 'Crow' me." He slapped the table. "We have two kids. Two psychos kidnapped a child from Walmart. Maniacs are running around in the goddamn woods grabbing women. Hell, taking them right out of the casino in broad daylight."

"It was night."

"Get a grip, you know what the hell I mean. Where's your brain, woman?"

"Don't insult me." Quill glared at him.

"Then stop being crazy."

"Crazy? You want crazy? I'll show you crazy." Quill jumped up and threw her coffee cup against the wall behind Crow. Shards flew around the room. Coffee slid down the wall and pooled on the floor.

Baby Boy came running out of the back bedroom. Crow leapt to his feet and grabbed his son. "It's okay, Baby Boy, it's okay. Come on, let's go back in the room and finish your movie."

Quill, still shaking with rage, got up, grabbed another cup from the cupboard, and filled it from the coffeepot. Sat down again. She watched coffee roll down the kitchen wall. This was the first time in all their years together that things had bordered on the edge of violence. She had scared herself with her reaction. She stared into the coffee cup.

Crow came back. Looked at the wall, the coffee, the pieces on the floor. He reached for the broom that leaned against the refrigerator.

"Leave it," said Quill, her voice like the icicles hanging from the eaves outside the kitchen window. "You want to know what I was doing? I'll tell you what I was doing. I went to get Lisa; her name is Lisa Jackson. Whoever took her from the casino, whoever had her, raped her, then beat her half to death before leaving her for dead behind the gas station in Little Sweden. Not only half dead, but with only her bra and panties on. They dumped her back by the trash bins. The only reason she is alive is because the cashier thought she heard a cat." Quill's voice broke. "Thought she heard a cat!" Quill was back to yelling, standing at the table, leaning across it, her face three feet from Crow's. "Do you hear me?"

Quill sat back down, hard. "Cashier went to see if the cat was okay. Instead, she found a woman. One of *our* women, Crow. Us." Her voice raised, then lowered. "Her friend Julie texted me this morning, asked if I would go get her. 'Cause Lisa refused to let the woman who was helping her call the cops. She got hysterical at the idea of men coming to get her. So yes, I went." She gulped warm coffee.

"Jesus Christ." Crow rubbed his hands over his face.

"She didn't have any clothes on, Crow." Quill was unaware of the tears streaming down her face.

"Fuck."

"When we said we'd call the cops she curled in on herself, a trapped cat. You've seen caged, scared animals." Quill took a breath. "And I froze, Crow. I didn't know what to do. Couldn't do anything. Gaylyn took charge. Your 'teenager' acted like she handled a war zone every day. She sent me out to warm up the car. I wasn't any good to Lisa at all." Tears rolled down her face. She choked back sobs.

Crow got up and went around to Quill. He pulled out a

chair next to her. Pulled her onto his lap. Cradled her in his arms as deep sobs racked her body. Baby Boy peeked out the bedroom door. His dad motioned for him to go back into the room. He did. He came back with his tablet and sat down in the doorway where he could watch his movie while keeping an eye on his mom and dad.

Quill's phone rang. It was across the room in the pocket of her coat, which hung on a hook by the doorway. She sat up. The phone stopped ringing. She wiped her eyes on the hem of her shirt and blew her nose on the greasy handkerchief Crow pulled out of his pocket. The phone rang again.

"I better get that." By the time Quill dug the phone out of her coat pocket it had quit ringing. Then it started ringing again.

"'Lo?"

"Hey, it's me, Gaylyn. The police are interviewing Lisa and they need the gym clothes you let Lisa wear."

"Oh god, I wasn't thinking straight—I threw them in the trash bin by the elevator. Hopefully no one emptied it."

She listened as Gaylyn relayed the message and male voices responded in the background. Meanwhile, she watched as Crow swept up the broken coffee cup and finished mopping up the coffee with paper towels.

Gaylyn came back on the phone. "I'm going to step out into the hallway."

The background noise abated, and Gaylyn relayed that the hospital would keep Lisa overnight. Gaylyn thought the doctors might be worried that Lisa was suicidal. She was on an IV drip with antibiotics along with an antianxiety med. They'd done a rape-kit assessment. The city cops had already interviewed her. The tribal cops were on their way to do their own interview. Quill should be prepared for them to call or visit her. Whoever had Lisa must have kept her drugged. She couldn't remember much of anything. She thought she was kept in a motel room but didn't know which one or in what town. And maybe they moved her from one place to a different one. She just didn't know.

"Did she say anything more about who these guys are?"

"No. Sounds like they all have three-letter names, and no one bothered to introduce themselves."

Quill stared bleakly out the door window. Gray clouds hung over winter gray trees growing out of cold snow.

Gaylyn continued. Lisa had finally asked for her mother. Once her mother got there, Gaylyn was going to catch a ride home with a cousin who was at the hospital visiting a family member with cancer. They would bring her back to the rez. "Seems like a stupid thing to do after all this but I need a long run and fresh air. You think we can do that?"

Quill looked at Crow cleaning up the "crazy" mess. "I'll have to get back to you on that." They hung up.

She checked her texts. There was a text from the school saying Niswi was complaining of a stomach ache and wanted to come home. Quill looked over at Crow, who was reading the same message on his phone.

"I'll go get her," he said. "She wet the bed last night. She never wets the bed. Not even when she was a baby. That's what I wanted to tell you this morning and didn't get a chance to."

"Oh no . . . She's scared. I'm sorry, Crow, I'm sorry but I had to go."

"You need to stop. Slow down, Quill. Stop and think. You

can't be putting yourself in danger. We got two kids here. They should be our number-one priority."

"They are. I know. I'm sorry. Not sorry I went but sorry for the worry I caused. I'm tired, Crow. Can you take Baby Boy with you? I need to be alone for a little bit. I promise not to go anywhere. Pinky swear, promise." She gave him a crooked grin.

Once her two guys left, Quill locked the door behind them. Something she and Crow never did. But today she did. She stripped and took a long hot shower. Put on clean clothes. Crow texted to say he would take the kids into Cloquet and get them burgers and malts.

She gathered all the dirty clothes from all the bedrooms and threw in a load of laundry. Put rabbit in the crockpot with potatoes, carrots, and onions. A half a cup of maple syrup. She swept all the floors. Mopped the kitchen floor to catch any last shards of coffee cup that might still be there. Took out a frozen loaf of bread dough to thaw. She would make biscuits to go with the stew for supper.

Then she filled a glass with water and sat back down at the kitchen table. She scrolled through her texts. Nothing new from Punk. Good—Quill wasn't ready to hear anything about Punk's love life. She texted Julie that Lisa's mom would be going to the hospital to be with her. That they were keeping her overnight.

Finally, she googled counselors for youth. A long list popped up, and her exhausted brain couldn't help her decide or take action. She called the Indian clinic and asked for a referral to a therapist who worked with Indian youth around trauma issues. They gave her a name and number for a counselor in Duluth. She called and took the earliest appointment available—two weeks out.

And with that she set her phone down, went to the couch, pulled the Indian-print throw over herself, and closed her eyes. As she drifted off to sleep, she reached into her pocket to make sure the beaded earring was still there. It was.

CHAPTER EIGHTEEN

The front doorknob rattling jarred Quill wide awake. She jumped off the couch and moved to the door even as Niswi yelled, "Mom, open the door."

"Sorry, I fell asleep."

Niswi tumbled in, pushing past her dad to get in out of the cold. Crow carried Baby Boy.

Niswi immediately turned on a computer game while Crow took off Baby Boy's snowsuit, mittens, and boots. "You okay?" he asked Quill.

She shrugged. "As good as can be expected, I guess."

Crow gave her a long hug. "I'm gonna go back out and work on the truck," he said, heading out.

Aiming for a measure of normalcy, Quill pulled a chair over to the kitchen counter for Baby Boy to stand on so he could help her make peanut butter cookies. Like the three-year-old he was, he sloppily dropped teaspoons full of cookie dough on a baking sheet. Niswi, engrossed in her computer game, called from her perch on the couch, "Ma, company." She pointed at a gray sedan pulling into the driveway.

Quill used a kitchen towel to wipe peanut butter off her hands. A man and a woman got out of the car and approached Crow. He gestured toward the house. Quill was already opening the door before they could knock. She waved at Crow to keep working.

After he visited Lisa in the hospital Patrick warned Quill in a text that someone from the Bureau of Criminal Apprehension would show up to question her after all that had happened. He explained that the tribe had some jurisdiction over the recent abductions but that the BCA was the state agency that dealt the best with crime scene investigations. They had tools and resources the tribe didn't, and the forensic kit from Lisa would be handled by them.

The two people at Quill's door introduced themselves as agents with the BCA and said they needed to ask her a few questions about the recent abductions of the two women from the casino and the missing woman known as Mabel Beaulieu. Quill brushed her hands down the sides of her jeans, feeling Mabel's earring that she had tucked into the corner of her left pocket.

"Come on in. Let me plug my son into the tablet." She walked Baby Boy into the back bedroom and turned on a children's movie for him. "Stay here till Mama comes get you." She patted his head. Back in the living room, she told Niswi to go watch the show with her brother or do her homework, "please?" Niswi side-eyed the man and woman on her way out of the room.

Quill took a pan of cookies out of the oven and used a spatula to put them on a dinner plate. She offered the agents coffee and set the plate of still-warm cookies in front of them. Told them to help themselves. She continued to roll peanut butter cookie dough into balls, then squash them flat with a fork on the cookie sheet. Neither agent took a cookie but they each sipped the coffee.

They started by asking her about the run in the woods. Clearly, Patrick had filled them in. What had she heard? Who had she told? They moved from that line of questioning to asking about Julie's attempted abduction from the casino. What did Quill remember? How did she know how to administer Narcan? Were she and Julie friends? Did she know Julie's cousin? The guard who tasered one of the men?

Quill became flustered, as the questions seemed to imply she was somehow guilty in the situation. Mid-answer to one of the questions, she smelled cookies burning and quickly jerked around and opened the oven. Relieved, she saw they were only a little crispy around the edges.

At the same time, Crow came into the house. He asked with his eyes, *Everything okay?* She answered back with her eyes, *Uh! What do you think?* Crow grabbed a coffee cup out of the cupboard and poured himself a cup. Offered more coffee to the two agents. Neither wanted more. Crow leaned his back against the cupboard, watched the agents and his wife over the brim of his coffee cup. Even before he said "Gotta warm up a bit," it was clear he intended to stay.

The agents pointedly ignored Crow and asked questions about where Lisa was found. Quill told them they would get better answers from the attendant at the gas station. They asked why she went to Little Sweden instead of calling the police.

Crow, standing right next to Quill, ever so slightly touched his elbow to hers. If the agents hadn't been looking directly at them, Quill would have slugged him on the shoulder. Still smarting from their earlier argument, she stepped away from Crow, and she shrugged in answer to the question. "I just knew a woman needed help," she finally answered.

The female agent asked, "Why did you throw away the clothes you gave Lisa to wear?"

Quill looked at the woman in disbelief. She took a bite of a burnt cookie.

Swallowing the cookie, she finally answered, "I was horrified. I couldn't imagine wearing those clothes ever again. I didn't stop to think there might be evidence on them you might need. Sorry, I just wasn't thinking."

Quill didn't hear Niswi sneak into the room. Didn't know how long she had been standing there listening. "Hey," she said, when she caught sight of her daughter out of the corner of her eye, "get back in there with your brother."

Niswi stared at the two strangers sitting in their kitchen, with their short hair, pressed clothing, and pale pink skin. She grabbed a handful of cookies off the plate. She looked at her mom, then her dad, and said, "'kay."

"One final question and we'll leave you to your family. We know it must be getting on to dinner time. Do you have any reason to believe that anyone in law enforcement might be involved?"

Quill and Crow looked at each other in shock at the question. "No. Why would you even ask that?" Quill asked.

"Part of our job is to investigate any police misconduct," the female agent answered. "Just covering all bases and possibilities."

Both Quill and Crow shook their heads no.

The male agent closed his little notebook and the female agent clicked off the phone she was recording the conversation on. They stood up together in a synchronized move without communicating that they were done and leaving. They thanked Quill for her cooperation and said that if they had more questions they would be back. They appreciated her help.

Quill and Crow stood in the kitchen and watched them leave. As soon as the door shut behind them, Niswi came running out of the bedroom. "Why is the FBI here? Whatcha do now, Mom? Were they FBI? They looked like FBI."

"What the heck? Why do you think I did something?"

Niswi said, "Yeah, right, Mom." And she scrambled to the couch to watch the agents drive away.

Crow went back outside to continue working on the stray pickup truck in the yard. It was late afternoon, but in the Minnesota winter, nightfall had arrived while the agents were there. From the front window Quill could see Crow illuminated by his mechanic's flashlight as he got ready to crawl under the car. She turned back to the kitchen and made drop biscuits for the rabbit stew cooking in the crockpot.

Niswi trailed after her with every step as she finished the laundry and put clean sheets on all the beds. Baby Boy, tired of his video, slammed small trucks and cars under the couch in the living room.

Quill went to the basement and pulled out a camping mat from their powwow gear. She laid it on the floor by Baby Boy's crib and piled a couple blankets and a pillow on it. "You can sleep here tonight again if you want," she said to Niswi.

Gaylyn texted her. *Do you want to run after supper?*

Let me check w/Crow. I'll text Punk and see how she's doing. Tell her she can watch us from her window.

She sent Niswi outside to call Crow in to eat. After everything that had happened during the day, she hesitated to bring
up the idea of running but finally ventured, "Gaylyn wants to
run tonight." Before Crow could shake his head no, she said,
"We need to run off some stress. Today was hard on us. You
could tie the sleds to the back of Betty Boop and pull Niswi
after the truck. You could be our spotter for a night run. Keep
us safe."

Niswi screamed, "Yeah, Dad!" She jumped up from her
chair, swung her fist down through the air. "Stoodis, skoden."

"Well, that was a setup," Crow said. But he bundled up and
went out and tied the sleds to the back of the pickup. He drove
slowly behind Quill on the run to Gaylyn's and then followed
the two women on the road around the village. Gaylyn asked
Quill if Punk had responded to her text.

"Nah, I suppose she's shacked up. And with her leg in a
brace she probably feels bad about not being able to join us."

Lots of childish shouts and giggles erupted from the sleds
as Niswi's friends hopped on with her as Crow passed by.

As they neared Punk's house on the next pass, Quill slowed
and said to Gaylyn, "I'm gonna run in and check on her. Catch
you on the next round." She waved to Crow to keep going, to
follow Gaylyn.

The driveway was empty and there were no lights on at
Punk's house. Quill knocked anyway. She reached up and
knocked on the glass of the front window. No response, not
even a movement of the curtains. When Gaylyn came back
around, followed by Crow with the pickup load of kids, Quill
rejoined the run.

"Maybe she's sleeping," she said to Gaylyn. "That leg must
hurt her more than she was letting on."

Later, with both kids asleep in their bedroom near Crow, Quill stood at the front window and looked out into the calm night of the village. She was finally feeling more at ease. A car drove by. She could swear it was the same battered white car she'd seen the other day. *Someone on the rez must have bought an old junker,* she thought as she backed away from the window and tidied up the kitchen.

The next day Quill's car was impounded by the BCA to be combed for additional evidence. Crow used his mechanic skills to get a beat-up old Ford Escort running for Quill to drive while she waited for the state to return her own vehicle.

Quill, on her way to get groceries for the week, couldn't resist driving by the casino. She circled through the parking lot to look for the black truck. It wasn't there. She wondered if the men had switched trucks or were lying low now that the police were investigating.

Quill stopped by the police station to talk with Patrick, find out if there was any news with the investigation.

"We've secured surveillance video from the service station where Lisa was found; however, it only focuses on the gas pumps." He added that the station didn't have any cameras on the sides or back of the building where Lisa was found. "Also, the BCA said some of it is out of our hands because many out-of-state pipeline workers come from states that don't require front and back license plates. And whoever is doing this, looks like they smear their plates with mud in a direct attempt to make it impossible to identify them." Patrick gave a rueful laugh. "The local teens—monkey-see, monkey-do—are now mudding over their plates, as if we won't recognize their faces."

He assured her the police were investigating, looking for evidence at the Little Sweden motel. "Apparently that place is a home base for a group of pipeline workers. We think the men who attempted to take Julie, and who took Lisa, kept her there. She gave us a description of one of the rooms she was kept in and it matches that motel, although it's kind of hard to say; these chains all tend to look alike."

"And Mabel?" She touched the earring still in her pocket.

"We're still looking. There is video going back to the night you heard her scream. I've got Cliff looking at the footage. So far there's no sign of her at the motel. We've been told the worst crime committed there was a drunken wedding party a few years back. And then there was a brawl where a local farmer caught his wife having some afternoon delight with a minister from a neighboring town. The personnel are lax on keeping security footage. They tape over it to save on overhead expenses every week. I don't know if we're going to find anything."

"You have to find who did this. This is making everyone around here nervous as all hell."

"Working as hard and fast as we can, Quill. We have limited manpower, and the BCA can't do anything more until they get forensics back. Given the state backlog, that could be awhile."

"Well, I hope to god no more of us go missing in the meantime."

Frustrated with everything Patrick had said, Quill once again drove through the casino lot. She racked her brain for something she might be able to do, something more than look at trucks. Nothing came to mind. She hit her hand on the steering wheel in frustration. *All these damn trucks are starting to look alike.*

For the rest of the week, Quill went about the everyday business of being a wife and mother but continually mulled over various scenarios as to what she could do to find the men who were terrorizing the community. She hated feeling powerless and living on the edge of fear that permeated the village, her home.

Niswi returned to her own bed after a few nights on the floor of her parents' bedroom. Quill still kept the therapy appointment for her daughter in Duluth. Gaylyn worked her casino job. Punk responded to texts, *Still laid up.* And *Having a regular honeymoon over here being taken care of by robo-cop.* Punk had holed up with boyfriends in the past, so Quill figured it was just a matter of time before she resurfaced, sore leg and all. Quill pushed aside the niggling fear she felt about the abduction of the women and realized she was lonely. After all the years of being friends, it was strange not to see Punk almost every day.

For the rest of the week she and Gaylyn and a handful of other women ran the village road each night. One of the more energetic elders would join them as they passed the elder housing, jog a few yards with them, and then walk back to the senior apartments. On the next lap the same elder would stand out on the roadway, an abalone shell in her hand, sage lit with its healing smoke filling the air. She used an eagle fan to smudge all the women as they ran by.

The entire community was still on edge following the abduction and return of Lisa. Rumors swirled as thick as the smoke from winter chimneys. People whispered about Mabel—where she might be, and what might be happening to her. Still, to have the village come to life with the women running—in the middle of winter, in the darkness of the night—eased people's fear a little. They could see one another and know one another were safe.

At the end of the week, Earline, the Elder Who Smudges, called Quill over. "Hey, my girl," she said, "we're proud of you. You've got the community out and showing their strength in spite of their fear. The elder women here decided to sponsor a run from the casino to Little Sweden and back in honor of Lisa and Julie. And Mabel Beaulieu. It will be a 'No More Stolen Women, No More #mmiw' relay run. I know it's kinda quick but it's all organized for us to go on Monday. The women's track team and the high school girls' track team are signed up to run."

Quill ran in place; she didn't want the cold air to cause her leg muscles to cramp. She felt her heart expand with gratitude.

The Elder Who Smudges continued, "We passed the hat and raised enough money to have fifty red kookum scarves printed. They got a silhouette of a woman running with an eagle feather tied in her hair. Figured you all could wear them as headscarves or tie them in your hair."

"What do you want us to do?" Quill gestured at the women running down the road.

"Just run. We got it organized, with a little help from our friends. We'll have some snacks for you along the way and the center will have grills going with hotdogs and hamburgers for when you return."

Quill felt a measure of relief. Her brain felt worn out trying to think of what she might be able to do to find the ones responsible for Lisa and Mabel. Running was something she knew how to do. Something she was good at.

CHAPTER NINETEEN

The morning of the run the sky was tinted a soft yellow. The winter air crisp. All things were in place. Quill would run. Crow, along with Patrick and Walt, Barbie's husband, would move runners from place to place as they relayed forward. After no response from Punk to her numerous texts, Quill finally got a text back: *Have fun.*

She texted back, *'Bout time you answered. No one's that much in love. Miss you. Don't think this is about fun though. Hurry up and get to walking.*

A thumbs-up text dinged on her phone.

Quill, Crow, and Gaylyn, with Niswi and a couple of her friends in the back of the truck, arrived at the community center parking lot. A couple hundred people milled around in the cold. Everyone wore red.

"Well, damn," Quill said. "We went from the three of us running to this crowd?" she said to Gaylyn.

Gaylyn shrugged. "Skoden."

They moved to a table where the women's track coach was busy signing up folks and handing out numbers for people to pin on their jackets.

Close by, the Elder Who Smudges handed out her red kookum scarves. She smiled and stood up straighter as Quill and Gaylyn approached. "Wondered when you two would show up. I shoulda ordered a hundred of these. You're the instigators here. Stuck three back into the box to make sure you got yours. Where's the third Musketeer?"

"Still laid up with her bum leg."

"Here, take hers. We got women from Grand Portage running. The Cities. Another group from Red Lake. A couple women paid me to order more. Maybe I'll start a little side business at the veterans' powwow this summer. Aye!" They all laughed. The women attached the scarves to their braids. Quill stuffed Punk's in her pocket and looked around the crowd on the off chance she'd shown up. Nope.

Right at 8:45 the women's hand-drum group started singing. At the end of the song the Elder of Long Prayers started to pray. She was dressed in all her winter regalia: the beaded hat, the appliquéd winter coat, the beaded mukluks on her feet, and today, beaded smoke-tanned moosehide mittens with mink fur around the cuffs.

Once again she prayed to all the directions and all the four-leggeds, and two-leggeds, and wingeds, and those that crawled, and those that swam in the water. She prayed for all the stolen women. She prayed for the spirit of Raven Lone Eagle. She prayed that Mabel Beaulieu's spirit would lead authorities to her. She prayed for the families of all the missing women and children. She asked all the manidoog to care for all the people. She prayed that the Creator would touch the hearts and spirits of the people who visited such horror on the women and children of their communities. She prayed for their healing. She prayed for a safe journey for the runners.

Quill looked around. Cliff stood on the edge of the crowd. When their eyes met he responded with a small head nod. In a small group of women near him, Quill saw Julie. She was bundled up in a winter parka. Migizi was standing with her, holding their baby in a beaded cradleboard, a star quilt shielding the baby from the cold. Julie's arm was around the shoulders of a woman whose face was framed by a fur hood on a parka and a red scarf tied across her face. It took Quill a second to realize the woman was Lisa. Their eyes met in recognition and Lisa gave a slight nod. Quill nodded back and nudged Gaylyn, who said, "Yeah, I saw."

A woman, one bundled so only her eyes were visible, squeezed up next to Quill. "Heard anything about Mabel?" she asked, her voice muffled behind the wool scarf she wore over her nose and mouth.

Quill studied her eyes. It was Suzy, the woman from the treatment center. Reflexively, Quill reached into her pocket and felt the small nub of the beaded earring fastened in there. "No," Quill answered. The woman sidled away.

Quill scanned the crowd and noticed a woman, her jacket unzipped, exposing a very pregnant belly. The woman was by herself, leaning against the beat-up white car Quill had seen driving around the rez. Quill wondered briefly who she was related to. Most likely she was pregnant by one of the young men from the village. That would explain her presence.

Just then the Elder of Long Prayers finished with "Miig-

wech, Daga bi-wiidokawishinaang wii mino bimaadiziyaang."
And the crowd came to life, everyone eager to get started.

"Hey, hey, hey," the Elder called. "Put your tobacco in the sacred fire before you head out." Within seconds the caravan of runners circled the fire burning at the back of the building, put tobacco into the flames, and the designated lead group took off running while the rest piled into pickup trucks and cars.

Quill and Gaylyn jumped in the pickup with Crow and the kids. They passed the head team of runners slowly, half of whom wore the red kookum scarves tied on their heads and the others over their mouths. Quill wiped the tears that threatened to spill from her eyes. She looked at Gaylyn, who quickly turned her head to face out the window. Quill softly punched Gaylyn in the shoulder and said, "Ah, come on. You know you wanna cry too."

"Shuddup."

They both laughed and Quill wiped her eyes again.

The women's hand-drum group rode in the back of a pickup and sang round-dance songs. The upbeat songs teased the women about finding a boyfriend, losing a boyfriend, sneaking out to dance at a 49, or riding in a one-eyed-Ford. They sang the Strong Women's Song, an anthem for Native women created in the 1970s to honor the Anishinaabe women who were kept in solitary confinement in the Prison for Women in Kingston, Ontario.

The morning passed quickly. Quill and Gaylyn ran when it was their turn. Niswi ran short distances with them. Closer to the town of Little Sweden, the women stopped running relay and ran as a pack. Quill tried to count them. She lost count at forty. The women, running in pairs, streamed toward the town. In an unplanned move, Gaylyn, with Quill keeping pace, led the women to circle the gas station where they had found Lisa. Quill felt a range of emotions, everything from rage to pride, as they circled four times, giving the women's war cry, *Lliillliillii.*

The attendant who'd found Lisa came out of the station and stood in the cold, tears streaming down her face. From there, still led by Gaylyn, the women ran en masse down the main street to the motel. Once again, unplanned, the women circled the squat building.

Four times they circled, while giving the women's war cry. On the second run, a trio of men stepped out a back door, vulgar grins on their faces. One of the men pretended to jack off with his right hand near his crotch. Gaylyn, with fist raised, led the women angrily toward them. With false bravado, the men laughed and backed into the building and slammed the door shut as they did so. On the third round, the women, who were carrying their kookum scarves or had them tied on their wrists, counted coup on the door like they did on the pickup trucks and big SUVs with out-of-state plates, or no plates, that sat in the motel parking lot.

Quill did not see the black pickup truck she was hunting. Again, she wondered if the men had changed vehicles or gone into hiding.

A news station from Duluth interviewed the Elder of Long Prayers and a couple of the more outspoken singers, who led the way into the parking lot in the back end of a pickup truck. The crew noticed Cliff, arms crossed, legs splayed; everything about him screamed "military intimidation." As they approached him with mic and camera, he turned his back to them and walked off.

As Quill and Gaylyn ran by, they saw Cliff's reaction to the film crew.

Gaylyn, barely out of breath, said, "I have no idea what Punk sees in him."

"Give him a break. Punk's in love," said Quill. "Maybe, like you, he just doesn't like cameras."

On the fourth lap around the motel, the women ran with fists high in the air, and their voices raised in the piercing *Lliillliillii*. They didn't stop to visit or use the bathroom or get a drink of water; they finished the lap and then headed back home. A few miles out, the college coach reorganized the women back into their running teams, and Quill and Gaylyn relayed back to the reservation. This time the hand-drum singers sang more prayer songs than round-dance songs. While the women ran with the same determination on the return, the tone of the run was more somber.

The women arrived back at the community center with the sun going down. They laughed about their sore legs and aching feet. For the first time since the woman's scream in the woods, Quill felt a sense of relief. A sense of her own power had returned with the run. The unease that had been coursing through her body was gone, or at least temporarily abated.

Kids ran in and out of the center, bringing the cold air in with them. Teenagers hung around the back of the building, smoking cigarettes and giving hickeys.

Out of respect to the runners who'd traveled the farthest to join the run and faced a long drive back home, the kitchen crew put food in containers to take on the road.

Quill and Crow sat with Gaylyn at a table in the gym. Barbie's husband ran home and returned with Barbie and their crew of kiddos. Quill waved for Patrick and Cliff to join them when she saw them come into the building.

"You could have been a star," Quill teased Cliff as he sat down.

Cliff blew air between his lips. "Not my thing." He tilted his head toward Patrick indicating he should be the one to speak.

"What did they ask?" Gaylyn turned to Patrick.

"They wanted to know why you all were running. Asked what I know about the missing women. I didn't have much to tell them other than everything is still under investigation. They should have interviewed you and Quill. You were the ones who got Lisa," Patrick answered before taking a bite of frybread.

"Nah," said Quill. "The BCA said to not say anything. Guess they're afraid we might jeopardize the case or something."

Different people from the community stopped by to chat. There was a lot of hand shaking and quick hugs all the way around. Finally, while a tired Baby Boy crawled up on his dad's lap, Niswi seemed to have gathered steam as she ran in and out of the hallway, playing tag with her friends from school. "Time to get the wild one home," said Crow, standing up with Baby Boy in his arms.

Quill gave Gaylyn a soft punch on her arm and said, "Catch ya later."

"Gotcha," Gaylyn replied.

At home, Quill was in bed, scrolling through texts and social media, reliving the day, when Crow came out of the shower. When he put his arms around her and kissed her, running his hand down her bare back, she groaned and laughed, "What makes you think I have energy for this?"

"Glad you're my wife," he answered, looking into her eyes. Soft caresses down her back with deep kisses turned into soft and slow lovemaking, after which they both fell asleep, tangled in each other's arms.

CHAPTER TWENTY

With Punk out of commission and Gaylyn working days at the casino, Quill was on her own to obsess about Mabel and the black truck that the men had piled Lisa into. With everything that had happened following that day, it was hard to believe it wasn't even a month since she had heard a woman scream in the woods. Even though she had no proof other than the earring she still carried in her pocket, she knew it was Mabel she had heard. Something told her she might never meet Mabel, which only fueled her determination to find the black truck that took Lisa away from the casino.

After the run to Little Sweden and back, Quill spent the next couple days driving the reservation roads looking for the black truck. One afternoon she drove toward Little Sweden, a few miles past the reservation boundary, and pulled off on a side road like the cops did, the front of the car facing the roadway. She drank coffee from a thermos and watched cars and pickups drive to and from the reservation. The only interesting vehicle she saw was the pregnant lady's beat-up white four-door leaving the reservation. When she finally pulled out of her hiding spot and headed back toward the village, she spotted Cliff's cruiser off on a side road. An unfamiliar car was pulled up alongside him, both cars with their windows rolled down. The cold air sent their breath up in white clouds so Quill couldn't make out who Cliff was talking with.

Later that afternoon, like every afternoon all week while Niswi was in school and Baby Boy was with his dad, she went to the casino and walked through the aisles of slot machines looking at the men who gambled. She walked by the blackjack dealers on the floor and peered into the high rollers room. She didn't know who she was looking for, but she couldn't stop looking. Older retirees who traveled from around the state and from across the Canadian border to waste away their Social Security checks were interspersed with younger men who were clearly pipeline workers. They were boisterous and threw money at the slots without a care, often making side bets against the machines and one another.

After a walk through the casino, she was headed back to her car in the parking lot. As she searched the rows for her own car a muscled hand grabbed her forearm and yanked her backward. She looked up into the angry bearded face of a white guy. His blue eyes pierced into her dark brown ones. "Who you looking for, bitch?" he snapped.

Quill tried to wrest her arm out of his grasp, but he held tight.

"You think we don't see you coming in here day after day. Never gambling. You the one got the police watching our every move?"

Quill twisted and turned, tried to get out of his grasp. She looked around the parking lot. Not another person in sight. She was a good distance from the casino's front door so security wasn't in hollering distance. Damnit.

"You better watch yourself, girl. Curiosity killed the cat, and you might end up like your little mohawk friend." His breath smelled like stale coffee. Quill, who hadn't zipped her jacket, pulled her right arm out of the sleeve of her coat, then slid out her left arm and took off running. The guy was left holding her pale blue down jacket. He dropped it on the ground. "Yeah, you better run." He laughed after her.

Quill quickly ran between two cars, sliding on packed ice, but she maintained her footing. She ran back toward the glass doors of the casino. The last thing she wanted was for the guy who grabbed her to know which car was hers. She could hear the man laughing and when she glanced back over her shoulder to see where he was, he was sauntering after her, back toward the casino.

Inside the casino, she saw an open elevator. *Get away* was the only thought that fueled her run to it. Inside the elevator an old man was wearing a small oxygen tank and his wife was hunched over a metal walker. Quill dashed in and slid to the side, out of sight, as the doors closed ever so slowly behind her. The couple looked at her strangely and shuffled closer together on their side of the elevator. It wasn't until she was on the ride up with them and her breathing slowed that she realized she could have stopped at the hotel reception desk for help or run to one of the security guards who stood by the door. Instead, she rode to the eleventh floor with the old couple and exited when they did.

Her breathing back to normal but her insides still shaking, Quill walked through the labyrinth of the casino's hallways. She followed signs that said ELEVATOR 2—SWIMMING. She smelled the chlorine of the swimming pool as she turned down one hallway. Midway down the hallway a door opened, and Cliff hurried out of a guest room. Without looking in her direction, without seeing her, he quickly headed in the opposite direction. Quill stopped and quickly pulled back around the corner. *What the heck is Cliff doing here in the middle of the day?*

And why in the hell am I hiding from him? Fear was making her do strange things; if anything she should have called out to him for help. Told him what had just happened. She realized she wasn't thinking straight. She leaned against the wall and listened to the sounds of the hotel. She could hear the faint sound of kids laughing as they splashed in the pool. She could hear an elevator ding and its mechanical workings grind. She peeked around the corner. The hallway was empty. The elevator sign on the wall pointed her in the direction Cliff had walked. She took a deep breath to calm her nerves and headed that way. Maybe she could still catch him and tell him about the guy in the parking lot.

When she got close to the door Cliff had exited, she slowed and stopped, off center to avoid being seen through the peephole. She listened to the low sound of men's voices, barely audible above the voices of a daytime TV show.

The ding of the elevator down the hall made her jump and she hurriedly walked toward the sound. She worried that Cliff was returning, and she didn't want to be seen standing outside the room he'd just left. Instead, a group of kids, all in dripping-wet swimsuits, came running past her, laughing, jostling one another as they ran down the hallway. Quill stepped out of their path, then continued to the elevator that would exit by the indoor swimming pool.

Back on the main floor, she walked slowly down a hallway, past the pool area, scanning all directions for Cliff but not seeing him. When she reached the main lobby area she again looked for Cliff, and more cautiously for the man who had grabbed her outside. As she scanned the reception area she wondered to herself, *What did the guy in the parking lot mean when he said, "You might end up like your little mohawk friend"?* Her only friend with a mohawk was Punk. *Where the heck did Cliff go?* She didn't see him or the man from the parking lot, although she did see Gaylyn's dad go into the buffet line. *Bet he's using his daughter's work discount to eat,* she thought uncharitably.

She approached security and asked one of them to escort her to her car—a not-infrequent request of them—and security, without hesitation, walked her out. Quill led them on a detour down a wrong row, while she looked behind herself frequently and at the surrounding cars, making sure there were no occupants in any cars near hers.

Finally, back at her rez-car Escort, she mumbled "Thank you" to the gray-suited guy, hopped in, and immediately locked all the doors behind her. She was freezing without her coat and turned on the car and cranked up the heat. As she watched the security guard's retreating back, she rubbed her arms with her hands to generate warmth and to calm her shivering. She briefly wondered again why she hadn't hollered to Cliff for help; he was a cop after all. But he was never really friendly toward anyone but Punk. And something about the way he hurriedly left the hotel room seemed sketchy now when she thought back on it.

Warmed up some, she looked around the lot again and didn't see a threat. She backed out of the parking spot, and on her drive out of the lot spied her down jacket still lying in the slush of the roadway. She pulled up alongside it, quickly opened the car door, reached down, grabbed it, slammed the door shut, and immediately locked it before driving out of the casino parking lot.

As she drove back toward the village, she turned in to the cop shop. Pulled her jacket back on. Brushed some dirt off the sleeve. Walked into the station and asked the guy sitting there if Patrick was in. She paced in front of the art on the brick wall, her footsteps echoing as she waited. When Patrick arrived, he came in from the outside. Cold air blew in with him. He led her to the interview room and left briefly to get them both a cup of hot coffee.

Quill blew on the drink before taking a sip. She told him about the guy who'd grabbed her in the casino parking lot. Described him. White, six-foot, bulky but not fat. Blue eyes. Light brown beard. He wore a black snowmobile suit. Patrick took notes. She asked him not to tell Crow. She didn't want to worry him. She didn't tell him the man's comment about "your little mohawk friend." She was starting to feel a bit crazy and again thought of Punk, whose own brand of craziness usually helped balance her out. She needed to talk to Punk and make sure she was okay.

She also didn't tell him about seeing Cliff leave a room in the casino hotel. She did ask if Cliff was working, and when Patrick said, "Yes, do you want to talk to him?" she said, "No, no, just wondering 'cause you always seemed to be working together when I talked to you before."

She quickly changed the subject to ask if there was any progress on finding Mabel, even though she herself had lost hope of them finding her. At the most, she hoped they would find whoever was responsible for her disappearance.

"None," Patrick said. He leaned back in his chair and sipped his coffee. Said it was a wearisome job that was taking a toll on the morale of the entire tribal police force. That he would go himself to check out this guy at the casino. Give him a talking-to. He cautioned her to watch herself, watch her surroundings.

After she left the station, she drove to Punk's. Still no sign of life in there. She pounded on the door and reached over and tapped on the living room window. Nothing. She tried the door handle. It was locked. That was strange; nobody locked their doors on the rez. But nothing had been normal since she'd heard the woman's scream in the woods. And Punk— she was used to Punk disappearing when she got into the honeymoon phase of a relationship, but this hookup with Cliff was running long, even for her. Not hearing any sound or movement from the house, Quill finally gave up and drove home.

That night, during the women's run, Quill knocked on Punk's door again. No answer, even though the lights were on in her house and Cliff was driving as spotter. She slowed down enough to run alongside his car. She motioned for him to roll down the car window. "What the heck is going on with Punk?" she asked him. "I haven't talked to her in over a week now."

He answered curtly, "At home, sleeping." He pulled his car ahead even as he answered.

Quill gave him the finger inside her mitten and caught up to Gaylyn. "You're right. He's an asshole."

CHAPTER TWENTY-ONE

As Quill ran she debated with herself whether to tell Crow about the man at the casino who'd grabbed her. She hadn't shared with him about trying to find the black truck or her walks through the casino looking for the men who might be abducting women. Not only would he worry, he'd be angry at her for putting herself in danger. She decided against it.

However, after the run, as they drank hot chocolate in the kitchen, Quill said, "I'm worried about Punk. Now she's not even answering texts or calls and when I stopped by her house—how long has it been? Over a week now right?—she didn't seem like her usual punkish, grin-in-your-face, 'go-get-a-tattoo-or-another-piercing' self. Tonight, she didn't answer the door, even though the lights were all on in the house. Cliff said she was home sleeping."

Crow told her to let it be. "Relationships change people," he said. "And even if you want to—no, 'need' to—run the Boston Marathon, that doesn't mean everyone around you has to have the same ambition. Friendships change. It doesn't mean there is anything wrong."

His answers didn't ease Quill's mind. The next morning she drove to Punk's house and pounded on the door. She walked around the house and tried to peer into the windows. Curtains were drawn over every window. *What the fuck?* Quill stood outside in the freezing cold. The comment from the jerk in the parking lot ran through her head again. *You might end up like your little mohawk friend.* Her gut, now clenched in a knot, told her no one was in the house. Where in the hell was Punk?

Quill got back into her car and drove to the elder housing, which was catty-corner across the road. She asked the gaggle of gray-haired women sitting in the dining area, with a view of Punk's house, if they had seen her in the last couple days. It was a unanimous no from all the elders.

As she was heading back to her car, Earline, the Elder Who Smudges, called her to come back. She stood right inside the entryway, her gray cardigan pulled crisscross on her chest. Quill rejoined her in the tight space. Earline pointed her lips in the direction of Punk's house. She said in a low voice, "I ran into your friend, maybe a week ago, at Walmart."

Quill waited.

"She didn't look so good. Hobbling around in that big leg brace."

Quill nodded.

"Looked like she was finally growing out her mohawk. Her black roots were showing."

Quill raised her eyebrows, beckoning Earline to continue.

"I don't want to gossip but you know that piercing she has over her eye?"

Quill nodded.

"It was ripped out."

Quill stared across the road at Punk's house, then quietly said, "Maybe she got tired of it and took it out."

"Nah. She had a butterfly bandage on it. I asked her what happened. You know how curious us old ladies can be. She said it got caught on something. Hurried away—hobbled, really—before I could get too nosy."

A senior with a walker stopped by the entryway and was eavesdropping on their conversation. "That new cop sure keeps tabs on your friend over there," she said, interjecting herself into the conversation.

"Yeah?"

"Doesn't give her room to breathe. His car is in and out of there all the time."

All three women stared across the road.

"I think he has a jealous girlfriend too. Some girl in a beat-up old car has been driving down this road a lot. Slows down when she passes the house."

"I had a boyfriend once," an even older elder who just happened to walk by chimed in. The entryway was getting real crowded. "Always checking up on me, always accusing me of sleeping around. He was the one cheating. The backside of my cast-iron skillet took care of him."

"Is he the one buried out in the woods over there?" one woman asked.

"Knock it off. Thought you said you wouldn't tell anyone."

The three old ladies laughed. Quill backed out the doorway. Thanked them for the information. She stood in the cold, her hand on her car door handle, as she looked across the road through the pine trees to Punk's house.

Automatically, Quill touched the pocket that held Mabel's earring. Quill's parents were the silent type. They didn't fight out loud. Quill never witnessed any violence in her home. If her mom was mad at her dad, her mom would dish up Quill's plate and her own, but not her husband's. When they were getting along, she always dished his plate up with the best piece of deer meat, the most mashed potatoes, and, if there was cake, the biggest piece. But not when she was angry with him.

Likewise, her father expressed his anger in his own quiet way. He would walk ahead of his wife instead of by her side. He would avoid eye contact, even when speaking to her. Quill remembered one fall. Her parents were angry at each other for over a month. Her father watched a football game every Sunday afternoon. Her mother had a favorite show she also watched on Sunday afternoons. She would sit down in front of the TV and grab the remote and switch to her show mid–football game. Her father never reacted. He never made eye contact. He sat quietly through his wife's show, and when the credits rolled he would grab the remote and switch it back to his game.

Quill never knew what instigated that fight or what resolved it. All she knew was that on Super Bowl Sunday her dad watched the game without interruption and her mother went back to dishing up his plate at mealtime. Her parents would be shocked at how she yelled at Crow. And at the recent times when Crow raised his voice to her. Truly shocked.

Quill felt again for the small nub of the earring in her pocket. The earring gave her comfort in the midst of craziness. A talisman that grounded her. Reminded her that her life was fine for the most part. That there were worse things happening in the world than the immediate things happening to herself.

She looked at Punk's house. She knew domestic abuse happened all the time on the rez. To her knowledge, Quill didn't have any close friends in that predicament. Or maybe she was so close she was in denial and didn't know about it. She recalled the gossip about Gaylyn's family. The talk about how her dad beat her mom. Threatened the kids. But Gaylyn never talked about it either. And she didn't seem to hide from folks. Quill wondered if Punk was hiding something from them, from her. Maybe the new boyfriend wasn't such a cool dude as Punk made him out to be.

Quill felt her phone repeatedly buzz in her pocket. She checked it as soon as she was in the car after turning on the engine and letting the heat blast away. There were three calls from Crow with no texts. She called him.

"What's up?"

"They arrested one of the pipeline workers. They got his DNA off Lisa. They're taking him to the jail in Duluth."

"Well, damn. When did this happen?"

"This morning. The police arrested him in North Dakota over a year ago, sexual assault, but the woman backed out of pressing charges. Patrick brought in a guy late last night. He was staying at the casino apparently. Patrick had the BCA send his picture to the attendant over in Little Sweden, see if she recognized him."

"It was him?"

"Well, he was one of the guys who was in and out around the time Lisa went missing. The hope is he will name names, give the cops some information. I don't know anything more than that. Figured you would want to know."

"Thanks, Crow."

"Yep. Love you."

"Love you too."

Quill hung up the phone. And sat with her hands on the steering wheel. A rush of emotions ran through her body. Relief. Anger. Hatred. Sorrow. She reached into her pocket and pulled out Mabel's earring and looked at it in the palm of her hand. Tears clouded her vision. She wiped them away with the sleeve of her jacket. "Are we ever going to find you?" she asked the earring before putting it back into her pocket.

She sent a text to Gaylyn and Punk and told them the news. Instead of texting Julie she called. The phone rang and rang. She was ready to hang up when Julie answered, out of breath.

"Hello?"

"Julie, it's Quill."

"Sorry, I was changing the baby."

"Did you hear the news?"

"No. What?"

"Patrick arrested one of the guys who they think abducted Lisa. He's in jail at the tribal station right now."

Silence. After a long pause, Julie finally spoke. "I guess they'll be calling me to see if I recognize him, huh?"

"I didn't think of that, but yeah, I suppose. Sorry to be the bearer of bad news."

"But it's good news, right? Maybe they'll sentence him. Do you think they called Lisa?"

"I don't know."

"I better wait. Let her hear from them. I want to be sure."

"Yeah. I suppose. How's she doing?"

"Rough. But she feels safer at home, up there in Grand Portage."

"Good. Listen, I better get going and get back to my own little one. I left him with his dad again."

"All right. Thanks. Are you running tonight? I might run with you if Migizi will watch the baby. Lose this baby fat."

"Yeah. I'm always out there."

CHAPTER TWENTY-TWO

When Quill pulled into the driveway, Crow was under the hood of a vehicle and Baby Boy stood in the car behind the steering wheel. Crow stood up and motioned for her to join him.

"What?"

"Gaylyn's in the house. Something's wrong. Not sure what."

"I told her about them arresting the guy. Maybe that's it."

"Maybe." And he ducked his head back under the hood. Baby Boy waved at her.

Gaylyn sat at the kitchen table, hands wrapped around a coffee cup. She still wore her winter coat and her mittens were beside her hands. If Gaylyn were the type to cry, Quill would have guessed she had been crying.

"Hey, kiddo, what's up?"

Gaylyn looked at her with dull brown eyes. "Have you seen Punk?"

"No. Not since I stopped at her house. Why?" Quill didn't bother to take off her coat. She sat with a thud on the chair across from Gaylyn.

"I think she's gone."

Quill's head was spinning. Too much was happening too fast. Quill took a deep breath. Exhaled slowly before asking.

"What do you mean, gone?"

"My dad . . ."

"Your dad what?"

"It's all fucked up, man. So fucked up."

Quill stood still in silence. Waited her out.

"He does meth."

"Yeah, so you said. What's this got to do with Punk?"

"My mom and dad were fighting. He said that if she didn't give him some money, he was going to sell my little sister to the pipeline workers. Like the new cop did with his new girl-friend."

"What?" Quill sat down hard in a chair.

"We haven't seen Punk. There's only one new cop."

"What the fuck? That's not possible. Come on." Quill pushed back her chair and headed for the door. Gaylyn followed.

"Where you going?" Crow hollered after them.

"Punk's," Quill hollered back.

At Punk's they jumped out of the car and pounded on the door. Hollered her name. Walked around the house and pounded on the windows. Quill even looked in the trash container that sat against the wall of the house. It was empty.

They stood at the front door. Looked at their tracks in the snow around the house.

"Let's go talk to your dad," Quill said, already moving toward her car.

"Are you crazy? He's out of his mind. You don't want to talk to him!"

"Get in if you're coming with."

Gaylyn jumped in and slammed the door shut behind her.

At Gaylyn's house, Quill was out of the car before her. At the front door before her. She did step back to allow Gaylyn to open the door and go in ahead of her.

Gaylyn's home was the basic HUD house, like all the rest of the homes in the village, with the same basic layout: walk in the front door, up a couple steps into the living room, where an open floor plan connected the living room to a dining area and then the kitchen with the sink, stove, and fridge. Down a hall would be one or two bedrooms and a bath. In the basement might be another bedroom and maybe a half bath.

Quill noticed how cluttered everything in the house was. Gaylyn must have tried to spruce it up a bit. Her kookum scarf was pinned to the pale yellow living room wall. A bright piece of fabric art in the middle of the chaos of poverty. A small shelf held several basketball trophies and one that appeared to be a track trophy. Clearly, athletic achievement ranked high in the household. Quill couldn't make out the name or year on the trophies from where she stopped right inside the doorway. Gaylyn walked into the middle of the living room. Stood stiffly and looked at her dad, who was tinkering with a car part at the kitchen table. Newspaper served as a tablecloth. In an ashtray sat a glass pipe, which he didn't try to hide.

Dishes were piled in the sink. There was a path of grime on the old linoleum floor from the front door to where the man sat. He was skinnier than Quill remembered from seeing him outside working on cars. An old landline phone sat on the kitchen counter alongside an equally old toaster and plug-in coffeepot. A small TV sat on a coffee table against one wall in the living room. A frumpy couch sat against the opposite wall, the back covered with a well-worn star quilt in shades of yellow and orange. Another attempt at some cheer in the room.

"Where's Ma?" Gaylyn asked him.

He gestured down the hallway toward the bedrooms of the house. Gaylyn walked back there. She left Quill standing by the door. Quill could hear a plaintive woman's voice respond to Gaylyn's.

Quill took a deep breath and walked toward Gaylyn's dad. She decided to plunge right in. "What's this I hear about the new cop selling his girlfriend to the pipeline workers?"

He didn't look up but kept his focus on the piece of metal he was scraping with a screwdriver. When he finally looked up at her, his glassy eyes darted from her to his work and back. One side of his mouth turned up in a grin. "Who said he was selling anything at all?" He lit up half a cigarette that was sitting in his ashtray. Blew smoke in her direction. Eyes darted up at her and back to the table. His leg jounced on the floor.

At that moment, Gaylyn returned from the bedroom. She threw daggered looks in her dad's direction. He hurled the screwdriver across the room at her. "Stitches for snitches, bitches." The screwdriver stuck into the linoleum floor three feet from where Gaylyn stood.

She grabbed Quill's arm and pulled her out the doorway. Back in the car she breathed heavily. "Told you, he's crazy. What did he say?"

Quill repeated the conversation. They sat quietly in the car outside the house until they saw Gaylyn's dad push back the sheet that served as a window curtain and peer out at them. Quill drove off.

"Let's go tell Patrick we want to do a wellness check on Punk. Tell him we haven't heard from her at all. She doesn't answer the door and we're afraid she fell or something."

"Stoodis then."

Quill typed into her phone. Waited until the phone number for the tribal police popped up. She called. When the operator answered she asked to be put through to Patrick. It went to voicemail. She left him a message.

Gaylyn slapped her hand on her leg. "Shit, I forgot, I gotta work. Can you drop me off? Trying to make enough to get my mom and sister away from that asshole."

"Sure."

Just as Quill dropped Gaylyn off at the casino her phone dinged. It was a reminder that in half an hour was Niswi's therapist appointment in Duluth. "Shit!" She pounded the steering wheel and for a mere second debated between the well-being of Punk and the well-being of her daughter. She texted Crow and asked him to have Niswi ready and waiting, she would be there in five to pick her up.

Quill, driving above the speed limit, took the back roads before hopping on the freeway into Duluth. Left two more messages for Patrick. They were only eight minutes late for the appointment. The therapist's office, and the therapist herself, could have stepped out of an old-fashioned television show. She was a tall blonde who wore full-skirted dresses cinched at the waist. Dim lights bathed the waiting room filled with swanky office furniture a few shades darker than the soft mauve walls. Upbeat quotes surrounded by flowers on canvas adorned the walls.

The therapist reached out a slim hand to shake Quill's. "Glad you could make it. Today, we'll go over the goals for Niswi's treatment plan."

Inwardly, Quill groaned. She had forgotten she needed to meet with the woman. She wanted to run back to Punk's house and break down the door if necessary. She wanted to call Patrick again, get him to check on Punk. Instead, she stood, frozen, watching the therapist watch her, then her daughter.

When Niswi smiled at the therapist she smiled back and opened a door next to her office door. The room inside was lined with toys, a furnished dollhouse, and a sensory table. "Niswi, can you play in here while I talk with your mom for a couple minutes?" She led Niswi into the room and then opened the door to her office, indicating for Quill to enter. "Make yourself comfortable," she said, pointing toward a small couch in her office.

When Quill sat she could see Niswi through a one-way mirror. Her daughter was already playing with the elaborate dollhouse. She checked her phone to see if Patrick had called or texted back.

"You seem rushed. Worried. Anything you care to talk about?"

"No, just a hectic day." Quill pushed loose strands of hair back off her face. "How is Niswi doing?"

The therapist asked how Quill thought Niswi was coping. Quill affirmed she was sleeping through the night and no longer wet the bed. When the therapist asked how things were at home, Quill froze. She didn't know how to answer. Being asked that question on this day—after the day spent with Gaylyn, waiting for a call from Patrick, needing to find Punk—made Quill feel protective and scared. And guilty, even though she knew she had done nothing wrong.

The therapist stayed quiet waiting for an answer, but it was a different quiet than riding in the car with a silent Gaylyn. Or the quiet she enjoyed with Crow when she helped him work on his cars. Those were familiar silences. The therapist's silence begged for words to fill it. And Quill struggled through her mind to find words to say. She ran her finger over a crease on her jeans and scrunched her forehead into worry lines, thought how shabby she must look to a woman who dressed as if she had just walked off the set of a daytime soap opera.

"What are you thinking?"

"What?"

"You look worried. Concerned."

"Just a lot on my mind. Sometimes life is just a lot. But I'm happy that Niswi is seeing you."

"Niswi told me you are training for a marathon."

Quill nodded.

"She's proud of you. You know that?"

"I didn't know that." Quill felt her phone vibrate in her pocket. She fought the temptation to pull it out and check who was calling.

"She is. She says she wants to be a runner when she grows up. Any news about the young girl taken from the restroom where Niswi and her aunt were? Niswi also did mention other women were kidnapped."

"No, I haven't heard anything more since they found Raven

Lone Eagle. I think we talked about that when I first brought Niswi here."

The therapist nodded.

"And yeah, another woman was abducted. But she's back home. I didn't know Niswi knew about all that."

The therapist said, "Little ears pick up everything," and Quill felt anger rise in her chest. She wanted to scream, *You think I don't know?* Instead, she smoothed the crease on her jeans one more time. The therapist went on to talk about the issue of missing and murdered Indian women. How present-day trauma on top of generational trauma reverberated through a community, especially one as small as the one where Quill and Niswi lived. Quill looked at the non-native woman sitting across from her. The calm demeanor, the designer dress and shoes, the textbook analysis of generational trauma, the measured pace of her words. Again, Quill fought the urge to scream, *You think I don't know?*

The therapist switched to a tone of gentle caring. She suggested that maybe Quill consider therapy for herself. "I understand how hard it must be to live in a community constantly in crisis."

As she voiced those words, Quill, who was staring at a picture of a glowing sunset over the therapist's left shoulder, saw Jimmy Sky jump off the bridge, and watched her smaller self run for help. She heard the woman scream in the woods and reflexively felt for the earring in her pocket. She saw Lisa sitting in the storage room huddled with snacks all around her and the look today on Gaylyn's face at her kitchen table.

Quill scanned the room. Instinctively, she found the exit door and in the one-way mirror the door to the room where her daughter played. She watched Niswi carefully put a doll on a bed and cover her with a tiny blanket in the plastic mini-mansion. Quill looked at the therapist. "We're fine for now," she said. "We should go if we're done talking about Niswi."

The therapist stared compassionately at her for too long a minute. "I would like to see Niswi a few more times. We need to make sure the progress we've made sticks. And if you change your mind, my colleague is an expert on working with adults who have extensive trauma." She opened a drawer in her desk and pulled out a business card. "Here, take this, and if you change your mind give her a call. Tell her I referred you."

Quill stuck the card in her back pocket. The last person to give her a business card had been a plumber from Duluth who'd come out a few years ago to fix their septic tank. He left a magnetic card that still stuck to the side of the refrigerator at home. The weird thoughts that crept into her head at times. She stood, zipped up her jacket, and said the first thought that popped into her mind. "I don't want to be late picking up her brother."

The therapist stood up and opened the door to the playroom. Niswi looked disappointed to leave, and Quill, once again, felt unsure of herself and guilty about her parenting. Quill was not the girly-girl type. Quill's own few dolls had spent lonely weeks and months on her closet floor until her mom gave them to a cousin. As an only child she was raised doing things with her parents—hunting and fishing with her dad, or going out into the woods to harvest the birch bark her mother needed to make her baskets. When she played with kids in the village they ran in the woods, they built forts in the trees, they played in the muddy ditches—physical adventures that required muscle and stamina. Quill watched as Niswi carefully put the dollhouse mom and dad down in front of the living room TV and waved goodbye to them before following her mom out of the therapist's office.

CHAPTER TWENTY-THREE

"I gotta check on Auntie Punk," Quill said to Niswi as she turned in to Punk's driveway. "Wait here, I'll be right back."

She jumped out as soon as she put the car in park. The snow-packed gravel on the driveway crackled under her shoes. Cold air seeped into the clothes she was wearing. The curtains were still pulled shut over the windows of Punk's house. No one answered as Quill pounded on the door with her closed fist and hollered Punk's name. The house was dark and felt empty.

Quill heard tires on gravel and turned to see who was driving past. The battered white car frequenting the reservation roads pulled in behind her green sedan, blocking her in. The early-evening dusk made it hard to make out the woman's face, but the energy she gave off was rage. Quill recognized her as the pregnant woman she had seen around at the various events.

Quill looked from the woman to Niswi and back again. The aggressive stance of the woman as she stepped out of her car made Quill reflexively look at the woman's hands to check for a weapon. Quill didn't know if she expected to see a gun or a baseball bat or a crowbar. The woman's hands were empty, and she spoke first. "Are you shacking up with Trent?"

Stunned, Quill stared at her.

"You got some fucking nerve sleeping with him, you fucking ho." The woman glared around the yard, looking at Quill's car, the house, the pine trees. "I suppose he didn't tell you that he already has a kid on the way." With those words she whipped open her winter coat to expose a well-rounded belly. "This is his baby. Did he tell you that, bitch?"

Shocked, and aware that Niswi was sitting in the car, Quill neither moved nor said a word.

"Has he told you how much he loves you? Maybe slaps you around a bit and then brings one of those single roses they sell at the end of the drugstore counter? I put up with his shit before he got shipped overseas. He came back and jacked me around some more. Crying how sorry he is and how the war fucked him up. But once I got pregnant, he left me alone. Said he came over here for a better-paying job. Said he was going to get a house for us." She eyed the yard again. "You stupid bitch. You know why he's shacking up with you?" She didn't pause in her tirade. "He can't afford to rent a place because he's been sending his paychecks back to me. We have a savings account for a new house. And our baby."

Niswi opened the car door, stepped out, and, wide-eyed, swiveled her eyes back and forth between her mother and the pregnant woman.

Quill, who still stood on Punk's doorstep, said softly, "Niswi, run, get your dad. Run. Get your dad."

"What'd you say, bitch?" the woman screamed. "Don't be pulling any sneaky bullshit on me."

"I told her to go home. She doesn't need to see this," Quill said. "Go on," she said more sternly to Niswi, who unfroze and took off running down the road in the direction of home.

"You nasty ho. I've been watching you."

"Look, I don't know what you think, and I don't know anything about your man. But if Cliff is your man, he's the guy who's been staying here—"

"I'm not stupid. I've seen his car parked here. Then comes and tells me he's only investigating a break-in. You look like a break-in to me."

"You can go by the tribal police station, up the road over there. About ten miles. That's where he works."

"Seen you all smiley at him at the center after the run. I've been watching you awhile now. You don't know who you're dealing with." The woman was clenching and unclenching her fists as she spoke.

"Look, find Cliff at work. The two of you can sort it out without involving anyone else." Quill almost rolled her own eyes as she realized her placating tone mimicked Niswi's therapist's voice.

"Shut the fuck up. Don't tell me what to do. And his name is Trent, not Cliff, you dumb bitch," the pregnant woman shouted. She turned abruptly and reached back into her car. When she stood back up, she held a handgun. She used both hands to point it directly at Quill.

Quill saw the back of Niswi running toward home and she

screamed, "Run!" And turned and slammed her whole body into the cheap HUD door of Punk's house. She didn't know if the sound she heard was the doorframe breaking or gunshots. She fell face-forward into the foyer, landing sharply as the lock on the door gave way. She clawed halfway to standing. She slammed the door shut as she saw the woman wave the gun back and forth. Just then a bullet ripped through the wood a foot above her head. Instinctively, she ducked. "Crazy-ass woman," she screamed. "I don't know who the fuck your boyfriend is!" she yelled. More gunshots.

Quill dropped to the floor. Dirt dug into her knees. She scanned the area directly around her. Saw Punk's mop and broom leaning against the wall. She grabbed both and stuck them between the base of the door and the bottom step of the stairs directly across from it. *Hope to god that holds,* she thought as she crawled up into the living room. The woman outside seemed more intent on shooting her instead of coming in to confront her directly. Quill tripped scrambling up the stairs. "What the fuck?" she gasped. "I'm too young to die."

She started to laugh, verging on hysteria; the picture of herself running when she saw Jimmy Sky dive off the bridge and the more recent vision of Niswi running to get her dad. *My kids.* The thought brought tears to her eyes.

"Where the hell are you, Punk?" Finally in the living room up the stairs, she scooted on her butt away from the door and lay down on the floor with the couch between her and the wall. *What the hell have you gotten yourself into this time?* She lifted her head and looked around the living room. Across the room, on the kitchen table, was a single wilted red rose, drooping in a makeshift mason jar vase.

A bullet hit the side of the house just as headlights swept through the window and floated across the opposite wall.

"Let me in, motherfucker!" The woman had finally reached the door. She pounded, screaming. Quill crawled across the living room floor to the end of the couch and hid, curled in a ball. "In case she gets lucky and breaks the broom handle," she said out loud.

The headlights on the wall were still. Quill listened for a car door to open. The woman kept pounding and calling her every vulgar name Quill had ever heard. She felt her phone buzz in her pocket; she didn't dare answer but stayed scrunched down, hidden.

Another set of headlights wavered across the wall, followed by a car door slamming. "Cassandra, what the fuck you think you're doing?" It was Cliff's voice.

The screaming and yelling between Cliff and the woman immediately escalated.

"Calm down, Cassandra. Put the gun away."

"I'll kill that bitch. You think I don't know about you and her?" She pounded on the house door. Quill tried to make herself smaller.

"Come on. We can talk this out. Stop before you get arrested."

"I'll arrest you, *Cliff*." The woman spat the name out. Quill, still crouched, raised herself up and peered out the window. The woman walked toward Cliff, or Trent, or whoever he was, gun pointed at him.

Quill saw another car door open in the yard and Crow came running to the house, as the two in the yard continued to scream at each other.

"Put the gun down, Cassandra."

"To hell with you."

Back and forth they yelled. Neighbors who had driven over when they heard the gunshots and yelling stood behind their open car doors as if that would stop a bullet if she did decide to shoot.

"Quill!" hollered Crow. "Answer me, damnit." Pound. Pound. Pound.

She stood and reciprocated on the glass window. More cars were pulling into the driveway. Two cop cars had their lights flashing. "Hang on. I'm okay!" she shouted. She ran to the opposite end of the couch.

The second she lifted the broom and mop handle, Crow pushed his way in. Slamming the door behind him, he pulled Quill into his arms. She could feel his whole body shaking as he held her tightly. Tears streamed down her face. She had to push back from him to get some room to breathe.

"The whole village is out there. Who the hell is that woman? She attacked Cliff. Started hitting him with that gun she has. Patrick finally grabbed her and took it away from her. She's pregnant and fighting like a zombie. I thought you got shot," Crow said, his voice tight with fear.

There were a couple knocks on the door. They ignored all of them until Patrick poked his head in the door. "You all right in here?"

Without looking at him, Crow hollered, "No one's hurt, just leave us alone for a bit."

Crow used his free arm to run his hand over his head in frustration, pushed his hair back away from his face. He pulled Quill down beside him on Punk's couch. He used one hand to dial his sister and ask her to go to their house and get his kids. If she could keep them overnight, yeah, that would be great.

They sat quietly for an indeterminate amount of time. Finally Crow spoke. "I can't do this, Quill. Niswi came running into the house screaming that someone at Punk's was shooting you. We can't do this anymore. I'm gonna take them and go stay at Barbie's for a while."

Quill pulled away. "What?"

"She peed her pants right in front of me, for god's sake."

"You can't take the kids and leave," Quill said incredulously.

"I'm going to. You keep running off on this wild mission to find these women, to rescue Lisa, and folks are saying you drive around the casino at all hours trying to find the men who are taking the women. Niswi could have gotten shot today."

"I was just coming to check on Punk. Punk's not even here." Her voice cracked. "This house is empty."

"Then where is she?"

"I don't know. That's why I came over here. Gaylyn heard something about the new cop selling his girlfriend. And we haven't physically seen Punk in forever. Or heard from her. Look around, she's not here. Where the hell is she?"

"Call her."

"I call her, I text her, there's no answer."

"If she's missing, let the cops deal with it."

"What cops? The one she's been shacking up with? Whose pregnant wife is out there trying to gun me down? Or the other cops who couldn't find Lisa? Can't find Mabel? I can't sit on my ass while the cops don't do their job. Fuck that."

Crow's voice cracked. "I thought you might be dead. You can't leave me alone. We have kids, for god's sake." He rubbed his hands over his eyes. "I won't make it. Let the cops do their job. Your job is to take care of the kids. Take care of us."

"That's not me, Crow, and you know it."

Crow looked defeated. "Then I'm gonna take the kids and go stay at Barbie's until this whole thing gets resolved." He paused. "Or you come to your senses."

"Oh Christ. Crow." Quill pushed away and jumped up. "And don't you dare think you can keep my kids from me."

Crow pulled himself together, determined, resolved. "I'm not keeping the kids from you. I'm keeping them safe. I don't know what else to do, Quill. You're not thinking straight." He stood up and reached for her.

"Fuck you." Quill turned away.

CHAPTER TWENTY-FOUR

E ventually, the murmur of excited voices outside drifted out of earshot as people who had come out to witness the shootout went home or to the community center to continue adding to the story of the night's event. Car doors slammed. Engines started. When headlights again illuminated the room, Crow reached one more time for Quill. She turned her back on him. He left.

Quill sank into the cushions of Punk's couch. "What the hell?" She burst into tears and wrapped her arms around her chest as her body trembled with fear. Adrenaline coursed through her with nowhere to go. "Where the hell are you, Punk?" She buried her face in her knees and wailed.

Finally, she pulled herself up off the couch and rummaged through Punk's kitchen, looking for any clue of where Punk might be, any sign as to what might have happened to her. She sniffed the coffeepot that was half full. No mold, and it didn't seem that old. From all accounts of the women at the elder housing, Cliff—or was it Trent?—had been staying here all along. The mess in the kitchen attested to that. Punk was more of a bougie, eat-some-leafy-green-health-food kind of a person. The dirty dishes piled in the sink and empty cans of hash and chili in the garbage under the sink were not Punk's.

The bedroom looked like a man cave. Shirts pulled off and left inside out. Trousers dropped where Cliff had stepped out of them. Anything wearable strewn all over the floor and easy chair. Punk's running suits hung neatly in the closet. Her panties and socks were neatly rolled and tucked in a dresser drawer. The Velcro brace Quill had last seen on Punk's leg stuck out from under the bed.

The bed sat in the middle of the room. On either side were bright pink nightstands. Quill opened the drawer on the neater side, obviously Punk's. Inside the drawer was a small pack of tissues, some false eyelashes kept neatly in a plastic case. Receipts. Odds and ends of hair scrunchies, bobby pins, and fake neon hair extensions. Eye shadow.

Quill moved around the bed. Opened the drawer of the other nightstand. Right inside the drawer, bare of all else, was Punk's sequined smartphone. She picked it up, turned it over and over. Hit the on button. It asked for a password. She pulled out her phone and texted Punk's. The sequined phone dinged.

Quill looked around the room. She even got down on her knees and looked under the bed. She went through each room of the house, each closet and cupboard. Anything with a door on it she opened, dreading the possibility of finding Punk. In the basement was a small chest freezer that she knew Punk kept stocked with deer and rabbit meat. She stood, her hand on the lid, for a good minute, every horror film she had ever watched where a dead body was kept in the freezer flashing through her head. She threw open the lid. The freezer was half empty. The butcher-wrapped packages all had neat black-marker labels of WABOOSE and WAAWAASHKESHI, all in Punk's handwriting. Quill slammed the lid down. Her arms and legs were shaking. She dropped to the concrete floor with her back against the freezer.

"Where are you, Punk?" she asked, then sat in silence waiting for an answer. Silence followed silence. She stared at the concrete blocks across the room. Her mind raced. *Gaylyn's dad said the new cop sold his girlfriend. The texts I've gotten from Punk haven't sounded like her. How long has she been gone? A week? More? When's the last time I saw her? Actually talked to her?* She counted days backward on her fingers. *Eight days?* They all blurred together for her.

Quill felt her body shake again as she thought of the torture Lisa endured before she was dumped like trash behind the convenience store. And that was only a few days. She pushed herself up and ran back to the bedroom, grabbed Punk's phone from where she had dropped it on the bed. *Maybe Patrick can get this thing open somehow? Or the BCA.*

She ransacked the house again, looking for anything with Cliff's name or the name Trent on it. Nothing. She stuffed Punk's phone in her pocket and stepped outside. The pregnant woman's white car sat in Punk's parking spot. She pulled the broken front door shut. Dug her own phone out from her jacket pocket and dialed the tribal police. "Hey, this is Quill. I'm over here at Punk's where that crazy woman was shooting at me earlier. Can someone come over here and board up the door so no one breaks in and steals her stuff?"

"No one's home?"

"No. Can you send someone? I'll wait till someone gets here."

The temp outside had dropped below freezing. She stomped her feet and blew warm breath on her hands while she was put on hold. Short of patience and freezing, she was about to hang up when the same voice came back on. "Someone will be there shortly. Leaving now."

Quill gasped. "Wait, wait, wait! Who's coming out?" Anxiety pumped through her body at the thought of Cliff pulling into the driveway.

"The janitor from the community center is on his way."

Quill exhaled in relief.

"I'm gonna wait in my car," she said, and clicked off her phone. At her car door, she bent down and picked up an empty shell that glinted in the snow. It went into her pocket with Mabel's earring. As soon as the janitor arrived she backed out around the white junker and left.

CHAPTER TWENTY-FIVE

Later at the police station, Quill paced the floor while she waited for Patrick to show up. When he did wave her into the room she now considered hers, he disappeared and returned with a cup of coffee.

"You okay?" he asked. He collapsed into a chair, shoulders slumped from the weight of the night.

All her words rushed out. "Crow said he's leaving me, taking the kids to his sister's. He says I'm not safe to be around. Why'd that woman shoot at me? Do you have her locked up?" Hot coffee splashed as she jerked around the room and kept pacing.

"Careful. Take a couple deep breaths and tell me what happened."

"Gaylyn said her dad said the new cop sold his girlfriend. When we went over there and I asked him about it, he threw a screwdriver at Gaylyn. Stuck straight up in the floor by her feet. I don't know if he missed intentionally. We haven't seen

Punk in days, so I wanted to go check on her. I thought she was lying low 'cause her leg was hurt. But there's no one at her house."

"What do you mean?"

"She is not at home, but I found her phone there. She really is gone." She pushed it across the table. "Maybe you all have some magic to get some information from it."

Patrick picked up the phone, turned it over in his hands, the sequins glinting in the light. He looked at her with skepticism.

"She's gone. Cliff, or Trent, or whatever the hell his name is, has obviously been staying at her house, but she's gone, Patrick. Gone. And where the hell is Cliff and his baby mama?" She looked around the room as if he might appear out of thin air. "Who the hell is he? And who the hell is she? That woman called him Trent."

"Trent, huh? I don't think that's the name he gave us when we hired him." He rummaged around in the file cabinet behind his desk. Pulled out a file. Thumped it on the desk. "You know what? His name is Trent. Says right here, Trent, but now I remember. He just said to call him Cliff, that he's always gone by Cliff. You know how it is with names around here, Quill."

He stared out the window into the dark of the night. "We all got there about the same time. Me, Cliff—you say she called him Trent, huh?—and Crow. Crow jumped out of his truck and ran to tackle her. But Cliff showed up at the exact same time and hollered at her. Then she and Cliff went at each other like cats and dogs. Her being pregnant and all." His eyes were wide in disbelief. "Good thing she ran out of bullets. She got in a few good whacks with the butt of the gun before Cliff was able to grab her arms and restrain her. At that point I was just doing crowd control. Seemed like everyone in the village showed up once they heard gunshots. I told Cliff to bring her here to the station." He too looked around as if Cliff might appear out of thin air. "He took the gun from her and stuffed her into his car. That's the last I saw of either of them. They never showed back up here."

Quill slowed her walk to take a drink of tepid coffee. "Crow's really pissed at me."

More coffee. More silence.

"Why can't you catch these guys?" Quill begged. "Gaylyn really does think Cliff sold Punk to guys from the pipeline."

When Patrick peered at her over his coffee cup, she continued. "Her dad does meth, you know."

"That shit's all over the reservation. We plug up one source and another takes over. To begin with, it was the Native gangs from the joint sending their soldiers up here." Disgust in his voice. "Then it was folks from south of the border—all that Hollywood cartel bullshit. Hooking up with the girls up here and stashing their drugs in the basements of our houses. A couple years ago we had some sizable drug busts. Damn shame it was our women who ended up going to prison, doing federal time 'cause of the RICO laws. While the men waltzed back south." He dumped his cold coffee into the sink. "You know, you're right. I brought that one guy in. He works for the pipeline. Hasn't given us any useful information. The lawyer from the corporation is keeping him pretty quiet. We're a small force here. And every time something big happens we have to wait for the agencies with more manpower to help out."

He lifted his cup to take a drink of his coffee. Realized it was empty.

An officer stuck his head in the room. "Need you for a sec out here, boss."

Patrick pushed away from the table. "Be right back."

Quill used what little energy she had left to sit in a chair and twist it to stare out the window into the dark. *Did Crow really take the kids to his sister's?*

She heard the door open behind her and in the window reflection she saw Patrick reenter the room, followed by Gaylyn. She quickly swiveled back. She noticed the two cups of coffee Patrick carried before she saw the look of devastation on Gaylyn's face, who also carried a white coffee cup.

"What?" She jumped up. Her heart dropped and her stomach grew queasy as she anticipated either bad news about Crow and her kids or about Punk.

Gaylyn looked at her with dull brown eyes. "My mom tried to kill my dad." She plopped into a chair. She ignored the hot coffee that spilled on her leg.

"Wait . . . run that by me again," Quill stammered.

"At home. She stabbed him. My little sister called 911. The ambulance came, took my dad to the hospital. He's gonna live," she said dispassionately, as she stared into the coffee cup, ran her finger through the coffee spill. "Then the cops showed up and arrested my mom. I didn't know what to do so I got into one of the cop cars and caught a ride over here. Asked for Patrick."

Quill's head was spinning. Too much was happening too fast in the world for her.

"My sister's still at home. It was self-defense. My dad . . ."

"Is she okay?" Quill stood up. "Should we go get her?"

"Nah. She's okay. She's not that little, just little to me."

Quill sat back down. Drank some coffee from the cup Patrick pushed her way. "Was he hurting your mom?"

Gaylyn looked sideways at Patrick, then back to Quill. "Can we not talk about it?"

Quill looked at Patrick. He was the cop in the room. The gatherer of evidence. The keeper of the law. "Yeah, no, we don't need to talk about it. Is your mom okay?"

"It's all fucked up, man. So fucked up."

The three sat in silence.

"So, she's in jail here?"

Gaylyn nodded. "He was out of it. On meth."

Quill blurted out once again, "I thought folks grew up and didn't do that kind of crap."

"He might be my dad, but he's never been an adult." She shook her head. "I didn't know where else to go."

They all sat in silence. Drank some coffee. Swiveled their chairs to look out the window into the dark and then back to the table.

"How long will they keep my mom?" Gaylyn asked in Patrick's direction.

"She's gonna get charged with attempted murder. She needs a lawyer. My guess is she'll be eligible for a public defender."

Gaylyn laid her head on her forearms.

Quill waited through the silence.

Gaylyn finally raised her head. "I have money saved; I planned to go to the Cities, once my little sister graduates high school. Take her with me and get a job down there. Away from this craziness. I hated the idea of leaving my mom with my dad, but I couldn't think of anything else. What if she goes to prison?" Her face was filled with fear. "What if when he gets out of the hospital he comes home? He can't do that. He can't. I'll kill him."

"Whoa. Whoa. Don't talk like that." Patrick's voice was filled with concern. "You can get a restraining order. Keep him away."

Gaylyn came alive. "Let's do that. He can't come back home. A restraining order would keep him out? Away from me, my little sister? I'm over eighteen. I can take care of her. Been taking care of her forever already."

"Good idea," said Patrick. "Wait here. I'll be right back."

Gaylyn put her head back down on her arms, shutting Quill out. Quill stood at one of the windows. She was starting to feel the exhaustion of the night as the adrenaline drained from her body. She was ready to crash.

When Patrick returned, he sat back down and pointed in some vague direction in the building for the tribe's Human Services Department. He slid a piece of paper toward Gaylyn. "Here. Give her a call. My cousin. She's an advocate. She'll walk you through all the forms that need to be filled out for an order for protection."

In a soft voice, raising her head slightly off her arms, never making direct eye contact with Patrick, Gaylyn asked, "Is my mom going to be okay?"

"Yeah. She's doing okay. We have a decent staff; they'll look after her."

"What's going to happen to her?"

"I honestly don't know. That's up to the judge. Ask my cousin about a public defender for her, okay? And here's my cell number." He wrote it on the back of the paper he had just given to Gaylyn. Quill typed it into her phone under his work number. "You girls go home. Get some rest. I better get back to work." He pushed away from the table. Leaned on his fists on the edge of it. Looked at them. Looked at the door. Gaylyn stood up, said a quiet thanks, and left. Quill followed.

"Can I give you a ride home?" Quill asked her retreating back.

"'Course."

When they pulled into Gaylyn's driveway, the sheet that served as a curtain over the living room window lifted and dropped quickly.

"My little sister. She must be worried, scared sick," Gaylyn said, then mumbled thanks over her shoulder as she got out of the car.

Quill waited until Gaylyn was in the front door before pulling out of the driveway. Quill could have turned right, the shorter distance to her own home, but she was compelled to take a left and drive by Punk's house one more time. She slowed to a crawl as she approached the house and noticed that the crazy pregnant woman's beat-up white car was gone. *Huh. Did she and Cliff return and get it? Or did the cops tow it?* There were so many tire tracks going in and out of the driveway that it was hard to tell which tracks were the most recent, especially with just the beam from her headlights to try to see in the dark. Next, she noticed that the front door was boarded securely and the glass windows of the house, with no light emanating from the inside, only reflected what little light was outside.

When she reached home, the same darkness greeted her. As

did the empty space where Crow normally parked his truck. Inside, as she wandered room to room, she noticed Baby Boy's favorite trucks gone and an empty pajama drawer, along with the absence of Niswi's school backpack in her room. A stack of Crow's T-shirts was gone from their bedroom. She threw herself on the rug on the living room floor and cried herself into exhaustion, followed by dark sleep.

CHAPTER TWENTY-SIX

Quill ran. She passed the tree where she had dropped to the ground in terror as a woman screamed in the woods. She passed the place where she had stopped to pick up a small beaded earring. She ran down the road where the community had walked after searching the woods for Mabel. Without her husband. With one of her best friends missing. After getting shot at. After her friend's mother stabbed her husband and went to jail, Quill ran.

She ran in the freezing cold. Her running shoes sank in snow up to her ankles in places on the winter path. Alternately, she screamed and cursed. Dared someone to try and stop her. Dared someone, anyone, to kidnap her. Tears ran down her cheeks. Sweat slid down her spine. She stopped counting laps on her third run through the woods.

Eventually, her tracksuit soaked with sweat, she returned to her car on the side of the road. She turned the heat on full blast. Stared down the road. Nothing in the universe moved.

The only sound was her own labored breathing and the sound of her car engine. In the dead of winter, no bugs, dragonflies, or butterflies flitted by. No rabbit hopped across the road. No deer walked softly through the snow, peered doe-eyed out from the leafless trees.

"Okay girl, whatcha gonna do?" she asked herself out loud.

"Find Punk. Kill Cliff. Drag Crow and the kids back home . . ." Maybe not kill Cliff. She doubted Crow would bring the kids to visit her in prison.

"Make a plan, girl, make a plan."

In the meditative silence of winter in northern Minnesota, Quill envisioned tracking down Cliff, getting him or his baby mama to tell her where Punk was, then rescuing Punk. She and Gaylyn had already rescued Lisa; Punk had to be nearby. She hoped. She prayed. A hawk flew across the road, coming within inches of the windshield. Within seconds, two eagles soared above the treetops. Quill heard their whistle through the closed windows and over the sound of the car engine. "Miigwech Migizi. Miigwech Gekek." Quill opened the glove box and grabbed her tobacco pouch. She rolled down the car window and offered a tobacco prayer to the bineshi that flew overhead.

She called Patrick on his cell. He picked up right away. "Anything new on Cliff? Trent? Or Gaylyn's mom?" she asked.

Patrick sounded tired. "Slow down, Quill. Cliff? Nah. I am still trying to figure out how we screwed up on that one. Hiring him, you know? Checked with cops up in Duluth and over toward Little Sweden and no reports of either his car or hers. One of my guys went up to the hospital in Duluth to interview

Gaylyn's dad. See if they can get any information out of him. Nothing on Punk. We're on it, Quill. You take care of you. Take care of your family."

"Yeah, right." Quill paused. "Thanks. Later." And hung up.

Quill briefly debated whether to go home and change out of her sweat-soaked running suit. Her winter coat, gloves, and scarf were on the passenger seat. She had a change of clothes in a duffel bag in the trunk, along with a couple blankets, candy bars, and water—the usual winter survival kit for living in northern Minnesota. So, instead, she turned around on the road and went north of the reservation. Almost every time she had seen the white car on the rez it was driving in that direction on the road leading out of the village or coming back from that way. She hadn't thought anything of it, but maybe the woman had rented a farmhouse north of the village somewhere? Maybe she and Cliff were holed up out there.

She drove to the boundary of the reservation, then spent a good two hours going up and down country roads, scrutinizing each homestead and deserted lake cabin. Each place seemed to have its share of abandoned cars and farm machinery sitting alongside barns and houses weathered with age. Barns with doors sagging and kitchen windows hung with lifeless curtains. Progress, and sandy soil, hadn't created prosperous farms up in this part of the state.

Early twilight was setting in, and just as she was ready to give it up and head back to the rez, she passed a dilapidated farmhouse. It sat at the end of a long, unplowed driveway with fresh tire tracks. There were a couple places where it looked like a car had gotten stuck in the snow but was either pushed or the driver gunned their vehicle down the road. One curtained window let dull light slip out. Quill slowed the car to an even slower crawl. In the fading light she could just make out the back bumper of a sedan. *It kinda looks like Cliff's, kinda not.*

She killed the headlights and let the car drift to the side of the road, where she put it in park and turned off the engine. She rolled down the car window only to listen to the silence of the winter air. Any of the usual outdoor sounds were absent, as sound was absorbed by the recent snowfall. The quiet made the winter night more eerie. If it were freezing cold, the snow would have created a crust that would crackle when rabbits hopped on it and the sounds would carry long distances. Not tonight. Silence.

She shut off the overhead light as she debated whether to get out of the car and approach the house. She didn't want the light to give away her position. She debated some more in her mind what to do or not do. She twisted the driver's side mirror so she could watch the house while she formulated a plan. If it was Cliff and his woman, she didn't anticipate they would give her a very warm welcome. She couldn't very well just knock on the door and ask, "Hey, where'd you stash Punk?" If it was someone else, she didn't have a story to tell as to why she was approaching their home.

She felt a presence before she heard a crunch on the plowed snow between the roadway and the ditch. Quickly, she reached for the rearview mirror, intending to swivel it so she could see the passenger side of the car while she checked the house from the driver's side mirror. Before she even got the mirror twisted in her hand, the passenger door jerked open. Cliff slid onto the seat, pointing a gun in her face.

"What the hell you doing?" His voice sounded like gravel. His eyes and the gun in his right hand glinted in what little light reflected off the snow outside. He growled, "Don't touch that door," and pushed the gun against her right shoulder as she reached for the door handle. She grabbed the steering wheel with both hands.

"Where is Punk?" she snarled back.

"Hell. Same place you're going, bitch. Scoot toward me." As he slid halfway out the passenger door, he grabbed her phone off the car seat and tossed it into the snow-covered ditch behind him, all the while keeping his eyes and gun pointed at her.

Quill quickly turned the key in the ignition as she slid toward him, thinking she might be able to speed off and knock him out the door. The last thing she heard was the engine turn over.

She came to shivering with cold, her back against metal and what felt like a tire under her left side. The right side of her face stung and was swollen when she touched it. When she felt the objects around her, she realized she was in the trunk of her own car. The small cooler of extra food was still by her feet, her extra blankets between her body and the spare tire. She wasn't tied up, just tossed in, so she had some freedom of movement. She searched frantically for the trunk's emergency-release lever.

Her heart sank when she remembered how old her car was. It was an old junker Crow got running, made before every car was required to have a trunk-release safety feature.

Once she stopped moving, stopped looking for a way to escape, cold and despair seeped in. She pulled the blanket around her shivering body. She couldn't hear anything outside. She didn't know if the car had been moved, how long she had been knocked out, or what time it was. *Get yourself together, girl.*

Her coat and other winter gear was still on the front seat of the car. She felt around until she found the duffel bag and within the cramped confines of the trunk pulled on every piece of extra clothing, layers on top of layers. It cut the chill somewhat and gave her more padding against the hard metal. She took a drink of water but decided against eating anything. She would need more stamina later, she thought as she shoved as many candy bars and granola bars as she could get into the many pockets of the different outfits she wore. In doing so, she felt Mabel's earring still inside one pocket. She wrapped herself in the blankets, cried for Mabel, for Lisa, for Punk, for herself. And waited.

She saw a thin line of light along the trunk lid before she heard the car approach. Her heart leapt with hope when she heard the car stop. Maybe it was a cop or some farmer stopping to check out a stalled vehicle. She raised her arms to pound with her fist on the trunk when she heard, "Just do as I say, you stupid cow. We wouldn't be in this mess if you just stayed in North Dakota like I told you to."

Quill heard a slap, skin on skin, and the sharp intake of a woman's voice.

Then Cliff again. "Shut the fuck up. Quit your whining. Get in there and drive. Follow me."

The car door opened and shut. The engine turned over. The

thread of light inside the trunk disappeared as Quill heard another car pull in front of hers. As the car turned corners on the country roads, she slid from side to side. Exhaust from the old muffler seeped into the trunk until she found the crowbar by the spare tire and knocked out the taillight on the driver's side. She put her face as close as she could get and breathed in cold fresh air.

Quill considered calling out to the woman driving, hoping for mercy, but figured if it was Cassandra, she might just try to shoot her again. She did twist around and try to push the backseat forward, thinking she could easily overpower a pregnant woman. It didn't work. She twisted back around to get fresh air from the broken taillight. *What the heck?* Tears came to her eyes again as she thought of Crow, Niswi, and Baby Boy. *Get your shit together and get out of this mess.* She wiped away the tears.

Eventually, the car was on a paved road going straight. The easy sway of the car threatened to lull her to sleep. Afraid of the carbon monoxide she pressed her face closer to the broken taillight, willed herself to stay awake. Unsure of how far they had traveled, she backed away from the fresh air when the car stopped and light again appeared in the crack of the trunk lid.

"Get out," she heard Cliff say to Cassandra. "Get your fat ass into my car and wait for me. I don't want to see your face until I take care of some business here."

Car doors slammed. The car turned a couple short corners, then the engine shut off. She willed herself to close her eyes and stay limp as a key was inserted into the trunk lock and the trunk opened. She wanted him to think she was passed out.

Not a threat. She wasn't prepared for Cliff to slap her hard across her face. "Wake up, bitch."

Instinctively, her hands flew up. Rage filled her chest. She slapped and struck back at him. He grabbed both her wrists in one hand, swearing while he did so, and used his free hand to choke her until she passed out again.

CHAPTER TWENTY-SEVEN

"**Q**uill. Quill." Punk's voice reached through the deep fog of Quill's brain.

"Hey, girlfriend, I been looking for you" were the words that exited Quill's sore throat.

"Shuddup." Punk gave a weak smile.

"Where the fuck are we?" Quill's head was cradled in Punk's lap.

"Little Sweden. Some hellhole. The motel we ran around." Punk's salon-finished nails were chipped and ragged as she held a cheap plastic cup to give Quill a sip of water. "Sorry you ended up in this mess. Apparently I have really poor taste in men."

"Stop it. Laughing makes my throat hurt. Water. What the hell happened?"

"Cliff . . ."

"Who isn't really Cliff—that woman carrying his child calls him Trent."

"Yeah, not surprised. He's scary dangerous. All sweet and

kind to rope me in, then wham, worst abuse I ever lived through."

Quill looked at Punk. Her mohawk was shaggy, with scraggly hairs growing over her ears. The elders were right. The earring over her eye had been ripped out, although the wound was healing. Her eyes carried a deep sadness.

"As far as I can tell, he messed up on some deal or other with some of these pipeline workers and they wanted women, girls actually, in payment." Punk gave Quill a sip of water, then stared into the distance. "I'm too old for what they want, which doesn't mean they don't take it." She tilted her head and squinted her eyes. "So are you." She set the empty cup on the floor beside her. "I'm scared."

"How do we get out of here?"

"I don't know. I've been locked in here most of the time. Unless . . ." Her voice drifted off and her eyes got vacant again.

Quill pushed herself to sitting. Everything in the room was dirty. The bedding was rumpled and stained. Tissues and empty water bottles fell out of the waste bin. Stale eggs in Styrofoam sat on the dresser. Punk's torn and stained pink running suit hung on her. She had lost the soft roundness Quill was accustomed to. As Quill pushed herself to stand, she patted her pockets. Some still held candy bars and health snacks. Mabel's earring was still safe. "He threw my phone in the ditch. We gotta get the hell out of here."

"How? That door is locked from the outside. They only open it to get in here." Punk remained folded in on herself on the grungy floor. "He just dumped you in here like you were trash."

"You think he'll be back?"

"Not tonight. It's when they first get off work that you really gotta worry. They eat, drink. Then the craziness starts. They're probably all passed out right now. And they leave real early for work."

Quill tried the door. It didn't open. She looked closer and saw that the door handle had been altered. It didn't lock from the inside like a normal motel door. It was indeed locked from the outside. She looked out the window. Four stories below, a service road ran behind the building they were in. Snow glistened in the darkened backyards that faced the road. Some had garages that opened to the service road, some had fences or privacy hedges. They were on the top floor of the motel and there was no way to slide the window open. She walked back across the room, pressed her ear against the locked door, and listened.

She had found Cliff's farm hideout when the sun was going down. With no idea how long she was knocked out for, she figured it was at least a forty-five-minute drive from the farm road to the Little Sweden motel. Maybe it was close to midnight? Maybe not? She'd lost track of time. She didn't hear any sounds outside the door. She looked out the peephole but all she saw was a distorted view of an empty hallway. Taped on the door was a yellow, weathered layout of the hotel marking the exits in case of fire. She found the circle that indicated YOU ARE HERE.

According to the map, right next door was a meeting room and then an exit stairway. Her heartbeat increased. "Punk! Lookit." She jabbed her finger on the map. "We can dig our way out of here."

Punk looked up from the floor. "Are you crazy?"

"Fuck no. I'm not hanging around here waiting to get

jumped. Come on, help me find something to tear a hole in this wall."

"We'll wake up the whole motel."

"Geezus, girl, come on." Quill started rummaging around in the room. "Get up. Help me move this dresser in front of the door. Block it. Come on, help me lift it. Move it quietly. If someone opens the door it will take them a bit to get to us."

Both women were worn out from the physical abuse they had endured, Punk more so than Quill. But urgency generated by the possibility of escape, fueled by adrenaline, gave them the energy needed to move furniture to get the door blocked. Finished, they sat, backs against the dresser. They rested and listened for noise outside the room. All was still quiet. "Help me get the towel rack out of the bathroom," said Quill when she'd caught her breath.

After a couple tries, and finally using all her weight to pull down on it, followed by a loud *crack!*, Quill freed the towel rack from the bathroom wall and handed it to Punk. "Here, use the sharp edge of that. Start scraping." She pointed to where the dresser had been.

Punk's tentative scrapes sounded like mice in the walls. She was afraid the noise she made would wake some of the men, but when no one came to investigate she started scraping harder. Quill used a plastic knife she found in the garbage to unscrew a long metal handle from the dresser drawer. Once she got it free, she used the metal handle like a knife and attacked the wall with a vengeance. Drywall dust covered them both. They would stop every few seconds to listen for any movement outside the room. It was a cheaply made hotel with no insulation between the walls.

"What are we going to do if we get out of here? There will

be men all over the place looking for us, and no one in this town seems to care 'cause they're making money off this pipeline." Punk spoke softly, her voice shaking, near tears.

"One thing at a time, girlfriend. One thing at a time. Right behind this motel are residential homes. We're going to cut straight across the road out there and hide in someone's backyard for a minute. I'll figure something out, okay?"

"Okay."

Once they broke through the drywall, they pulled chunks of it off until they created a hole big enough to crawl through. Then Quill sat on her butt and kicked the wall out on the other side.

Both jumped when a man's voice from below hollered out. "Shuddup! Hump the bitch someplace else. Some of us gotta work in the morning."

Both women sat silently, frozen, listening for any movement or noise from any other part of the hotel.

Punk started to cry softly. Quill whispered, "Shh, shh," in her ear. "It's okay. Listen. No one's coming. We're getting out of here."

"We'll get killed."

"We'll get killed if we stay. We're gonna get out," Quill comforted Punk.

After what seemed like hours listening for any sound that indicated someone was coming to find out what the noise was, and with no one appearing, Quill whispered, "Now, go!" Quill pushed Punk toward the hole.

Quill followed Punk. Once through, she hurried to the thin stream of light she could see from under the door. "Come on," she whispered back to Punk.

They walked quickly, softly, to the exit stairway and ran four flights down. Freezing air engulfed them as they rushed outside. The door slammed shut behind them. Neither woman looked back. Quill ran directly to a garage she saw across the service road without a fence attached to it. She had to wait until Punk caught up with her, then both women ran alongside the building into the backyard. A security floodlight flashed on. Quill pushed Punk back against the garage wall into darkness.

They squatted down. "Let me think," said Quill. She got up and walked back alongside the garage. There was no indication of life at the motel, no indication anyone had noticed they were gone. She walked back to Punk.

"Come on. We're going to run to the gas station. The attendant there found Lisa. She'll help us."

"I don't know if I can."

"You will—it's not a matter of can."

Quill restrained herself from running full out as Punk limped along behind her. They followed the garages, fences, and trees that lined the road where it was the darkest. Every few houses, they stopped. Punk's leg wasn't healed properly; she had also been without good food and had been abused. The short run to escape was taking a toll on her.

"We're almost there," Quill said when they made it past the motel and were standing in the shadow of a tree. A semitruck rolled past, blowing even colder air at them. Punk crouched, quaking, until the truck's taillights faded down the road.

Quill pulled her to standing and gave her a push to get her moving across the road.

A worn sign on the gas station door said the place would

open at 5:00 A.M. Quill cupped her hands and peered through the window at a digital clock that read 3:43. "We can't wait till it opens," she said to Punk as she pulled her around to the back of the building out of sight of any cars that might pass.

Punk's teeth were chattering from the cold. "If they find us, we're dead. If we stay outside, we're going to freeze to death." Tears once again rolled down her cheeks.

"Listen to me. We gotta keep our shit together. You've been through hell. I'm gonna get us out of here one way or the other. Here. Put this on." Quill pulled off one of the running jackets she had put on in the car trunk. "Squeeze behind the garbage bin, out of sight, and out of the windchill. I'll be right back."

Quill ran back across the street to where a snowmobile sat between two garages. She felt across the dash in the dark and luck was with her: a key was in the ignition. She straddled the machine, turned the engine over, and almost flew backward off the sled as she hit the throttle and five hundred pounds of metal jerked forward.

The roar of the motor and the smell of exhaust filled the winter air. She glanced back at the motel, which was still shrouded in sleepy darkness. She drove to Punk, accidentally killing the motor as she hit the brakes too hard. "Get on," she whispered loudly to Punk.

Punk scrambled onto the seat behind Quill. Both women jerked backward as once again Quill hit the throttle harder than she needed to. Punk hung on for dear life as Quill steered the machine down into the ditch alongside the pavement and headed in the direction of home.

CHAPTER TWENTY-EIGHT

Neither woman was dressed for the winter temps. Quill was driving the snowmobile at top speed, which only increased the windchill. The last time she had driven a snowmobile, Crow had signed her up for the powderpuff derby in a snowmobile rally west of Duluth. He had made sure to borrow the necessary winter gear for her. This time she had no snowmobile suit. No helmet. And without gloves, she found she had to switch hands while she drove, in order to blow warm air on her free hand, hoping to avoid frostbite. She couldn't feel her face. The only warm spot on her body was her back, where Punk clung to life.

The town of Little Sweden was no longer in sight behind them when Quill, in a frozen daze, almost hit a vehicle that was half buried in snow in the ditch. Unfamiliar with the snowmobile gears, she once again killed the engine as she swerved to avoid the car.

Punk bounced off the machine into the snow. "I think I'm gonna die right here," she said.

Quill pulled her up to sitting. "Nah. We got life to live. Get up. I didn't rescue your ass to leave you out here to become a chunk of ice."

Punk was a shivering mass as Quill lifted her onto the snowmobile before she waded through snow up to her knees around to the driver's side of the car. The doors were sealed shut with snow. Whoever had run into the ditch had needed to roll down the window to get out. Quill crawled through the open window. Found a couple blankets and a stash of stocking caps on the backseat. On the back floor were some bungee cords. In the front seat, a pair of gloves were on the passenger-side floor. A box of farmer's matches were in the glove box, along with two chocolate bars and a pair of kid's mittens. Someone else who knew how to pack a car for winter driving.

She put a couple stocking caps on Punk's head, put the kid's mittens on her hands, and used one bungee cord she'd found on the back floor to hold a blanket in place around Punk's body. For herself she pulled on a full-face stocking cap, strung another bungee cord around her upper body to hold a blanket around herself, pulled on the gloves, and started up the snowmobile. She couldn't feel her feet at all.

As they jounced through the ditches Quill plotted their next move. Her phone was in a ditch somewhere north of the reservation. No one was home at her place. She had given Punk's phone to Patrick. She didn't think either of them could survive a ride beyond the village, which was closer than the tribal police station. "Gaylyn is our best hope," she said out loud to herself.

She pushed the snowmobile at top speed until they reached

the reservation and were at Gaylyn's driveway within an hour. When Quill shut off the engine and jumped off the snowmobile, Punk fell forward on the seat. Gaylyn must have heard the machine pull into the yard because she opened the door just as Quill reached it.

"What the heck!" she said as she pulled Quill into the warmth of the house.

"Get Punk," gasped Quill as she fell onto the sagging couch in the living room. Without taking off any outer wear, she immediately pulled off her shoes and socks, curled into a fetal position, and rubbed her feet. She couldn't tell which were colder, her feet or her hands.

Gaylyn carried Punk in and gently laid her on the end of the couch.

"You gonna live?" she asked Quill. When Quill nodded yes, Gaylyn added, "I'm gonna get some pans of warm water, not hot, to warm her up. You both got frostbite."

Gaylyn doctored the women's extremities until both felt the sting of pins and needles that told them blood was rushing to the frostbit areas. Punk passed in and out of consciousness while Quill told Gaylyn all that had transpired. "I think if we can get out to that farmhouse we can catch him—catch Cliff."

"Um, you just told me both he and the crazy woman have guns. Don't you think we should call Patrick?"

"No. They haven't arrested him. Have they done anything? No. It would be wasting precious time when I know where he and his woman are holed up. I'm going; you want to come with or not?" Quill started to pull on her damp socks. "Does your dad have a hunting rifle? We got two at our house."

"Hang on, girlfriend. And what's your plan, ride out there

on a snowmobile? Shoot him with Crow's deer rifle? Come on, there's gotta be a better plan than that. My car is out here, just filled up earlier tonight. Don't put on those wet socks." Gaylyn went into one of the back rooms and returned with a pair of dry socks that she tossed to Quill. She also carried a .22 rifle. "Found a pocket full of ammo, but all I've ever tried to shoot is rabbits. Not saying we should shoot someone; I'm trying my best to stay out of jail to take care of my sister. Don't need to be roommates with my mom."

"What about Punk? She needs medical care. I hate to just leave her." Quill was torn between helping her friend and getting the guy who had caused all the chaos, turmoil, and hurt in their lives. "I know where these two are, we should try to get them now. Let Punk sleep. She's safe here, and as soon as we get back, we'll take her into Duluth to the hospital."

"You're probably right. She might be scared if she wakes up and there's someone else here and not us. My little sister's here if she does wake up. Better to let her sleep, keep her covered and warm until we get back."

Quill recognized that neither she nor Gaylyn seemed to be thinking right, but running on fear, she was driven to action.

Gaylyn drove Quill to her house, where she quickly pulled her own winter gear over the running outfit she was wearing, grabbed a hunting rifle and ammo from a locked safe in the storage room under the basement stairs, and hopped back into the car. "I'll tell you how to get there. I drove up and down these roads north of the rez until I spotted his car mostly hidden behind the house. I think I can get us right to the spot," she said as she put ammo into the rifle she held between her knees.

"Go straight. Turn left. Right around this curve up here. There. There. Shut off your headlights. There it is, up there on the left."

Gaylyn killed the headlights and drove a couple hundred feet up the road until they were past the driveway. Morning twilight was beginning, although the sun had yet to peek above the eastern horizon.

Quill spoke in a soft whisper. "Looks like we've got an hour, two at the most, before sunrise. We can sneak up on them in the dark. This is about where I was parked when he grabbed me. Didn't see him coming. But look, that's my car, sitting as pretty as you please right there by the house. Asshole."

"What's our plan?"

"Get 'em."

"Come on, Quill. He's army, he's got guns, and he's psycho. And it sounds like the woman is too." Gaylyn's whisper was harsh.

"But they're asleep. And not expecting us. Otherwise, my car wouldn't be sitting out there for the world to see. He thinks he's safe. Thinks me and Punk are sitting in that rotten motel room and that he's gotten away with it. I'm not letting him skip out of here without paying for the damage he's done to Punk. To all of us. Turn off the overhead light and get out without slamming the car door."

Quill led the way. She with a hunting rifle and Gaylyn with her .22. They walked up the road a few feet, then walked down into the ditch and across a field to approach the house from an angle, and circled it. Quill motioned for Gaylyn to stay back around the corner from the farmhouse door. She went to her own car, crouched down, and as quietly as possible opened the driver's door. The inside light popped on. She reached in quickly, shut off the light. Felt around the ignition. The key was there. She popped the trunk lid. The trunk light didn't come on in the old junker. Gently, she closed the car door without letting it latch. She lifted the trunk lid wide open and felt for any possible weapons. Just a lug wrench, which she threw into the snow. She stood, rifle ready to fire, half expecting Cliff to come charging out the house door.

When no one appeared she ran back to Gaylyn and pulled her behind a weathered well house that stood at the end of an old-fashioned clothesline. She was starting to shiver again in the cold. "Hang on a sec. I'm gonna disable the distributor coil from the crazy woman's old junker so she won't be able to follow us. If he comes out, holler 'Police!' and shoot at the tires of his car."

Before Gaylyn could protest, Quill crouched down and ran to the white car. She felt through the grille until she found the hood latch. It screeched as it opened. All her hours under the hood of a car with Crow worked to her advantage in the moment she reached in and yanked the distributor coil out.

She ran back to where Gaylyn stood in the shadows, gun aimed at the cars. Softly, through chattering teeth, Quill said, "Go on back to the side of the house so you're closer to the door. See those rocks that kinda mark where people should park? I'm gonna get one and throw it at the door, make some noise. When he comes out, I want you to yell, 'Police, get on the ground!' If I need to, I'm going to fire a round over his head. We're going to put him in the trunk of my car and drive him back to the tribal police station."

"What about his woman?"

"I'm not going to worry about her. She can rot in hell for all I care." As soon as Gaylyn moved into place, Quill hefted a good-sized rock at the wooden door. It sounded like a cherry bomb on the Fourth of July when it cracked the door.

Within seconds, Cliff, barefoot in boxer shorts and a worn white T-shirt, with the hair on his head standing up like a rooster comb, flung the door open.

Gaylyn, with a deep growl Quill didn't recognize, hollered, "Police, on the ground, hands behind your back!" She had the .22 pointed above Cliff's head. He made the slightest move to turn back into the house and she fired into the doorframe right above his head. "Get down!" she hollered again. This time he dropped to his knees, hands on his head.

Quill approached with the hunting rifle at the ready.

"Who the hell are you? What the fuck you think you're doing?" he snarled at Quill. He started to rise up and Gaylyn fired another round into the door above him. He jerked back down.

Quill couldn't tell if she was shivering from the cold, adrenaline, or fear. "Get up. Over to the car." She kept the gun trained on him. "You left me and Punk to die. I don't need a reason not to shoot. Move."

"Don't try anything. I can shoot you from here," Gaylyn said, and trained her rifle on him.

He winced as his feet walked across ice-cold gravel. He moved slowly to the car and Quill could tell he was trying to stall. She pushed him with the barrel of the rifle when he tried to slow down. "Cassandra!" he finally hollered at the top of his lungs.

The pregnant lady filled the doorway, white nightgown billowing in the wind like some horror movie scene. "Trent!" she hollered at the same moment Gaylyn took another shot at the house door. The woman quickly retreated.

"She's going for a gun, Quill. Get him in the car."

Quill fired into the air over Cliff's head. He jerked down. "Get in the trunk!" she screamed.

He did. As she slammed the trunk lid down and ran to jump in the driver's seat, she saw Cassandra standing in the doorway. A pistol was pointed in her direction while Gaylyn circled in front of the woman, her .22 ready to shoot again as she backed her way toward her own car, which sat back up on the road. Quill rolled down her window. "Run!" she yelled to Gaylyn.

Gaylyn turned and ran. Cassandra fired but missed. In her rearview mirror Quill saw the pregnant woman waddle to her car. Quill laughed out loud, knowing the car was not going to start. To cover the cursing and banging coming from the trunk, Quill turned the radio up full blast as well as the heat. When Gaylyn reached her own car, she did a quick K-turn and followed Quill.

When she got to the tribal cop parking lot, Quill pulled up in the "No Parking" fire lane. She got out and waited for Gaylyn to arrive and exit her car.

"What the hell." Gaylyn looked at Quill. Both women were bundled in winter gear. Thick scarves wrapped around their necks. Gloves on their hands. Winter boots on their feet. Both had long dark hair sticking out wildly from under their stocking caps pulled low over their ears. Nothing moved in the brightly lit lot where three cop cars were parked. The women could see their breaths in the cold winter air. A *thunk, thunk* came from the trunk of Quill's car.

"You got a body in there?" Gaylyn asked.

And both women dissolved into laughter. The kind of laughter that builds and builds. The kind that causes one to double over and say, "Stop, my stomach hurts."

Quill was the first to pull herself together. Leaning against the trunk of the car, between laughs, she gasped, "We gotta get him outta there. He might freeze to death, and then I will be charged with murder." They laughed again. Quill finally straightened up, pulled her stocking cap down as far as it would go on her head, tied her wool scarf in a knot, and said, "For real now, I'm gonna go in and tell them who we got here." She took a deep breath and walked into the police station.

"What in the goddamn hell were you thinking?" Patrick threw his duckbill cap across the room and slammed his hand so hard on the table that Quill and Gaylyn jumped in their seats. Patrick was as red in the face as Quill had ever seen an Indian turn. "What the hell? You can get charged with interfering with an ongoing investigation. Tampering with evidence. Assault." His open hand hit the table again. He stared hard at both women. Spit flew at them as he yelled. "Assault with a deadly weapon."

"He kidnapped me." "Assaulted and raped Punk." Both

women spoke in unison. "And Punk, half dead, had to call us to help her because you two ran off to chase after Cliff," Patrick yelled at them.

Quill, wrapped in a blanket, still shivered from the cold, but mostly the fear, now that she was in a safe place. "I knew where he was. I knew how to find him. I didn't want him to get away. You didn't know where he was. Where to look. I did."

Gaylyn gripped a cup of hot coffee in both her hands. They were in the same interview room with Patrick they had been in when they came to talk to him about Mabel screaming in the woods.

Patrick, both hands on hips, turned his back to them and stared out the window. Bright sun glistened off the snow on the pine branches that ringed the tribal police station.

"Where's Punk?" Quill asked softly, afraid the question would set Patrick off on another angry tirade.

"Hospital. Duluth."

Long silence ensued. Garbled noises came from the two-way radio on Patrick's hip. He turned away from the window, walked out the door, and slammed it loudly behind him, making both women jump again.

They spent the rest of the day being interviewed by state cops, local cops, tribal cops, and BCA. Quill recounted her capture by Cliff. The women's escape from the motel. Quill's theft of the snowmobile and items from the car in the ditch. The frozen ride Quill and Punk took to the rez. Gaylyn's aiding and abetting Quill's capture of Cliff by pretending to be the police and forcing him at gunpoint into the trunk of her car. Cassandra, as they left her behind, her screams punctuating the winter silence with all the ways she would kill them as soon as she could.

Quill never stopped shivering. Gaylyn eventually resorted to sullen monosyllabic responses. Escorted bathroom breaks were few and far between. A fast-food meal, with cold French fries, was brought in at some point.

As sunset approached, the officer visits slowed. Quill rested her head on her folded arms on the table and dozed off. Gaylyn doodled squiggles and beadwork patterns on a lined pad of paper someone had left behind.

Eventually Patrick, with tired worry lines etched on his face, came in and sat down quietly. He slid Quill's phone toward her, touched her arm gently with it to wake her up. "One of the officers found this in the ditch. We've been charging it for you. Wanna see if it still works?"

Quill barely raised her head. Used her middle finger to turn it on. Gaylyn held back a chuckle. The phone pinged to life. Quill sent a text to Crow. *Suppose you've heard. Please come home.* She closed her eyes and put her head back down on her arms.

Patrick cleared his throat. Quill opened her eyes. Gaylyn stopped doodling. "Cliff's in jail. Cassandra is in the hospital in Duluth. Early labor and all that. She's in police custody. Some things still need to be straightened out with the snowmobile, but I'll see what I can do. It'll take a week or two to sort through all the different issues here, but for now you two are free to go."

"We didn't do anything," exclaimed Gaylyn. "What do you mean, issues to sort out?"

Patrick threw his hands up. "Calm down. Just saying, a lot

has happened. Your car is impounded for evidence. Go home, rest, sleep. Whatever you need to do to take care of yourselves. I'm glad you're safe. I'll be out front to give you a ride home when you're ready." He pushed his chair back, stood, and exited. He left the door open this time.

CHAPTER TWENTY-NINE

Quill entered an empty house and crawled into bed without getting undressed. Sometime during the night she jerked awake when she felt Crow get into bed next to her. He pulled her tightly into his arms without saying a word and she fell right back to sleep.

When she woke midmorning, Crow was working on a tribal vehicle out in the front yard. She didn't know what to say to him so she puttered around all day. Swept the floors. Took a bath. Changed into clean clothes. Crow came in occasionally for a fresh cup of coffee but neither spoke. He left around suppertime. Quill stood at the front window and watched him drive off. She assumed he was going to Barbie's, where the kids still were. She didn't know how to have a conversation with him about all that had happened.

A couple days later she got a call from Punk. She was going to be home; she figured she'd get there around two in the afternoon. Could Quill call Gaylyn and then both meet Punk at her house? She didn't want to be there alone right away.

"Of course," answered Quill. At one-thirty she put on her winter gear and told Crow, who was once again working on a car in the yard, that she was going to walk to Punk's.

He looked up with guarded sadness in his eyes that wrenched Quill's heart. "Be safe" was all he said.

Gaylyn was already at Punk's on the front steps. Quill joined her and waited until a medical taxi pulled into the yard. Punk got out, dressed in a new black running suit.

"What the fuck?" were Punk's stunned words when she saw her new door with two security locks. She burst into tears. "How could I be so stupid?" she wailed as she entered the house. She went directly to a chair at the kitchen table, sat, and buried her face in her arms, sobbing softly.

Quill asked Gaylyn to make them all fresh coffee. Gaylyn also dug around in the cupboards and fridge and set out plates of commodity cheese, venison salami, crackers, and Oreo cookies. When the coffee was ready, Gaylyn and Quill each pulled out a chair to sit on. Punk still sat with her head on her folded arms, crying softly. Quill went to the bathroom and returned with a roll of toilet paper that she set down by Punk's arm. Without lifting her head, Punk grabbed a handful of tissue off the roll, wiped away her tears, and blew her nose. "How could I be so stupid?" she repeated, and put her head back down on her arms without looking at either of them.

While they waited for her tears to subside, they took turns slicing off pieces of venison and cheese and eating it on crackers. For the longest time the only sound was the crunching of crackers and sipping of coffee.

Quill was reaching for a cracker when Punk jerked herself upright. For a long moment she stared at the dead, dried flower in a small vase on the center of the table. She reached out, grabbed the vase and with all her might threw it at the far wall. Glass and flower petals smashed and scattered as it hit. She pushed away so abruptly her chair fell over behind her.

She rushed into a back bedroom and returned with an armful of men's clothes. She marched through the smashed glass and dried flower bits. She struggled with the door to get it open, and when she finally did, she forcefully tossed all the clothes out into a snowbank. She bent down and tossed out the men's shoes that were sitting by the doorway. She made three more trips to the bedroom and back; each time she brought more men's clothes and shoes. Then, apparently finished with the bedroom, she went to work emptying the bathroom of men's cologne, a toothbrush, and a handful of razors. They got tossed into the snow as well.

Gaylyn and Quill watched silently, nervously. Drank their coffee and ate more slices of venison and cheese. Gaylyn killed off the Oreos. Done with the bedroom and bathroom, Punk opened a drawer in the kitchen and pulled out a knife. Gaylyn's "Whoa" didn't stop her. She sliced through an expensive Native artist's painting that hung on one wall. Shredded it. Tossed it out the door. An Indian pottery vase went out next. CDs and videos were broken in half and tossed. Last, she grabbed the blue and orange geometric-print Pendleton blanket off the couch, stabbed the knife through it and slit it in half before tossing out the door. To which Quill said, under her breath, "Hey, I wanted that."

After tossing the blanket, Punk whirled around the room, scanning for any object she might have missed. Not seeing anything, she returned, uprighted her chair, plopped down, and said, "Well, guess that takes care of that. Any coffee left?"

Gaylyn poured her a cup.

Punk wailed, "You guys must think I'm the stupidest person around."

To which Gaylyn replied, "No, my dad's stupider."

"That crazy woman shot at me," Quill said, looking into her coffee cup. They took turns reliving each moment of the past few weeks. Hushed voices. Angry voices. Scared voices. Going over all the "what ifs" and "whys" and "how comes."

Punk told them how angry Cliff got at her for "showing off" with her flashy outfits and hair. She had bought a red outfit to wear to the Lone Eagle gathering. They had argued about her going. He grabbed her and twisted her leg. Said she would never run again. She screamed so loud Cliff thought he'd finally broken it. "I tried to text you a bunch of times that night, but I guess you were asleep," she said to Quill.

Quill thought back. She remembered ignoring texts from Punk about wanting to chat because she had her mind on the other missing women at the time: Mabel, Lisa.

Punk continued with her story. After she cried in pain all night, Cliff took her to the clinic the next morning. He begged her not to tell anyone. He needed his job with the tribal police, he said. Swore it would never happen again. Bought her flowers. Cleaned the house. Made her good food. After that night, he only hurt her in places no one would see, that was, until he ripped her eyebrow piercing out. She felt small and ashamed and hadn't known how to tell them. And then he started to control her phone too. "Sometimes I would text you during the night. You know, those texts that just said hi. Or a laughing or crying emoji."

She continued, giving them more details. She had really believed he loved her because he was always so kind and loving

after each act of violence. Brought more flowers and the painting and the Pendleton. How stupid could she be? The women
assured her it wasn't her fault. No, she wasn't stupid.

"And then," Punk continued, "I found out he was the one
who was selling meth to some folks here on the reservation."

"My dad," chimed in Gaylyn.

"I overheard a conversation he was having on the phone. I
pushed him to tell me 'cause I heard the word 'meth.' He said
that after he got out of the service, when he lived at Turtle
Mountain, he was in a rough way, PTSD and all that, doing
and selling drugs. He screwed up big-time on some drug deal.
He moved over here after he convinced the men he owed
money to that he would pay them with girls from this reservation. He knew the pipeline was coming this way. As a vet he
had preference getting hired on the police force."

"Oh, Jesus Christ," said Gaylyn.

"I found out from Patrick that Cassandra is his wife. He
told her a whole other story about coming over here. You
know? That the pay was better and they could save money if
she stayed and lived with her mom until the baby came. From
my time in that hellhole it seems Cliff set up the whole thing
with Lisa and Julie. Possibly Mabel too. But I don't know for
sure. At a minimum, with all three women, he looked the
other way as a cop and gave false information to sabotage the
investigation. I was confined to the house. He controlled my
phone. And then, I guess when he figured out Cassandra was
over here trying to find him, he took me over there."

All imaginable swear words floated throughout the air in
the kitchen.

Out of words and stories, the women sat in silence. They

all jerked involuntarily when they heard tires on the driveway. Gaylyn peeked out and saw it was Crow. Quill broke the silence. "He probably got worried waiting for me to come back. Punk, why don't you sleep at our house for the night, maybe a couple nights, until you feel safer? The kids are still at Barbie's and you can sleep in Niswi's bed. I'll run out and tell Crow."

The other women hurriedly cleared the table, rinsed off the dishes, put the food back in the fridge, swept the glass off the floor. Punk grabbed a change of clothes.

Everyone piled into Crow's pickup. It was a quiet ride with a stoic Crow. Gaylyn was dropped off first.

"Are you sure this is okay?" Punk asked.

Crow nodded yes.

At the house, Crow went straight to their bedroom.

Quill asked Punk, "You all right, need anything? You can stay up and watch movies on the TV if you want."

Punk sat on the edge of the couch. "I'm fine. I can watch something on my phone. You sure he's okay with this?"

She apologized over and over for causing them so much trouble while Quill tidied up the living room and kitchen.

Crow came out of the bedroom and told Punk, "Knock it off, of course you're welcome here. Go to bed and stop worrying. It's safe here," he said to her as he locked up the house—something they never did—and when he and Quill went to bed he closed the bedroom door—another thing they never did.

They undressed quietly. Crow pulled on a pair of sweats, "just in case," he said. Quill kept on a T-shirt and panties for the same reason. They slid into bed and grabbed each other in a tight embrace. Crow, in a low whisper, told Quill how scared he'd been when he saw the woman waving a gun around and shooting at the house Quill was in. "And then Patrick told me all the rest that's happened since. I need some time for things to get back to normal." Crow's voice cracked.

Quill kissed him to shush him. She told him how worried she'd been that Cassandra might shoot her. Thank god she ran out of bullets. She talked about how bad she felt for Punk and all that happened to her. Almost happened to herself. How Gaylyn's assessment of Cliff was dead-on right from the beginning. How she herself hadn't wanted to believe that Cliff would hurt Punk; she didn't know the signs, didn't know what to look for. She hated herself for that. Crow shushed her, told her it didn't make any sense to blame herself, but she did have to stop getting herself in dangerous situations before his heart gave out.

She replied that she didn't try to get into trouble. Maybe she was cursed? Maybe she'd angered the spirits in this lifetime, or in a previous lifetime, and this was all payback for an incident she couldn't even remember. Maybe she should have worn a ribbon skirt to the march when Raven Lone Eagle was missing.

Crow told her to knock it off. His kisses went from soft shushes to deeper, longer kisses. Quill's body responded. The terror of all that had transpired, the possibility of losing each other, fueled their lovemaking. They made love fiercely, quietly, desperately. Spent, they pulled their "just in case" garments back on and fell asleep in a tight embrace.

The next day, Punk wanted to return to her own house right away. Crow, before he headed out to jumpstart someone's car, convinced her to give herself time, there was no rush. She was welcome at their house. Crow's sister was going to keep the kids a few more days.

Midmorning, Patrick knocked on the door. Quill invited him in and directed him to a chair at the table. Poured him a cup of coffee. Patrick asked Quill if she wanted to press charges against Cassandra. He could charge her with assault and terroristic threats. They were already charging her with discharging a firearm in the village.

"Nah. Just make sure she and her demon spawn go back to wherever she came from," Quill answered.

Patrick looked at Punk. "Are there any other charges you want to file against Cliff? We're already charging him with numerous kidnapping and trafficking charges." He looked uncomfortable; he cleared his throat and looked into his coffee cup. "If he ever hurt you, or forced you to do anything, um, sexual, against your will, according to state and tribal statutes you can file those charges too if you want."

Punk shook her head no.

"Think about it," Patrick said, finally looking up. "When—if—it goes to trial, both of you will have to testify. He might just plead guilty. Some of the men from the motel have already been charged with sexual assault based on DNA. The camp lawyers are scrambling for plea deals, and we think some of the men have skipped back to their home states."

After he left, Punk went into Niswi's room to lie down and Quill sat at the table to scroll through social media. She hesitated and questioned her judgment, but she finally texted Barbie and asked how her kids were doing. Barbie replied that everything was fine, they were having fun with their cousins. *I know my brother,* she texted. *Just give him some time and space. He might just need time with you. The kids ask for you.*

Niswi has heard stuff at school. I told Crow she needs to see you. Soon.

Quill took some frozen stew from the freezer, thawed it in the microwave. She did some dishes, threw in a load of laundry. She was sweeping the floor when a knock on the door made her jump.

She looked out the front window to see Earline standing in the cold on her front steps. She quickly went down and invited her in. She looked up and down the driveway; the only car out there was her own. She asked, "How did you get here?"

"I walked." Earline unwrapped a scarf from her neck and pulled two stocking caps off her head. "We've been exercising over at the center. Watching you young ones run got us thinking we better move it before we lose it. Thought I'd come by and see if everything's okay after all the commotion around here lately."

"You want some coffee—or I got tea?" Once her guest was seated with a hot cup of coffee between her two hands, Quill checked on Punk, who was sound asleep. She gently pulled the bedroom door shut.

Earline asked if anyone got shot. Everyone at the elder housing heard the gunshots. Saw all the people standing in the headlights over at Punk's. When no ambulance showed up they figured everyone survived, but she wanted to make sure. She lowered her voice. "We all heard about Punk. Is she okay?"

Quill assured her everyone was as fine as they could be— hurt, shook up, but on the mend.

Earline reached into a cloth shopping bag she carried in with her. She pulled out short branches of cedar. She counted out four sprigs of the cedar and handed them across the table to Quill. "You've brought good changes to the community, my girl—with your running, and looking out for the women. And now catching that dirty cop. Often when there is good, the not-so-good tries to push its way in to get attention. Cedar helps keep all the good around us. I hang it above the entry-way to my apartment, and one small branch in the middle of a wall for each side of the home. I use thumbtacks. Do young people even have thumbtacks?" She took a sip of coffee. "Have your old man smudge the whole house with sage before you hang it up." She counted out four more sprigs of cedar. "These are for your friend. The one across the road from me." She counted out four more. "And these are for the other young woman who hangs out with you. And, oh, this is for you." She laid a folded piece of red cloth on the table. "One of the women at Lone Eagle's march noticed you didn't have a skirt. We made you one."

Quill's throat tightened and she felt tears threaten to well up in her eyes. She unfolded the fabric. It was a beautiful red skirt with varying shades of blue ribbon from the hem up to the knees. A slit on either side of the skirt would reach her knees, revealing an underlayer of a flowered red fabric. A beautiful skirt made exclusively for her.

"She put those slits on the sides so you can run in it if you want. It's got pockets too." Earline finished her coffee. She chuckled. "She put the underskirt so when you run, no one will see your bare legs. You know how traditional some people can be." Quill swore that the elder rolled her eyes. "Wouldn't want anyone to see your bare legs." With that pronounce-ment, she folded up her shopping bag, pulled her coat back on. "I should head back. The biddies at the center will be afraid I froze to death in a ditch on the way over here. They'll be calling Patrick to come find me."

Quill insisted on texting Crow and asking him to give Earline a ride back to the center. The two women rehashed the recent events while they waited for him to arrive. Punk slept through it all.

After Crow dropped Earline off at the center, he called Quill from Punk's yard and told her he had picked up all the debris. The only evidence of all the drama was a couple bullet holes next to the doorframe of the house. "Nothing that a bit of putty and paint can't fix."

CHAPTER THIRTY

Once again, life settled back into the slow, "Nothing ever happens here on the rez" routine of life in the community. Crow brought Niswi and Baby Boy back home. Early each morning, windows snapped from darkness to light, followed by the sounds of children laughing as they ran to catch their buses. Crow pulled more cars out of ditches, put used tires on vehicles to replace worn-out, already-on-their-last-tread used tires, and kept the tribal vehicles running. Niswi completed therapy.

Punk kept her mid-length shiny black hair. She teased that she might become goth and start to wear black eyeliner and black lipstick. Every once in a while, she would rat it up and call it her Amy Winehouse look. She switched her phone to a new number because Cliff took to calling her from the jail. She confided in the women that she was afraid and had trouble sleeping.

Gaylyn and her little sister started to take Punk to a

domestic-violence support group. Punk took an extra step to allay her fear and bought a German shepherd/black Lab mix from a dog trainer in Duluth. Once a week Gaylyn drove Punk and her dog, whom she named Assassin, to Duluth to attend obedience classes. The dog's nickname became Asin, or "rock" in Ojibwe. Asin got certification to be an emotional-support animal. Where Punk went, Asin went. On a leash, he ran with the women a lap or two of the village each night. He slept at the foot of Punk's bed.

The women continued to run each night. Quill, determined to train harder, started to run to the casino and back on Saturdays and Sundays. She told Crow the village laps weren't helping them build up speed or stamina.

The women missed the deadline to register for the Boston Marathon. They hadn't known they needed to fill out the proper forms with run times for registration when they had completed the Grandma's Marathon in Duluth the previous summer. The three women vowed to stay focused, stay on track, and together they sat around Punk's kitchen table and registered again for the Grandma's Marathon, which would happen in the early summer, and for the Twin Cities Marathon in the fall. Qualifying run times could get them into Boston the following year.

They asked Earline if she would order more scarves. They would chip in the money and also help her man a booth at the reservation powwows over the summer. The money raised would pay their entry fees into the different races.

The holiday season came and went. On social media there were the usual holiday breakups and resultant drama, and the usual number of overindulgence drinking arrests and three opioid overdoses; thankfully, no one died. People's pages filled with photos of happy children's faces at family gatherings. Families at holiday meals together, trees decorated and presents piled high.

With state and federal employees getting holidays off, and then the tribe adding on a day or two of their own, not much happened in the court system. Gaylyn visited her mother in jail four times a week. She said her mom looked better than she had in years. While the food wasn't great, she at least received regular meals. Her cheeks filled out and she joined the exercise program a church group organized for the women inside.

Julie and Quill talked by phone about once a week. Julie said that Lisa seemed to be doing a little better. She had some physical complications because of the attack, but she wouldn't tell Julie exactly what they were. Lisa wanted Quill and Gaylyn to come up to Grand Portage in the spring. An elder planned to hold a healing ceremony for her and she wanted the two women who rescued her to attend. Quill said, "Of course, let me know when."

Over time the horror people felt about the women's abductions faded. It was replaced by a new headline story out of Winnipeg about a preteen girl found in the Red River. Gossip online and at bingo wondered if it was the same people, border-crossing to avoid detection, who were committing the crimes. People speculated there might be a serial killer, or killers, targeting Native women on both sides of the border. There were few arrests and few convictions. An undercurrent of heightened awareness and fear permeated the community even when things seemed to be going well.

Still, life went on. There was always humor and connection with family, and while most people on the reservation decorated for the season and made multiple trips to Walmart for presents to pile under a lighted tree, Quill and Crow did a low-key holiday celebration.

They didn't do a tree, although they strung lights across the front eaves of the house. Anything to break the winter darkness. They loaded up the kids on Christmas Eve and visited Crow's brother, and his mom and dad also showed up. Crow ordered ahead of time and had peaches and different fresh fruits from Georgia delivered to his brother's home to be divided among the family members. All the cousins played outside, the men watched sports on the big-screen TV, and the women talked about kids and partners and the traumas and dramas of the season until it was time for a run to the local casino for Coverall at bingo.

At that point Quill and Crow, who were teased good-naturedly by the family about not being traditional Indians because they didn't gamble, rounded up the kids for the drive back home. Before they pulled out of the driveway, Barbie's husband flagged them down, said, "Hold on, got a present for yous," and opened the trunk of his car. He pulled out three packages of skinned and frozen rabbits and transferred them to the trunk of their car. He stood in the driveway and watched them drive off.

Baby Boy fell asleep before they got on the freeway. Niswi rode with her forehead pressed against the window and looked up at the night sky. She excitedly shared what she had learned in school about Ojibwe constellations. She called out Biboonkeonini, or the Wintermaker, when she found the constellation commonly known as Orion in the winter sky. Next, she found Maang, the Loon, better known as the Little Dipper. When they turned off the freeway, Crow pulled over, and while Quill sat in the car with their sleeping youngest, he and Niswi stood in the still night air and looked up at the stars.

Noon on Christmas Day, they drove to Quill's mom and dad's and ate roast moose with all the fixings. Quill's mom fixed her husband a plate, which Crow acknowledged by gently tapping Quill's leg under the table with his foot. His eyes said, *See, this is how it should be.* After her mother made a plate for Crow, she dished up food for everyone else. Crow nudged Quill's leg under the table again. She kicked him playfully.

The women planned a run for New Year's Day. They put a post on social media inviting women who ran with them to Little Sweden and back to join them. They organized short runs of 5K and 10K around the village roads and a longer one from the village to the casino and back. Once Earline heard about the plan, she convinced the women at the elder housing to borrow the grill from the community center, which was closed for the holiday. The women cooked up hotdogs, hamburgers, and frybread. Earline enlisted members of the Veteran's Club to sell her kookum scarves for her.

It became a community celebration. Crow convinced someone to deliver two porta-potties for the runners. About thirty women came who'd run previously. With reserved rooms at the casino hotel, they had kids in tow and left partners at the casino to gamble. Many said they planned to stay for the New Year festivities at the casino.

The time of daylight in Minnesota grew longer going into the new year. Gradually, sunrise arrived earlier and sunset later. The January thaw, a normal winter occurrence where the temperatures rise an average of 10° F above the temps a week before, arrived a bit early.

The warmer temps weren't enough to melt the snow; in fact they created the right weather conditions for a few more inches of snowfall. The additional warmth of the moisture in the air created large, waterlogged, storybook snowflakes. The kids caught them on mittens and showed one another the perfection of the no-two-ever-alike snowflakes.

After the tragedies of the winter, the few degrees of warmth created energy among the women runners. There was the promise of winter ending and the promise of the darkness abating as minutes of daylight were added to each day.

On one of the milder days, Crow was putting a new used muffler on someone's car in the front yard. Quill was in the kitchen making peanut butter cookies with Baby Boy when she saw a car pull into their driveway. A man and a woman got out of the car and approached Crow. He gestured to the house. A feeling of déjà vu washed over Quill as she opened the door before they could knock. They reintroduced themselves as agents with the BCA and said they needed to ask some follow-up questions about the missing woman named Mabel Beaulieu. Quill brushed her hands down the sides of her jeans, feeling Mabel's earring tucked in the corner of the left pocket. She motioned for them to come in and sent Baby Boy off to the bedroom with a tablet turned on to a children's movie.

As at their previous visit, she set a plate of still-warm cookies on the table and gave them coffee. Again, neither took a cookie but each sipped the coffee.

They asked her repeat questions about her run in the woods. They asked about Julie's attempted abduction from the casino. About her rescue of Lisa and Punk. How did she know where to find Cliff? How did she and Punk get out of the motel room? Why did she impersonate a police officer and stuff Trent, the man she called Cliff, into the trunk of her car instead of calling the police?

Quill, again, felt increasingly flustered, as the questions seemed to imply she was guilty in all that happened. Once again, she smelled cookies burning and quickly jerked around and opened the oven. At the same time, Crow came into the house. He asked with his eyes, *Everything okay?* Her eyes answered back, *Uh! What do you think?*

Just as they had during their previous visit, the agents pointedly ignored Crow, who leaned on the cupboard drinking coffee. They continued with questions about why she had gone to get Punk instead of calling the authorities. After several more rounds of inquiry that all sounded and felt accusatory, Quill looked side-eyed at Crow, silently asking him, *How do we get rid of these idiots?*

Quill didn't hear the school bus arrive. Niswi stormed in the door, laughing, but stopped stock-still at the edge of the kitchen when she saw the two strangers sitting at the table. Grabbing a handful of cookies off the plate, she looked at her mom and dad and, without being told, said, "I'll go to my room."

As before, Niswi's entrance seemed to cue the agents that it was time for them to leave. Both stood in a synchronized move and thanked Quill for her cooperation and said that if they had more questions they would be back.

Quill and Crow stood in the kitchen and watched them leave. As soon as the door shut behind them, Niswi came running out of the bedroom. "Okay, Mom, what did you do now?"

"What the heck! Why do you think I did something?"

Niswi smirked. "Get real, Mom."

Crow went outside to finish putting the muffler on the car in the yard. It had grown dark outside. Quill could see Crow illuminated by his mechanic's flashlight as he got ready to crawl under the car. She stood by the window looking out. The visit from the agents had unsettled her nerves. She wondered how long and how many times the events of this winter would come back to haunt her and her family. Eventually, she turned back to the kitchen and made drop biscuits for the moose stew cooking in the crockpot. She felt anxious as the feeling of wanting to run, to get away, crept back into her being.

Quill breathed deeply as she felt her anxiety begin to spiral out of control. She dug around in her junk drawer and found the business card given to her months ago with the therapist's number on it. She decided it was time to stop treating everything that happened to her as "Shit happened on the rez and you just kept going." She called the number and left a message requesting the soonest appointment available.

Spring crept into the village. The snow melted and the temperatures climbed to the low sixties. Quill was home alone. There was a knock on the door, and Earline, dressed in an oversized thick wool sweater, a little ragged from years of wear, kookum scarf tied around her neck, poked her head in and said, "Anyone home?"

Quill invited her in to sit at the kitchen table. She put out coffee and a plate of peanut butter cookies.

Earline sipped coffee and ate a cookie before saying, "We're having ceremony soon. Spring ceremony. You and your girl-friends should come. Some of the weight that you carry, I think it slows you down when you are running. Coming to ceremony might lift some of the weight off your heart."

"I don't know, Auntie. I'm . . . I don't know, not very tradi-tional, you know."

"Well, think about it, my girl. Ask your friends. But you come, even if they don't. It's the old ways that have kept many of us with one leg on the way out of this world halfways sane over the years."

Quill went quiet, not knowing what to say. Earline drank her coffee and switched the conversation to gossip about goings-on in the village until Crow pulled into the yard. Then she said, "I'll see if that man of yours can give me a ride to the grocery store and back home. You got a good one there." She winked. "Wish I'd found him before you." They laughed.

Quill watched them drive off. She knew Crow wouldn't be gone that long. She quickly changed into running gear. Put Mabel's earring into the pocket of her jacket with a pouch of tobacco and jumped in her car. She drove back to the trail in the woods where she'd heard Mabel's scream. Even in the warmth of the spring day, she shivered as she looked down the trail into the woods. Where she stood the ground was spongy, not completely thawed from the spring warmth. She could see far into the woods because the trees did not have their leaves yet. The brush, closer to the ground, was also bare, with only tiny leaf buds not yet open.

She felt the earring in her pocket and started to jog down the trail. The farther she ran the more solid the ground was. She looked at her watch, and when she reached the three-and-a-half-mile mark, which told her she was at the spot where she first heard Mabel's scream, she stopped and made a tobacco offering. Then she continued to run until she found the spot to turn to the right on the deer trail that would join up with the hunting road.

It was silent in the woods. The sun's spring heat barely reached the path she ran on. She was deep on the deer trail, deep in the runner's zone, when she saw a black pickup truck on the trail in front of her. Fear coursed through her body. She stopped short. Froze. She looked frantically around in the woods. The vehicle had not been there any of the times she had run this trail. There didn't appear to be anyone in the cab. Still, she hollered, "Hello!" Bear spray raised, ready to attack. Nothing. Her logical brain asked, *How the hell did that get here?* and, *This isn't a road; this is a deer trail.*

She approached the vehicle cautiously while scanning the trees around her, prepared to defend herself or run. *What in the hell was I thinking coming out here alone?* She peered into the cab of the truck. It was empty, no one there. No one in the bed of the truck. When she looked up the trail, any tracks left by the vehicle were filled in with snow. Only broken low branches gave any indication of how it got there. Someone had removed the license plates. When she saw a faint flower still visible in the dust on the tailgate she started shaking, positive it was the truck she had marked in the casino parking lot. Someone ditched it. She might never know who.

She took off running full-speed when it dawned on her that, even with Cliff in jail, the man who drove this truck must still be out there preying on women.

She kept running until she reached the hunter's road, her eyes constantly scanning the woods around her and behind her. She was alone in the woods until a hawk flew directly in front of her. When she looked up to see where it flew, she saw two eagles. They whistled down at her. Their presence eased her fears as she turned on the hunter's road in the direction of the main road. She checked her watch and stopped where she first found Mabel's earring. She took the earring out of her pocket and rolled it softly between her thumb and forefinger. "I'm sorry, Mabel. I wish I knew where you were and how to bring you home. I don't know all the right things to say or do, but maybe Earline is right. I will go to ceremony and call your spirit home. I will do it for you. For all our women still out there, waiting to come home. I brought your earring back for you."

Quill pushed the post of the earring into the bark of the nearest tree. The earring was so small no one would ever see it; only Mabel would know where to find it.

AUTHOR'S NOTE

Pocahontas was between nine and eleven years old when she first encountered John Smith. Sacajawea was probably twelve or thirteen when she was taken on the Lewis and Clark expedition. These two young women are probably the most recognizable names among the Native American women who have been kidnapped and trafficked. The majority of the women and children trafficked today remain nameless, and the country unaware of them.

The U.S. Department of the Interior's Bureau of Indian Affairs offers this 2017 statistic: "Approximately 1,500 American Indian and Alaska Native missing persons have been entered into the National Crime Information Center (NCIC) throughout the U.S. and approximately 2,700 cases of Murder and Nonnegligent Homicide Offenses have been reported to the Federal Government's Uniform Crime Reporting (UCR) Program. In total, BIA estimates there are approximately 4,200 missing and murdered cases that have gone unsolved."

Highway 16 in British Columbia, Canada, is known as the Highway of Tears because so many First Nations women have disappeared from or been found murdered there. A 2014 Canadian report identified 1,181 Indigenous women and girls who went missing or were murdered between 1980 and 2012, although Indigenous groups estimate the number to be closer to 4,000.

The "man camps" that spring up to provide temporary housing for the labor that arrives to work for extractive industries such as mining operations and oil pipelines create an environment that fuels the most recent atrocities on and near our communities. Native women and children are targeted because the men who occupy these camps know that local law enforcement agencies will not have the resources to stop them or to prosecute them, often because of legal conflicts that exist between tribal, state, and federal criminal jurisdictions.

Each of us who identify as female, who have female children or grandchildren as well as young female relatives and friends, are conscious of the fact that there are still targets on our backs. But even our young men are not safe. We dread late-night phone calls, we insist that our family members tell us where they are going and who they are with, and we don't fall fully asleep until we know that they are all home safe. It is a present-day, on-the-edge-of-trauma reality.

Today, #mmiw and variations of that hashtag (such as #mmiwg and #mmip) signal solidarity, in order to gain attention for and stop this crisis. The red handprint, usually across the face, is another symbol utilized. Red paint, red dresses, red ribbons—red because it is believed to be the one color that spirits can see.

This novel, *Where They Last Saw Her,* is an imagined story, one about women taking charge and putting their hearts, minds, and bodies on the line to care for and about one another. It was and is First Nations/Native American women who raised the battle cry across Canada and the United States and said, "Our women are disappearing. Our women are being killed and we will do something about it."

ACKNOWLEDGMENTS

Chi-miigwech to all the kwe who dream big, who are repatriating their minds, hearts, and bodies. You make me proud—each of you, all of you. Land back: water, not oil.

Special thanks to the kwe in and near Duluth. You inspire me and make me laugh.

Thank you to Jacqui Lipton, my agent; to Jenny Chen, thoughtful and insightful editor; to Mae Martinez, assistant editor; and to Beth Pearson, copy editor, who I think caught every single one of my errors. Thanks to each of you for paying close attention to the Ojibwe language (all errors in spelling or definition are mine) and to the nuances of the manuscript that make sense to me but maybe don't always translate into the broader culture.

To my writing group and to all the other women who follow this journey I am on—miigwech.

And, as always, to my children and theirs, who have always paid the price for this wild dream I have, much love.

WHERE
THEY LAST
SAW HER

Marcie R. Rendon

Random
House
Book Club

Because
Stories Are
Better Shared ™

A BOOK CLUB GUIDE

QUESTIONS AND TOPICS
FOR DISCUSSION

1. Quill, despite living in a society that often renders her and other Native American women invisible, refuses to be a silent bystander to crimes in her community. How does her defiance shape her role in the narrative and her interactions with the other characters?

2. How do Quill's friends Punk and Gaylyn, as well as her husband, Crow, and her family challenge and/or support Quill on her journey to seek justice for the missing women?

3. Discuss the significance of Quill's decision to take action by investigating the disappearances of the Native

women. How does her personal history and background shape her motivations?

4. What themes resonated with you most while reading the book? How do these themes shine a light on larger societal or cultural challenges?

5. What does the book reveal about the challenges faced by Native American women, particularly in terms of their visibility, and the difficulties that they encounter when seeking justice?

6. The novel harshly criticizes bystander culture. Could you identify scenes or characters that embody this indifference? Why do you think Quill chooses not to be a bystander?

7. Discuss the role of the pipeline construction and its impact on both the community and on the disappearances. How does the book shed light on issues of environmental justice and the exploitation of marginalized communities?

8. Explore the themes of trauma and resilience in the book. How do the characters cope with the trauma they experience? What messages does the author convey about healing and growth?

9. How does the title *Where They Last Saw Her* encapsulate the essence of the book? If you could retitle the book, what would you change it to and why?

10. Now that the story has ended, how do you see Quill's and her community's futures unfolding? What lasting changes might she have brought about in her fight against crime and indifference?

MARCIE R. RENDON, citizen of the White Earth Nation, is one of *O: The Oprah Magazine*'s 31 Native American Authors to Read Right Now and a McKnight Distinguished Artist Award winner. Her debut novel, *Murder on the Red River,* received the Pinckley Prize for Debut Novel and was a finalist for the Western Writers of America Spur Award, Contemporary Novel category, and her second novel, *Girl Gone Missing,* was nominated for the G. P. Putnam's Sons Sue Grafton Memorial Award. Her script *Say Their Names* will be produced by Out of Hand Theater in Atlanta, Georgia. And her script *Sweet Revenge* had a staged reading at the Playwrights' Center in Minneapolis, Minnesota. The creative mind of Raving Native Theater, she curated Twin Cities Public Television's *Art Is . . . Creative-NativeResilience.* Rendon received the Loft Literary Center's Spoken Word Immersion Fellowship with co-creator Diego Vazquez for their work with incarcerated women.

marcierendon.com

ABOUT THE TYPE

This book was set in Sabon, a typeface designed by the well-known German typographer Jan Tschichold (1902–74). Sabon's design is based upon the original letter forms of sixteenth-century French type designer Claude Garamond and was created specifically to be used for three sources: foundry type for hand composition, Linotype, and Monotype. Tschichold named his typeface for the famous Frankfurt typefounder Jacques Sabon (c. 1520–80).

RANDOM HOUSE BOOK CLUB

Because Stories Are Better Shared

Discover
Exciting new books that spark conversation every week.

Connect
With authors on tour—or in your living room. (Request an Author Chat for your book club!)

Discuss
Stories that move you with fellow book lovers on Facebook, on Goodreads, or at in-person meet-ups.

Enhance
Your reading experience with discussion prompts, digital book club kits, and more, available on our website.

Join our online book club community!
 randomhousebookclub.com

Random House Book Club ™

Because Stories Are Better Shared

RANDOM HOUSE